500

Under the Covers

D0869894

Books by P.J. Mellor

PLEASURE BEACH

GIVE ME MORE

MAKE ME SCREAM

DRIVE ME WILD

THE COWBOY
(with Vonna Harper, Nelissa Donovan, and Nikki Alton)

THE FIREFIGHTER
(with Susan Lyons and Alyssa Brooks)

NAUGHTY, NAUGHTY
(with Melissa MacNeal and Valerie Martinez)

ONLY WITH A COWBOY
(with Melissa MacNeal and Vonna Harper)

Books by Crystal Jordan

CARNAL DESIRES

ON THE PROWL

UNTAMED

SEXY BEAST V
(with Kate Douglas and Vonna Harper)

Books by Lorie O'Clare

PLEASURE ISLAND

SEDUCTION ISLAND

Published by Kensington Publishing Corporation

Under the Covers

CRYSTAL JORDAN
LORIE O'CLARE
P.J. MELLOR

APHRODISIA

KENSINGTION BOOKS
http://www.kensingtonbooks.com

APHRODISIA BOOKS are published by

Kensington Publishing Corp.
119 West 40th Street
New York, NY 10018

All Kensington Titles, Imprints, and Distributed Lines are available at special quantity discounts for bulk purchases for sales promotions, premiums, fund-raising, and educational or institutional use.

Special book excerpts or customized printings can also be created to fit specific needs. For details, write or phone the office of the Kensington special sales manager: Kensington Publishing Corp., 119 West 40th Street, New York, NY 10018, attn: Special Sales Department, Phone: 1-800-221-2647.

Aphrodisia and the A logo Reg. U.S. Pat & TM Off.

ISBN-13: 978-0-7582-3807-8
ISBN-10: 0-7582-3807-X

First Kensington Trade Paperback Printing: October 2009

10   9   8   7   6   5   4   3   2   1

Printed in the United States of America

Contents

Naughty or Nice

Crystal Jordan

Acknowledgments

Michal gets to go first in all my acknowledgments. The best friend speaketh and so it was and so it shall remain.

Next must be Dayna Hart, who so generously lent her name to my heroine. And Kate and Jerry, who let me steal their Disneyland joke and give it to my hero.

Special gratitude goes to those who critiqued or listened to me whine while writing this story (and, quite possibly, all my stories): Loribelle Hunt, Rowan Larke, Jennifer Leeland, Gwen Hayes, Karen Erickson, Robin L. Rotham, Gemma Halliday, and Bethany Morgan.

And since this story has sexy tattoos in it, I have to give a nod to my tattooed gurus: Eden Bradley, Lilli Feisty, R.G. Alexander, Adriana Parker, and Jeana Perry—best friend of Adriana and the very nice tattooist who let me pepper her with questions while she inked Michal.

The final word of thanks—and all other things writing-related—must go to the fabulous agent, Lucienne Diver, and the splendiferous editor, John Scognamiglio.

1

The scalding water hammered against Dayna's skin. The shower's heat was nothing to the fire that swept through her body. Clenching her teeth against the ache that built to a fever pitch inside her, she tried to suppress the need as she so often did. How long had it been since she'd gotten laid? Too damn long. What would Nathan think if he knew how unsatisfied she was physically? A small smile quirked her lips. Her boyfriend—no, she caught herself, her *fiancé*—would likely try to debate her out of it, explaining that physical desires were fleeting, but emotional compatibility and similar life goals were what mattered. That's what lawyers did—they debated.

As much as she agreed with him, and as perfect as they were together in every other way, her hormones weren't feeling very reasonable right now. She shuddered, biting back a frustrated sob. Her nipples tightened to painful peaks, and her sex throbbed. She leaned her forehead against the slick tile wall, letting the water sluice down her. The feel of it running over her flesh was almost a caress. Almost.

Sucking her lower lip between her teeth, she pressed her

hands to her lower belly and squeezed her thighs together. It was no use. Nothing would quell the rising ache except orgasm. Dragging in a sharp breath, she slipped her fingers up her torso to cup her breasts. A low moan threatened to slide from her throat, but she swallowed it. Nathan might hear her and come to investigate. *This* was something she didn't want to explain, justify, or debate. She'd rather he would decide to join her and slam his cock inside her until she screamed.

Pinching her nipples, she rolled them between her fingertips. Goose bumps rose on her skin and made her shiver. She turned to press her back to the wall, letting the water pelt over her chest and thighs. Her heart rate kicked up a notch, and her breathing sped to soft gasps. She closed her eyes, painting the fantasy in her mind. His big hands palmed her breasts, lifting them to suck the tips deep into his hot mouth.

Back bowing hard, she sought closer contact with those talented lips and tongue. She slipped her hand down her stomach, dipping into her heated pussy. In her daydream, it was his hand that stroked her, moving his fingers over her slick folds until she had to stifle a soft cry. Her breath caught, and her eyes popped open when he shoved two long digits inside her. Snapping her hips forward to meet the thrust of his hand, flames burst inside her. The slide of the water over her skin added another layer of sensation to those pummeling her.

Her dream man pulled back to look at her, watching her twist against the lashes of pleasure. His green gaze slipped down her body, and she felt it pass over her as if it were a physical touch. Her brow furrowed. No, Nathan had dark eyes, not light. She adjusted the fantasy, shower mist blurring the man's face. Yes. Perfect. Now it was just pure feeling, the fingers moving inside her, the water on her flesh, the heat and desire that raged through her. A shudder shook her, desperation slamming into her. She needed to come so badly.

"Oh, God," she breathed.

He angled his fingertips until he hit just the right spot, until she couldn't hold back a moan. Her thighs locked, and her sex clenched tight. Tingles broke in waves down her limbs. Her head rolled against the slick tile as orgasm exploded through her. Her pussy flexed around the thrusting fingers that worked her until she couldn't breathe, couldn't think. Her hips arched again and again, wanting more, seeking *more* of what she'd needed for so long. *Yes. Oh, yes.*

The hinges squeaked on the bathroom door. "Dayna, are you all right?"

She jolted, every muscle in her body going rigid. Reality intruded, and the fantasy dissolved, swirling down the drain like so much shower water. She pulled in a steadying breath, her heart pounding in her ears. "Fine . . . I'm fine. Just finishing up."

Grabbing a bar of soap, she washed herself quickly. Shit, shit, shit. Had he heard her moaning? Heat suffused her face as embarrassment flooded her. Her muscles shook with the aftereffects of orgasm. And still it wasn't enough to sate her. She turned her face into the shower spray. The water had gone lukewarm, she'd been in there so long. She sighed. Damn. Shutting off the spigot, she hopped out and hurried to dry off.

"Okay . . . hurry up in there. I'm trying to book our flight for Christmas." The door shut behind him with a quiet *thunk*.

And *that* was a discussion she seriously wanted to avoid. Nathan had proposed just before Thanksgiving, and he thought now was a good time to meet her family. Just the prospect made her belly cramp. Nathan was from a socially prominent family. He was a lawyer being groomed to step into the family game of politics. While she appreciated his drive and ambition, his work meant he had to be decisive, and when he made a decision, it was difficult to change his mind. There were times when she thought he crossed the line into being judgmental, and she didn't think her relatives had a hope in hell of making a good first impression. Not with a man whose own family was politely distant and who was raised by a nanny.

He just . . . wouldn't understand why her mother had enough divorces under her belt to put Elizabeth Taylor to shame, or why Aunt Rainbow thought she was psychic, or why her younger brother, Sam, had had so many wild nights he'd ended up a single father who ran the local bar. Dayna loved her family; she just seriously doubted her fiancé would be very forgiving of their flaws.

Stepping out of the bathroom, she saw Nathan propped up in bed with his laptop across his thighs. Case files were spread across the bed. She scooped his papers over onto his side of the mattress and climbed under the covers.

"The plane tickets and car rental are booked. We fly out on the twenty-first." He put his hand on her arm, and her insides clenched, goose bumps rising on her still sensitized skin. Would he? But, no. As much as they had in common, she and Nathan *didn't* share a lot of physical chemistry. She gave the mental shrug she'd been giving since they'd started dating almost a year ago.

"Okay. Don't forget to get chains for the tires. The roads can get icy that far north," she said, wincing. A lot more than the roads got weird that far north. Her little hometown at the foot of Mount Shasta was a totally different world from Los Angeles. Panic fluttered inside her belly again.

Reaching for calm, she grabbed the notepad on her nightstand and started a new list of things to do and pack before they left. She had dozens of lists. Lists for her work, lists for Nathan, lists for shopping—she even had a master list of the lists. Now she added the packing list to the master list.

"I already took care of the tire chains." Of course he had. She checked that item off her list. Like her, Nathan planned ahead and stuck to the plan. It was what she loved about him.

She smiled quietly and read through her list for the week ahead, settling deeper under the covers as the heater kicked on.

Nathan's cell phone rattled across the nightstand as it rang. It was ten forty-five at night, but it wasn't unusual for his work to interrupt their evenings. So why did a dart of anger shoot through her when he grabbed his phone and walked out into the living room? She stomped down on the wayward emotion. It was irrational to be irritated by things that wouldn't change.

And it wasn't like her to be so irritable, so restless. Frankly, it scared her to death. Whenever her mother had been dissatisfied with her life, it had meant another man, another move, another place for Dayna and her brother to have to start over again. *Please, God, don't ever let me become that.* Dayna was happy with her life. She'd worked damn hard to get everything just the way she'd always dreamed. Perfect man, perfect apartment, perfect car, perfect job. Flipping to a fresh page in her notebook, she started brainstorming a list of new ideas for upcoming books. She had a proposal to write for a novel for young adults before New Year's, and she wanted it done before she left for northern California. There was nothing she found more satisfying than her work. Everyone should love their job this much.

She had it all. But the nagging whisper in the back of her mind always said something was missing. She shook her head. It was pointless to go down that mental pathway. She was happy, damnit. She wasn't throwing it all away for no good reason. Her sex life wasn't *that* important.

While Sam was as freewheeling as her mother and as crazy as their flower-child aunt, Dayna had always wanted to be normal. Not to be the girl whose nutty family was gossiped about in their little town. Not to live under a microscope because she was different. Now she had that. With Nathan.

She just had to survive the holidays—a week, give or take,

and she'd be home free to live the quiet, dependable, perfectly organized life she'd always wanted. No problem.

A face flashed through her mind, and she almost whimpered in pain. Jake Taylor. Of course. Sam's best friend would be there for the holidays. He always was, and he always got a perverse amount of enjoyment out of antagonizing the men Dayna brought home. It had been that way since she'd started dating in high school. He was worse than her brother. A lot worse. The two of them were very bad boys and always had been, living hard and wild with too many women and too much booze. They'd cleaned up a bit in the last few years, but Jake was still a tattoo artist, and he had the ink on his muscular body to prove it. He had the face of an archangel and the body of a classic sculpture, but underneath all that pretty was a man who'd been in a lot of trouble and had had a childhood she knew was anything but angelic. She just wished he didn't have to be quite so in-your-face all the time. Or so in the face of every guy she'd ever dated.

She closed her eyes and wished for death. There was no way she was going to survive this.

Damn, she was beautiful.

A rueful grin curled his lips. Hadn't he always thought she was gorgeous? Jake's smile widened as he watched Dayna unfold her long legs from the passenger side of a silver SUV. Shoving the sleeves of his undershirt up to his elbows, he propped himself against the pillar of her aunt's porch, the evergreen boughs and red ribbons wrapped around it scratching his skin. He lifted his mug of coffee from the porch rail and enjoyed the show of Dayna walking across the snowy yard toward him. Everything about the woman said class and style, from the fashionable boots to the expensive scarf. Snowflakes clung to rich brown hair that swung in a bell against her jaw, and her pretty breasts bounced with each step. His body reacted to her, his cock hardening uncomfortably. Nothing new there. He'd been hot for her since he was old enough to notice girls. He shook his head and snorted, a cloud of steam erupting in the cold air.

A grin he couldn't stop kicked up one side of his mouth as he watched her pull the ever-present list out of her purse. The habit was as endearing as it was annoying, and he loved to harass her about it. She really did need to loosen up before she blew a gasket.

It took him a moment to notice the lanky man following his wet dream up to the porch. So that was the new guy. The fiancé. Jake's jaw clenched, a small dart of jealousy shooting through him. He ignored it, shoved it away. Something else that wasn't new—he felt it whenever Dayna brought a guy around, even back in high school, but doing anything about his jones for his best friend's sister was asking for trouble he didn't want. And he'd been in enough trouble in his life to know.

He could hear the other man's voice clearly across the yard. "Dayna, you have to be kidding. We can't stay here. It looks like something out of *Deliverance*. It's probably as freezing in there as it is out here."

"Really, Nathan. I lived here for years—it's fine. Give it a chance." Dayna flicked a glance over her shoulder at the man, tucking her list back in her bag. "Besides, it isn't even that cold for this time of year."

Nathan looked like he was sucking on a lemon when he swept Rainbow's cabin with a contemptuous glance. Annoyance fisted in Jake's gut, and he dragged in a calming breath, smelling the evergreen boughs they'd decorated the porch with. This home was vibrant and bohemian, like the woman who owned it. Maybe a little run-down, but that just made it comfortable. People weren't afraid to mess up anything in this house. Jake loved it here. The Sharps were as close to family as he'd ever had, and he was more grateful than they'd ever know that they'd taken him in and loved him no matter what. Not many people would have done that for the town drunk's kid.

"You mean it gets worse than hell frozen over here? You wouldn't stay here under any other circumstances, and you know it. Why compromise your standards? We'd be more comfortable at a hotel." The guy's arms pinwheeled a bit when he slid on a small patch of ice. *City boy not used to walking in the snow*. Figured. Looked uptight, too. He skidded again.

Jake arched a brow, stroking a hand down his goatee to cover a smile. It was mean, he knew. He didn't give a damn. He only had to put up with the man until they left after New Year's. The stiffs Dayna dated never lasted from one visit home to the next. Thank God. Fiancé or not, this guy wouldn't last either. Dayna would never be stupid enough to go through with it. Not with someone so disrespectful of Rainbow's house. Dayna worshipped her aunt, eccentric or not.

"Well, if it isn't the wild one himself." Dayna's wide hazel eyes crinkled at the corners when she smiled up at him. The smile was forced; he could see the stress lines around her mouth and eyes. From what little he'd seen, it must have been a hellish trip.

"In the flesh." Jake spread his arms and gestured down at himself.

Glancing up, he caught the disapproving look on Nathan's face when he saw the tattoos lacing their way up Jake's forearms.

"Hi, I'm Jake Taylor. Good to meet you." He offered his hand to shake, and Nathan hesitated a long moment before he took it. Jake smiled, and if a tiny part of him enjoyed making the other man squirm, he would never admit it to anyone.

"Nathan Bradford." His handshake was firm, even if he couldn't quite keep his lip from curling in disgust as he got closer to the tattoos. "You're the brother's best friend, right?"

Jake kept the smile on his face and resisted the urge to

squeeze hard enough to hurt. "That's right. Since the sixth grade when the Sharps moved to town. I've known Dayna a long time."

"Well . . . that's nice." Nathan's dark eyes narrowed, and he lifted his free hand to curl over Dayna's shoulder.

"Yeah, it is." Jake noted the possessive movement and dropped the other man's hand before he gave in to the need to break it. He jerked his chin toward the front door. "Penny and Rainbow are inside. Sam and his son, Toby, will be over in a bit. They're delayed."

"Isn't Sam's wife coming with them?"

That question let Jake know exactly how little Dayna had told Nathan about her family. Yeah, she liked to keep the Sharps her dirty little secret. He shook his head. She had it all wrong—it was the "normal," supremely uptight assholes she brought home that she should be ashamed of. She really needed to cut herself and everyone else some slack. Well, except Nathan. Him, she just needed to cut loose.

"No wife," Jake said. "When he was two, Toby's mom dropped him off on Sam's doorstep. Hasn't been back since."

It was Toby's arrival that had cleaned up Sam's act. Before then, he'd been even crazier than Jake, and the two of them had done just about every stupid, illegal thing short of killing a man. And they'd had a hell of a lot of fun doing it. They'd just been lucky enough not to get caught. Now they were both respectable. Well, as respectable as two tattooed, motorcycle-riding men could ever be.

"Ah. Dayna neglected to mention he was a single father." Nathan glanced at her, and she offered a weak smile. She winced when Jake spoke again, giving him the kind of look that begged him to shut his mouth. He ignored her.

"There's a lot to learn about this family." He doubted Nathan would be around long enough to do so, which was just fine by Jake. He pasted on his most helpful expression. "Like I said, Penny and Rainbow are inside—that's Dayna's mom and aunt, in case she forgot to tell you that, too."

Over Nathan's shoulder, Jake watched a car pull in behind the silver SUV and an older man step out. Penny's new boyfriend. Jake saluted him with his coffee mug, and he waved back. The front door swung open, and Penny hurried out, towing a small suitcase.

Ah, hell. Jake had a nasty feeling he knew where this was going, and he winced. Diligent, dutiful Dayna wasn't going to take this well. He braced himself.

"Hi, honey!" Penny set the bag down and swept her daughter into a hug.

Dayna squeezed her briefly, pulled back, and looked at the suitcase. "Going somewhere?"

"Why, yes." A brilliant smile wreathed Penny's face. "I've been invited to spend Christmas in Vail."

Eyes widening with a hint of panic, Dayna glanced between her mother and Nathan. "But . . . but we came up so Nathan could meet my family. You know that, Mom."

"Yes, but apparently my boyfriend just can't live without me for even a few days. It's going to be an adventure." Penny's hazel eyes twinkled with girlish glee. "Don't be upset, honey. Aunt Rainbow is here, and Sam and Toby. And Jake."

"Jake isn't a relative."

She threw up her hands. "He's like another younger brother to you!"

"No, he's not," Dayna said at the same time Jake blurted out, "No, I'm not."

Penny stood on tiptoe and smacked a kiss on his cheek. "Well, you're like another son to me."

"Thank you, Penny." He stooped down to hug the older woman, shaking his head and chuckling at the irrepressible force of nature that was Penny.

"Merry Christmas. Have fun!" She scooped up her suitcase,

scooted around her daughter, and met her boyfriend in the gravel driveway.

"She's really leaving?" Nathan had the kind of dumb-founded expression on his face that Jake had only seen on men right before he'd coldcocked them in a bar fight.

Dayna's lips flattened, her eyes swirling with hurt and anger. She pinned her gaze on the floor. "Yes."

"Is that normal?"

"Pretty much," Jake said and ran a hand over the back of his neck, his gut twisting at the pain on Dayna's face. She'd just never been able to accept that while her mother was a good person, she was never going to live up to the ideal Dayna had built in her mind. It was a shame for both of them. He met Nathan's gaze and gave a brittle imitation of a smile. "Like I said, there's a lot to learn about this family."

"*Ooo*kay, the snow's falling faster, so let's get Nathan started on learning about the family." Dayna shot Jake a killing glare and stomped on the toe of his boot as she walked past. Lucky for him, they were steel-toed.

This was going to be a very long holiday.

2

Nathan had taken one look at her aunt's rustic cabin and demanded they stay elsewhere. An hour of phone calls later, and he had been frustrated to find every bed and breakfast, inn, hotel, and motel in a fifty-mile radius was booked. What did he expect? It was the holidays.

Dayna just wanted the ground to open up and swallow her. She escaped the awkward fits and starts of conversation downstairs by retreating to her childhood bedroom. She needed some quiet time. A lead knot had settled in her belly, and she fought the need to throw up. Every one of her worst fears about bringing Nathan here had come to life. She collapsed beside the bed and pressed her shaking fingers to her eyelids. Nathan didn't just dislike her family, it was hate at first sight. And it was mutual. Aunt Rainbow said his aura was pitch black and his chi was blocked. Her brother hadn't voiced an opinion yet, which wasn't a good sign, because Sam normally never stopped talking. Even Toby—her normally sweet-natured nephew—had started crying the moment Nathan had looked at him. How had it all gone so wrong so fast? Bitterness coated her tongue, making her want to vomit even more.

Her mother had certainly been at her flaky best today. Icy tingles raced over Dayna's flesh just thinking about it. She was so angry her skin flashed cold and then hot. Her fingers shook, and she clenched them into fists.

Not again. She couldn't believe her mother had run off with some guy again. Why did she have to be so irresponsible and *selfish*? Was it so much to ask that she stay in town for one holiday and meet Nathan? Did Dayna mean so little to her?

Yes. That was what she'd always feared. Her mother was beautiful and charming but completely wrapped up in her own wants and needs. She was never satisfied with what she had; she always wanted the next best thing. Her mother loved her—she just didn't love her *enough*.

Thank God for Rainbow. Who would have ever thought that a flower child would be the best thing that had ever happened to her? But she was.

Dayna lurched to her feet. This wasn't helping. Going over and over it in her mind wouldn't fix this. When she stepped out into the hall, she looked around for a moment, uncertain where to go. She didn't really want to deal with her family and Nathan, but she also didn't want to be alone with her thoughts. She really wanted to have Aunt Rainbow hug her, stroke her hair, and tell her everything would be all right because she'd had a vision that said so.

A laugh straggled out at that. Dayna pulled in a deep breath, wiped her eyes, and turned for the stairs. Time to face the music and enjoy her holidays as much as possible, no matter how much everyone seemed to dislike each other.

She met Jake on the stairs; he was carrying a limp Toby against his broad shoulder. "Just laying him down in Sam's old room."

"Okay." Scooting around him, she ignored the shiver of awareness that went up her spine when she brushed against him on the narrow staircase, trying to beat a hasty retreat. She didn't want to see the condemnation in his green eyes at Nathan's behavior. Her head was spinning, and she didn't think she could handle much more.

"Dayna." His voice froze her on the bottom step. She didn't turn around when he spoke again. "I have to say, you could do better. That guy is an asshole."

Well, that was Jake, wasn't it? Mr. Opinionated. But she wasn't in the mood. She spun to face him, planting her hands on her hips. Lowering her voice to a hiss that wouldn't wake Toby, she glared up at him. "You know what, Jake? *Shut up.* I'm having a shitty day, and you are not helping. So just leave me alone unless you have something to say that will actually help."

His dark blond brows rose. "He called Rainbow crazy. She cried. I doubt that'll help, but you should know."

Oh, that was just *it*. She had had enough. The anger, frustration, and helplessness building inside her since Nathan had insisted they come here for Christmas exploded. She clenched her fists tight and the muscles in her body shook. Grabbing her coat and Nathan's off the pile on the couch, she stomped into the kitchen where Nathan and Sam sat in silence at the table. Her aunt had disappeared.

"Nathan," she snapped. He jerked and stood to face her. She shoved his coat against his chest. "I need to speak with you outside. Now."

Wariness flashed in his dark eyes, but he put on his coat and followed her to the front porch. The bitterly cold wind made her skin tighten as she rounded on him. "You know, it was your idea to come here for Christmas. No one forced you."

"I know, but—"

She cut him off. She didn't want to hear excuses for more

uncivil behavior. "Did you actually call my aunt crazy? To her *face?*"

After having her mother bail out on her yet again, it pissed her off to have anyone speak ill of her very supportive aunt. Crazy she might be, but she had always been there when Dayna needed her. No way in hell was some guy who didn't even know Rainbow going to come in and judge her.

A muscle twitched in Nathan's jaw. His nostrils flared with annoyance. "I may have mentioned that her ideas were a bit far-fetched—"

"Crazy, Nathan. You called my aunt crazy."

His long fingers pinched the bridge of his nose. "Dayna, she thinks the base of Mount Shasta holds an entrance to a magical underground land."

Her shoulder jerked in a shrug, her temper completely un-appeased. "She's a little eccentric."

The incredulous look on his face just made her anger flare hotter. Now he was looking at Dayna as if *she* were insane. "A little—"

"You know what?" she bit out. Her hand sliced through the air. "I believe in an omnipotent, omnipresent, omniscient being in the sky who watches over the whole world and will judge me by his personal moral code when I die. I also believe he forsook his only son so I could be granted forgiveness for any wrong I have done or will ever do. To someone who doesn't believe the same way I do, that would sound pretty weird, wouldn't it? If I celebrate my beliefs with a Christmas tree, and my aunt cele-brates hers by burning a Yule log on winter solstice, then I'm going to accept that she has as much right to her beliefs as I do to mine. You don't have to agree with me, you don't have to agree with her, but you do have to treat her *and* her beliefs with respect in *her* house. So try for a little bit of understanding, Nathan. Isn't that what Christmas is all about?"

He sighed. She hated it when he did that. It made her feel

like an idiot even when she *knew* she was right. Gritting her teeth, she spun on her heel and paced the length of the porch. She knew this would be a mistake. He just wasn't the type to get why she loved her family.

"You have to admit she's not normal, Dayna. Be reasonable."

She threw up her hands. "Normal. Is that all you care about? How people appear? How successful they are?"

"That's pretty rich coming from *you*, Dayna. You want everything in your life to be perfect. Normally." Irritation twisted Nathan's face, and the way he spoke made her feel like a scolded child.

She hissed at him, "I'm not the one being nasty and calling old ladies names."

He stabbed a finger in her direction. "You know what? This entire discussion is cr—"

"Crazy?" A saccharine smile curled her lips. "You really seem to like that word today."

Shaking his head, he took a step back. "Who are you?"

"What?"

"This"—his gesture encompassed her—"is not the woman I asked to marry me. I feel like you're an entirely different person here. I feel like I don't even know you. Have you been hiding this side of yourself all along?"

Yes. Her brows snapped together, rage and . . . fear coursing through her veins like ice water. Her hands fisted, and she shook her head in a denial. Of him or herself? She didn't know anymore. "How can you possibly say that? You're the one who's been rude to my family."

He folded his arms and made that sigh that set her teeth on edge. "Fine. I'll apologize to your aunt."

"It's not about my aunt." She propped her hands on her hips and narrowed her eyes at him. "You're not really sorry—you just don't want me to be upset."

A snort was his answer to that. "In any other situation, you wouldn't be upset. You'd agree with me that she was crazy."

She resumed her pacing. "Rainbow is *family*, Nathan. It's different. I don't expect you to understand that."

"I see. Then maybe we should take some time to rethink where we stand with each other."

Stopping, she turned to face him, wariness and unease sliding through her. The knot in her belly expanded even further, twisting tighter. "I don't understand."

"I don't expect you to." He arched a brow, and now it was he who offered a mocking smile. "What I'm saying is maybe we were too hasty with taking our relationship to the next level. I thought I had a partner who was on the same page as me, who understood me. This new side of you makes me reconsider."

Everything inside her shook, and she didn't know what to say, what to do, how to react. It wasn't like her. None of this was. "What are you saying?"

"It's really very simple. I'm going back to civilization to think." Bitterness tinged his voice. "You should do the same while enjoying the holidays with your *beloved* family."

Her head spun again, and she felt dizzy and nauseous. "So you're just going to leave me then? Just like that?"

Just like her mother. He was one more person who would bail out on her. It didn't matter that he'd always seemed reliable and dependable—perfect, even. Things had gotten rough, and now he was leaving. She couldn't live like that. Not anymore. Not ever again.

"I think it's for the best," he reiterated.

Tears burned her eyes, but she shook her head. "Maybe you shouldn't reconsider. Maybe we've said all we have to say."

"Fine. Good-bye, Dayna." He plucked his keys out of his pocket, walked to the car, pulled her suitcase from the trunk, and set it on the driveway.

She opened her mouth to call the words back. That wasn't

what she wanted. Yes, it was. No, it wasn't. She didn't know what she wanted. She didn't know anything anymore. No sound emerged from her throat.

Then it was too late. He was gone. Everything had changed in less than a day. Her perfect life was over.

This was the worst Christmas ever. She buried her face in her hands, waiting for the tears to fall, for some relief to the pressure growing inside, but her eyes were dry and gritty.

It only added to her misery when the door slammed shut behind her, letting her know someone was going to see her at an all-time low.

"Ah, hell. I'm sorry, Dayna. Don't cry." Jake. Of course it was Jake.

"I'm not." She shoved her fingers through her hair and curled them into fists before letting her head fall back. "You heard that?"

"Yeah." At least he didn't bother to lie. It was a small comfort. "Listen, I—"

"Dayna?" Her aunt's voice sounded from inside.

Dayna shook her head, letting her hands drop to her sides. "I need to get away from this house." She choked on a laugh. "No, what I really need is a stiff drink."

"That I can arrange." Jake reached out, taking her hands in his. His touch was gentle, and the expression on his sharp features was kinder than she'd ever seen from him.

It only made her feel worse, and she had to blink rapidly to push back the tears that wouldn't fall only moments before. She swallowed, wanting nothing more than to erase this day from existence. "I don't want to go to a bar. If I get trashed there, someone will tell Aunt Rainbow or Sam or my mom when she gets back, and I'll never hear the end of how Nathan wasn't worth it."

"Yeah, I get that." He nodded, squeezing her fingers. "Your

hands are cold. You should be wearing gloves out here." He rubbed her hands between his bigger palms, warming her.

That tingle of awareness she'd felt on the stairs rippled over her skin again, and the way his brilliant green gaze slid down her body only increased the sensation. She shook her head, denying it. Thinking like that really *would* be crazy.

His breath made white puffs in the air. "I have a bottle of Jack Daniel's back at my place with your name on it."

Her mouth opened and then closed. Damn, but she needed to not have to think, to worry, to overanalyze *everything* for once, and she couldn't come up with one good reason not to accept Jake's offer. "Okay."

He'd matched her shot for shot until they both couldn't see straight, until neither of them was thinking clearly, until it had seemed like the most natural thing in the world to kiss her, to strip her bare, and stretch her out on his bed.

She'd been with him every step of the way, yanking at his clothes, sliding her hands over his skin, whispering his name, biting his ear, begging him to fuck her hard.

It was better than he'd ever imagined, even in his wildest adolescent fantasies.

He watched her arch on his sheets, her dark hair a stark contrast against the white fabric. She reached up to spread her fingertips on his chest, and he damn near groaned at how good her hands felt on him. He filled his palms with her breasts, lifting them to suck each rosy nipple into his mouth in turn. Somewhere in the back of his whiskey-soaked mind, he knew it was wrong to touch her, but he couldn't seem to piece together why. When she wrapped her slim fingers around his cock, he didn't give a damn about the *whys*, he just knew he had to have more. More of her, more of this. More.

Jesus, he'd always wanted more when it came to Dayna.

"Hurry, Jake," she breathed, pumping his dick hard enough to make his jaw lock. He lunged for one of the condoms he'd dropped on the bedside table, ripped it open with his teeth, and sheathed his cock with shaking fingers.

She threaded her fingers through his hair, pulling him down for a kiss. Nipping at his bottom lip, a husky little laugh rippled from her. He slanted his head, caught that sexy sound in his mouth, and licked his way between her full lips. Their tongues twined, each fighting for control of the kiss. He nudged her thighs apart with his, settling between them. The head of his cock prodded her slick opening. Wrapping her legs around his hips, she pushed her feet down on the backs of his thighs. His breath hissed out at the feel of her soft, soft skin rubbing against him.

Fire fisted in his gut as he pressed his cock into the hot depths of her pussy. The snug sheathing almost made him come, but there was no way he was letting this end so quickly. Rocking himself inside her, he felt the slow drag of his hard flesh in her damp heat. A shudder racked his body, but he picked up the pace, shoving his cock deep with each push. Her slim fingers curled over his shoulders, the nails digging into his muscles. A little sting to sharpen the pleasure. He almost smiled.

The smell of her enveloped him, spicy roses and hot sex. The sensations burned themselves into his memory, and he knew he'd never get the feel of her off his skin, the taste of her sweetness out of his mouth. He didn't want to.

The sounds she made as he ground his pelvis against hers made his head feel as if it were going to explode. "Damn, Dayna."

"Jake, Jake, *Jake.*" She twisted in his arms, desire flushing her pale cheeks, making her eyes sparkle. A low laugh bubbled out of her as she tightened her vaginal walls around him. "Oh, my God, this is good."

A growl pulled from his throat. He gripped one of her thighs, hitching it higher on his hip so he could thrust deeper.

He couldn't get enough of her. "Baby, you have no idea how long I've wanted to do this."

"How long?" she gasped.

An evil grin he couldn't stop pulled at his lips. "Since I was old enough to get a woody."

"That's crude." The giggle she gave was as drunk as he felt. He laughed with her, every movement pushing him higher than he'd ever been.

Waggling his eyebrows, he let his smile widen. "I am crude, rude, and socially unacceptable."

"I noticed that about you." A little grin parted her full lips. She ran a fingertip down from his shoulder to circle his nipple. Then she flicked it hard with her nail, making him jolt. "You're a very bad boy."

Reaching between them, he rolled a finger over her clit in time with his thrusts. He wasn't gentle, working her hard. Her moans drove him on, told him how close she was to orgasm. He pressed down directly on her clitoris, and she arched against him, sobbing as her pussy milked the length of his dick. She shuddered, her fingers gripping his arms tight. "Yes! Oh, my God. *Jake!*"

Gritting his teeth, he jerked his cock from her slick sheath to keep from coming and ignored her cry of protest. Wrapping his hands around her trim waist, he rolled her over and pulled up her hips so he could plunge into her from behind. "If I'm a bad boy and you're in bed with me, sweetheart, what does that say about you?"

"That I'm having a *reeeeeally* bad night?" Flipping her short hair out of her eyes, she winked at him, another giggle breaking free.

"Or maybe you're just a little bit bad tonight." He cupped his free hand over the soft globe of her ass, rubbing in small circles. She arched her torso, pressing back into his touch.

She smirked at him over her shoulder. "You'd like that, wouldn't you?"

"Hell, yes." He flashed a grin. She had no idea how bad he'd like her to be. But she'd get a little taste tonight. He drew his hand back and smacked her ass hard. "I'm liking it a whole lot."

Her breath hissed out, a shudder running through her body. "Me, too."

"Well, if you want to try something naughty . . ." He slid from her body, and she moaned, her sex clenching around him to keep him in.

He replaced his cock with his fingers, stroking into her wetness and then trailing his finger up to the pucker of her anus. He worked his way in, slicking her with her own juices until he could slide easily.

"Oooh." She moaned with each press of his fingers, shoving herself back to meet his strokes. "That really is naughty."

"You were always the good girl I wanted to do bad things with." Jesus, the booze had loosened his tongue even more than it had her inhibitions. Why else would he tell her things he'd kept to himself for almost two decades? It wasn't like him to be so revealing in bed.

Her head dropped forward, her back arching. The softest whisper reached his ears. "I never knew."

"You do now." And he needed to shut his mouth and just enjoy this one night with her. It was all he was going to get, so he might as well revel in his teenage wet dream come to life and stop with the confessional. Spreading her cheeks wide, he nudged the head of his cock into her ass. He pushed in slowly, groaning at the incredibly tight fit of her around his dick. It was so damn good, he wasn't sure how long he'd hold out before he came.

She dropped lower, bowing her back and pressing her face into the pillow. It muffled the whimpers that erupted from her mouth, but he still heard them. He didn't bother to hide a smug grin. If she liked how naughty this was, he had a lot more in store for her.

Starting now.

He slapped her ass again in time with his quickening strokes, spreading short, stinging swats over the soft cheeks of her backside and down her slim thighs. She moaned, moving to meet his hand. The skin flushed under his palm, ripening to a rosy hue. He liked that. Liked that he'd left a mark on her, liked that she'd be feeling this and remembering every time she sat down tomorrow how she'd moaned and begged and screamed his name. She wouldn't be bruised, but the sting would last for a bit. Oh, yeah. He liked that thought.

A shudder shook her slim body. "Jake, I've never—"

"Let a guy spank you while he fucked you up the ass?" He smacked her again to emphasize his point.

She choked on a laugh. "Yeah."

Each plunge into her body drove him closer to the edge, and he knew he wasn't going to last much longer. Cupping his palms around her ribs, he pulled her up until her back pressed to his chest. She reached back and fisted her fingers in his hair, pulling him down for a kiss. He suckled her bottom lip, scraping it with his teeth. She shivered, working her hips in time with his.

Running his hands up her torso, he lifted her breasts and let them bounce down. They moved with each thrust of his hips. He rolled her nipples between his fingers, pinching and tugging lightly. She laid her head on his shoulder, her back bowing to push closer to his palms. He let one hand slip down over the soft swell of her lower belly, dipping between her legs to stroke over the wet, heated lips of her pussy.

"Now this is going to be really naughty." Then he drew his hand back and smacked her hard little clitoris.

"Jake!" she gasped, sucked in a breath, and snapped her head around to look at him. She choked and shuddered, arching her torso.

Glazed shock was in her gaze, and he swatted her again. Harder. She panted, moaning each time he made contact with her slick, swollen flesh. Letting her head fall back against his shoulder again, her fingers clamped over his forearms, and her nails dug in. The way her inner muscles tightened around his cock made him groan. He knew she was close, and so was he. "Jake, I—"

"Come for me, Dayna. Now." He slammed his hips forward, shoving deep into her ass. He delivered a series of hard slaps to her clit, and she screamed, twisting in his arms. Her anus clenched around his cock, and that was all it took to push him over into orgasm. He came in hard jets, groans ripping from his chest.

They collapsed forward onto the mattress, and he propped himself on his forearms so he wouldn't crush her. As he sucked in air, his lungs burned as if he'd run a marathon. Leaning to one side, he reached between them to slide his cock from her body. They both groaned at the glide of flesh. Dropping his forehead against her back, he felt how shivers still rippled through her body. He smiled, kissing the back of her shoulder.

He heard her swallow hard. "Jake."

Moving until he'd settled beside her, he tucked her hair behind her ear so he could see her flushed face. "How're you doing, sweetheart?"

"I'm . . . I think I'm okay." Her hazel eyes were still a bit stunned, and she blinked up at him slowly.

He chuckled, pressing a kiss to her forehead. He ran his hands over her bare back, just for the pleasure of touching her. "Good."

"Yeah, it really was." She sighed, and her eyes closed, her body relaxing by degrees. He lay back against the pillows, sliding an arm under his head. His fingers drew lazy patterns over her skin.

"Dayna," he breathed. Damn, it had never been so good, so sweet, with anyone else. But no one else was Dayna. She was special. A warning went off in the back of his mind. No woman should be allowed close enough to be special, but sleep was already dragging him under, fuzzing his thoughts. He'd worry about it later. He sighed and closed his eyes, contentment he shouldn't feel winding through his chest. Dayna curled against his side, her satiny flesh sliding over his. Her hand rested over his heart. He still had a smile on his face when unconsciousness claimed him.

3

―――――――――

Dayna yawned and stretched, rolling onto her side. Damn, she ached. Why did it feel like she'd strained every muscle in her body? Then reality returned, and her eyes flew open. Empty condom wrappers littered the nightstand and floor like garish confetti. Jake threw his leg over hers, his arms wrapping around her from behind.

"Oh, my God." Shock rocketed through her as memories of the night before flooded in. She'd had just enough alcohol to throw her control out the window, but not so much that she didn't remember every erotic detail of fucking her brother's best friend.

Holy shit, what had she done?

No, what was she still *doing?*

Jake's chest pressed to her back, pushing her torso forward a bit until her ass cradled against his groin. His long cock prodded at the entrance of her pussy, stretching her as he slid in one hard inch at a time. Her breath hissed out, and she clenched her teeth. The way he had her legs pinned together under the weight of his made his penetration sting, but her body was already heating and responding to his, morphing the burn of it into dark ecstasy. She couldn't think; every thought, every protest, every reason she shouldn't be doing this was ripped away in the whirlpool of sensation that sucked her down into the abyss. She scrabbled for the fleeing edges of her sanity. "Condom," she gasped.

A sleep-roughened chuckle answered her. "I put it on when I knew you were awake. We're covered. Or, I am, actually."

Her fingers fisted in her pillowcase, and she breathed through her nose to push through the pleasure-pain as he worked the entire length of his long cock into her dampening core. She whimpered. "Oh, my God, that's tight."

"Tell me about it." A harsh sound burst from his throat, and his thigh tightened around hers. He eased halfway out of her and then pushed back in.

Shivers skittered over her skin, fire and ice racing in the wake of the pain. God, she was so wet. The angle would be impossible if she wasn't. Arching her body, she tried to free herself from the leg pinioning her. His arm held her in place, his palm stroking over her breasts, tweaking each nipple in turn. Desperation burned through her as the craving sharpened. She moved one hand, clamping it over his knee. The crisp hair stimulated her palm. "Let me loose."

"No." He kept up that same slow, deep rhythm. It pushed her right to the edge without letting her fall over.

"Then *move*. Go faster. Harder. Something." Her nails sank into his flexing muscles, frustration clawing at her like a wild thing. "Damnit, move your ass, Taylor."

"Sorry, sweetheart. No dice." The light calluses on the pads of his fingers rasped against the underside of her breast, adding another sensation to those threatening to overwhelm her. His lips brushed over the back of her neck, his short goatee tickling her skin and making her shiver.

"Please."

His fingertips swirled up to tease her nipples until she wanted to scream. She bit her lip, raking her nails up his thigh. He just chuckled, prying her hand off his leg. "What's in it for me? You're just going to pretend this never happened as soon as we're done."

It was true. She knew it. He knew it. Her chest heaved with panting little gasps. She shook her head, denying his words. At this point, she was willing to sell her soul to make him let her come. "I—"

Burying his cock deep inside her, he stopped moving. "Don't even bother trying to deny it. I know you too well. You're a perfectionist."

Tears burned her eyes. He held her down, wouldn't let her escape what he was saying, what he was doing, what he was making her feel. Terror exploded inside her, whipping together with the desire and pain and desperation. It was too much. She didn't know how to take it all in. She shouldn't be doing this, shouldn't want this, yet her body wouldn't be denied. A sob caught in her throat. "P—please, Jake."

"Has being so focused on perfection and being so uptight made you happy?" He twisted her nipple hard, demanding a response.

Her lips pressed together, and she didn't say anything. She tried wriggling again, but she couldn't budge an inch. Damnit. Her muscles burned as she strained, sweat sliding down her skin in moist beads.

"I know you don't want to hear this." His tongue flicked out, trailing a line of fire down her shoulder. "Maybe you should try loosening up a little, see if that gets you different results."

He was right about one thing—she didn't want to talk about this, didn't want to listen. She jerked against his hold, pulling his hand away from her breast. It didn't stop the harsh throb of need between her legs or the way her vaginal walls clenched around his hard cock. Clinging to what little remained of her control, she managed to get out, "I'm not like you or my family, Jake. I like order and consistency. I like getting up and going to bed at decent hours; I don't like to drink all night. I know to you that seems boring, but I like to know where and when I'll be sleeping every night."

He *tsked* low in his throat. "There's a difference between keeping your life sane and keeping it so sane you're borderline OCD." He leaned close so he could speak softly in her ear, his voice dropping to a rough, silken purr. "And admit it, losing a little control last night, being a little naughty, was a lot of fun, wasn't it?"

"It was irresponsible. Hell, it's still irresponsible, considering you're inside me." And not as far inside her as she wanted. Guilt, anger, and self-disgust rolled through her. A tear slipped down her cheek. This wasn't her—the Dayna she knew herself to be would never do this, not with the least appropriate man on the planet. What was *wrong* with her? "This is crazy."

He rewarded that comment with a quick swat to her thigh. She squeaked and twisted, but it got her nowhere. This conversation was *not* what she wanted to be doing right now. She wanted him to stop. She wanted him to never stop. She needed to forget everything but the desires within her, needed him to fuck her senseless the way he had the night before. A hot flush burned her cheeks at the reminder of how wild it had been. Tingles spread down her limbs. She wanted more of that, and she knew she shouldn't. Madness. This was complete and utter madness. What the hell was she doing there? She'd been engaged to one man yesterday, and this morning she was in another man's bed.

"I can make you feel this good every night you're here, sweetheart." Every word was a deep, hypnotic rumble of sound. He could tempt a saint to sin with that voice. His fingers slid over her ribs and up until he fondled her breasts again. "It'll be a Christmas you'll never forget. I'll make sure you're on Santa's naughty list next year."

She shivered, fighting the pull of him. This couldn't happen again, no matter how good it felt. It was totally and completely irrational. It was something her mother would do. But her body didn't give a damn what her mind knew. His dick slid out of her one slow inch at a time before stretching her channel again as he filled her. Her nerve endings rioted, screeching for more. As she closed her eyes, her body quivered.

"No." She licked her lips, desperately trying to follow the thread of the conversation. "We can never do this again."

"You don't really want me to stop now, do you?" that black-magic voice continued, and his thrusts into her pussy picked up speed. Just a little. Just enough to make her body shriek with want. He opened his mouth over the sensitive spot where her shoulder met her neck, scraping his teeth over the tendon there. "Do you, Dayna?"

"No," she whimpered. If he didn't fuck her hard soon, she was going to die. Lava flowed through her veins, made her heart pound. Catching his hand again, she guided his fingers down her stomach and between her legs. He obliged by stroking her clit at the same leisurely pace as his cock. She hissed out a breath. Who knew the wild child had this much control in bed? Damn him. "Just this once. Just one more time. Make me come."

And then she said nothing more because his leg freed hers. She opened her thighs, arching against him as he shoved deep inside her pussy. The slap of skin against skin and their harsh breathing were the only sounds she heard. She closed her eyes, tears leaking from the corners at the intense sensations rolling through her. He rubbed her clit in a fast, grinding rhythm that made her mouth open in a silent scream. He slammed inside her twice more before her whole world coalesced into blinding white light behind her lids. Her pussy contracted, pulsing around his cock. He kept moving within her, and each stroke set off another wave of orgasm. Her tortured lungs sobbed for air as it went on and on, shoving her beyond any pleasure she'd ever known before. His groan echoed in her ear as his big, hard body locked tight and he seated himself deeper than he'd ever been.

She shattered, everything within her crumbling as she screamed. Some distant part of her mind wondered if she'd ever be the same again. It should have scared her, but it didn't.

"I'm sorry, Jake." Guilt flickered through those hazel eyes, making Jake grit his teeth and clench his fingers on the steering wheel just to hang on to his control.

Dayna regretted sleeping with him. It pissed him off. A lot.

Baring his teeth at her in a rough semblance of a smile, he tried to pretend it didn't matter. "So you're going to try to get back together with him when you get home?"

"I was happy with him."

And that sent him over the edge. He snorted. "Oh, give me a break. You are so bored with your life you don't even know what to do with yourself."

Her eyes widened with shock and then narrowed in anger. "I am perfectly happy—"

"If you're so fucking happy, Dayna, why did you spend last night in my bed?" He arched an eyebrow at her, daring her to contradict him. "If you were so in love with that jackass, you would never have slept with me, let alone come more times than I could count."

"So now you're calling me a slut?" Her face went ghostly pale, and then angry splotches colored her cheeks.

"You're about as far from a slut as possible." He shook his head, wanting to shake *her* and then take her over his lap and spank her. The thought of spanking her brought vivid memories of the night before roaring back, and his cock hardened in an instant. Shit. "You're so uptight, I'm amazed you unwound long enough to get off, let alone that many times."

She shoved the passenger door open. "Gee, if your morning-after routine is always this sweet, it's no wonder you end up dropping so many of the women you're always juggling."

"That isn't true, and you know it." *Sam* had always done the one-night-stand thing, but Jake was more of a serial monogamist. Dayna knew about his parents, knew why he'd never been one to sleep around on a woman. So now it was his turn to glare, and before she slammed the door, he spat, "Besides, I didn't hear you complaining last night."

No, she'd screamed, clawed at his back, and begged for more. He watched her disappear into Rainbow's cabin as he backed out of the driveway. Damn, this morning had started out with such promise and gone to hell the moment Dayna had gotten out of his bed. It made him want to snarl. He'd been waiting for *years* to peel back the layers of the good girl, knowing underneath the cool exterior he'd find fire hot enough to incinerate. Even then, she'd blown his expectations out of the water last night. He wanted more. Everything inside him craved it.

Crave. He paused, his insides tightening. His father had craved his mother, and look where that had landed him. No, Jake would never love or need a woman like that. He jerked his chin to the side. He wasn't his father, and he knew Dayna was leaving. He knew exactly what he was doing. This wasn't about needing her, it was about sex, pure and simple. *Great* sex with the sexiest woman he'd ever had the pleasure of fucking.

Now that he'd had her, he wanted more. She thought it was a mistake? Too damn bad. He knew exactly how good it was with her, and he was determined to get back in her pants as often as possible until she left. He grinned, rolling his shoulders as he turned down Main Street. Every storefront in the downtown area was decked out in twinkling white Christmas lights, including the shop he'd opened four years ago—*Taylor Ink*. He drove past, glancing in at the darkened interior. It was closed right now. He would open again for shortened hours a few days after Christmas but wouldn't go back to regular hours until New Year's Day.

So, until Dayna left, he had nothing better to do than her. Plenty of time to focus on loosening her up. It would be good for her to let go a little, and amazing for him to slide his hands over that smooth, creamy skin. And as a tattooist, he knew world-class skin when he saw it.

He also had a few very intriguing ideas on how to strip her of a little bit more of that control of hers. He stroked his fingers down the steering wheel, imagining her curves under his palms. Hell, he could do whatever he wanted with Dayna, and there was no danger of things getting deeper. He wasn't her type, and she sure as hell wasn't his. There was plenty of chemistry, but she wanted a nice guy. Hopefully not a dickhead like Nathan, but a *nice*, established guy. If possessive jealousy fisted in his gut, he ignored it. That just wasn't how things could go with Dayna. No, it was just some carefree fun. She needed some of that, and he was more than willing to help her out.

This was the safest risk he'd ever taken.

It had to be because he knew exactly what loving a woman could do to a man. It could eat him alive. Jake's shoulders stiffened, the muscles tightening as ugly memories he didn't want came rushing in. He shook his head. No woman was worth what his mother had done to his father. She'd left his dad, left them both, when Jake was six—Toby's age. When she'd skipped town with another man, Jake's father had crawled into a bottle and never managed to drag himself out again. Jake had watched his old man get drunk and stay drunk every single day until the day he'd wrapped his truck around a telephone pole. Jake had been eighteen and two weeks out of high school.

Yeah, his dear old dad had been a great example of what *not* to be. Jake never wanted to let a woman close enough to hurt him like that, but he also didn't wanted to be like his mother— a cheater. When he was with a woman, he was with her. After seeing what his father had gone through, he didn't believe in infidelity. He might not want *forever* with one woman, but while his affairs lasted, he didn't stray. He had fun, they had fun, but Jake was always the one to walk away. Always.

It wasn't that he didn't let anyone in. He had the Sharps. They'd been his family since he was twelve years old. He'd do damn near anything for them, but he could love them without risking his soul. That suited him just fine. He had the best of all worlds.

Sucking in a breath, he shoved the old ghosts aside and focused on how amazing his life was now and how mind-blowing the next week was going to be. A smile formed on his lips as the image of Dayna's slim body arching in pleasure came to his mind. He was one lucky bastard, and he knew it. Whistling tunelessly, he made the turn that would take him out to the lake . . . and his house.

4

"I like this one! No, this one!" Toby ran in a frantic zigzag pattern through the Christmas tree farm. Tugging her notebook out of her bag, Dayna checked the tree farm off her to-do list for the day. Toby had insisted they couldn't get a tree until Dayna was there to help pick it out. She grinned, footsteps crunching through the snow as Jake, Sam, and she followed the boy. She filed away little bits and pieces of the day to go in her next book. Maybe she'd talk to her editor about a holiday story.

She drew in a deep lungful of cold, crisp air, looking out over the little town spread across the mountainside below her. Snow blanketed the ground, fat flakes drifted in lazy swirls from the sky, and icicles decorated the edge of every roof. It was picturesque. She'd forgotten how pretty this area could be—she'd always focused on how much she wanted to get away and start her own life. She rolled her eyes at herself. She'd done such a stellar job with her life lately.

All her efforts had been focused on not thinking about breaking up with Nathan yesterday and *not* thinking about what she'd done with Jake last night, but it was all crashing in on her now. The pain of losing something she'd wanted so much. The self-loathing for losing control. The guilt. Her stomach heaved, and she swallowed hard to keep down the lunch she'd had at Rainbow's. God, she really was worse than her mother. At least her mother was thoughtless; Dayna knew what she was doing and did it anyway. Self-disgust crawled through her.

"Dad, look at this one!" Toby poked his little head out from behind a Douglas fir and then disappeared again.

Sam laughed. "Hey, rugrat. Wait up!"

Dayna tucked her scarf tighter around her neck as she watched her brother slog through the ankle-deep slush after her nephew. Toby looked just like Sam had at that age. Same eyes, same smile, same endless energy. She chuckled. Her brother deserved to have to deal with it from someone else.

Their footsteps had faded before she realized they'd left her alone with Jake. Rainbow had eschewed the delights of wading through the snow looking for a tree to stay home and cook dinner. Dayna tensed when she felt the heat of Jake's muscular body envelop her from behind. "Just the two of us."

She swallowed, but her mouth had dried, and she couldn't make a sound emerge from her tight throat. Goose bumps rippled down her limbs, heat flooding her body. The sensation was a sharp contrast to the chill of snowflakes catching on her eyelashes and kissing her bare cheeks and lips. She shivered.

A loud crack followed by a dismayed shout sounded to their left as a tree trunk snapped and an evergreen went down. A red-faced man emerged from the branches shaking his fist at a woman standing beside the tree. His voice slurred the way only copious amounts of alcohol could manage. "You stupid cunt!"

Jake growled and shifted in their direction when the woman planted her palms on her ample hips and snapped back. "Well, if you'd let me call for some help, it would have been fine. You can just do it all by yourself if you're going to talk to me like that."

She turned and flounced away while Jake pulled Dayna into the trees away from the still cursing drunk. Dayna tensed, worried for a moment that the drunken display might remind Jake of his father—one of the few things that could put Jake in a really dark mood. He was willing to drink in bars and at his house, but she'd never seen him drunk in the middle of the day. The few occasions she'd met his father, he'd been soused, regardless of the time of day. Jake was usually careful, except for last night. Looked like they were a bad influence on each other.

Clearing her throat, she tried to lighten the moment. "Well, Merry Christmas to him, too."

Jake coughed, shrugging his tense shoulders in an obvious attempt to shake off the moment. He offered her a tight smile. "You know, I've never understood using *cunt* as an insult."

"Why not? It's certainly derogatory." She winced.

His dark blond brows rose, and his grin widened to a more genuine one. "Yes, but why would I use a word that describes the happiest place on Earth as an insult? He might as well have said, '*You stupid Disneyland.*'"

A laugh exploded out of Dayna at the incredulous look on his face. No matter how long she'd known him, it constantly amazed her what came out of Jake's mouth. Tears welled in her eyes as her fit of giggles wouldn't stop. She wrapped her arms around her belly, trying to contain the chuckles, but she ended up slipping in the snow. It just made her laugh harder as Jake caught her from behind to keep her on her feet. "Oh, my God. I can't believe you said that."

His hands cupped her hips from behind, pulling her back against his chest. His voice lowered to that silken purr he'd used in bed. "I haven't been able to stop thinking about you all day."

Just like that, the laughter strangled in her throat as molten heat spread through her limbs.

"Don't say that," she whispered. All her regrets came crowding back in. What was she thinking to have a drunken one-night stand with her brother's best friend? She should slap his hands down and step away from him. But she didn't. Her insides had begun melting the moment he touched her, and her thoughts centered on the pressure of his fingers through her clothes, the memories of those big hands sliding over her naked skin. She dropped her head forward, her hair swinging into her face. "Don't—"

"Why? It's true." He nuzzled the nape of her neck, pushing her scarf out of his way. Fire exploded through her at just that light contact. Her breath caught. She'd never reacted to anyone the way she was reacting to him. How had this happened so fast? She'd never thought of Jake this way. He was Sam's best friend, he was every shade of wicked, and he was simply not the kind of guy she ever got involved with in any way. Until last night. It was like a switch had flipped, and now there was nothing she didn't notice about Jake. His dark, masculine scent, his deep voice, the heat of his touch whenever he brushed up against her. Which was often.

"Last night was fun." His breath heated her skin when he spoke. "Don't you agree?"

"Fun." She huffed out a laugh, a cloud erupting in the cold air. "That's not really my style. *You're* not my style."

Kissing her neck lightly, he flicked his tongue over her skin. "You tried me *and* fun on for size last night. We seemed to fit then."

"Temporary insanity?" Her muscles were loosening, molding her curves against his harder planes. They fit perfectly even through the bulk of their winter clothing. He was right about that. Her body clamored with the need to try him on for size again, her sex dampening as the craving twisted tight within her.

"Your insanity is my gift from the world. I must have been a very good boy this year. Thank you, Santa."

She glanced over her shoulder at him, arching an eyebrow. "Did you actually just say 'good boy' in reference to yourself?"

Winking at her, he slid one hand around to her lower belly and pulled her back until her ass rubbed against his erection. "Hey, I'm a successful local business owner. I pay my taxes. What else do you want?"

Her mouth formed a moue. "Honey, you're a tattoo artist. That hardly makes you a choirboy. Face it, you're a very naughty man."

"You know firsthand." His hips moved subtly against hers, and her lips fell open as she sucked in a shuddering breath.

"Yes, I do." God, was he naughty. They were in a *Christmas tree* lot. There were children nearby, including her nephew. And she was ready to turn in his embrace and beg him to fuck her. No. She wouldn't let that happen again. One night was stupid but understandable. More than that was unacceptable. She forced herself to focus on the arms wrapped around her. She pried one off her waist and spun away.

Her fingers slipped on his arm, pushing up his sleeve enough to see the whorls of ink on the inside of his wrist—the symbol for infinity with her family's first initials twining around it. Jake had designed the art and tattooed his own arm almost a decade before. He'd added Toby's initial to the design and done Sam's forearm at the same time a few years ago. Then her mother had asked him to add it to her ankle to celebrate her retirement. Dayna was the only adult in the family without the tattoo—Aunt Rainbow had had him put it at the top of her impressive cleavage on her sixtieth birthday, and she used it as an excuse to flash people whenever she wanted. A wry smile curved Dayna's lips and shook her head. Rainbow loved causing a spectacle.

Turning his wrist, Jake caught her hand and her attention. He pulled her around until she faced him, offering up a smile that made his handsome face flawlessly gorgeous. "What could it really hurt, Dayna? Go a little crazy for the whole week, not just the night. It doesn't have to mean anything other than two healthy, single adults enjoying some incredible chemistry."

He stroked his thumb over the pulse point in her wrist, just above the edge of her glove. She swallowed, fighting a shiver. His gaze locked with hers as he brought up her captured hand, brushing his soft lips over her skin. That wasn't where she wanted that talented mouth. Her hormones did a little tap dance at the thought of his lips against hers. He was an amazing kisser. He didn't rush; he savored the play of their mouths together. Insidious heat wound through her, flushing her cheeks. She stared at his mouth, remembering. "Jake."

He was reaching for her, his features tight with lust, when Sam's voice sounded through the trees. "Hey, you two. Toby found the one he wants. He's standing guard so no one else claims it."

"I'll bring my truck around," Jake called back. He gave Dayna a final, heated glance before he turned toward the entrance of the tree farm.

Her breath whooshed out, relief and regret twisting tight inside her. Turning on legs that felt too weak to hold her, she followed the sound of Toby's high-pitched giggle until she spotted her brother and nephew next to a Scotch pine. "Oh, it's beautiful. You're such a good tree picker, Toby."

He beamed up at her, wrapping his little arms around her leg to hug her. "This is gonna be the best Christmas ever, Aunt Dayna."

Sam's phone beeped, and he pulled it off the clip on his belt. "Damn."

"What's up?" She looked up at him.

He shook his head. "Just got a text message. One of the other bartenders has a pregnant wife, and she just went into labor. We knew it was coming soon, so I'm going to have to go in and cover the last half of his shift."

"Do you need me to take Toby?"

"Nah, I can drop him off with Rainbow on my way." He scooped up his son and tucked him under his arm like a football. "You stay with the tree so Jake can get the right one loaded. We'd never hear the end of it from the rugrat otherwise."

"No problem!" she called over her nephew's squeals of delight.

"Thanks, sis. I'll pay for it on the way out." He kissed her cheek and headed for the entrance. He waved Jake in the right direction from the main road as he passed.

Dayna grinned and shook her head. The smile widened at the rumble of Jake's big red pickup truck as he navigated the narrow muddy track that ran through the trees. That was one pretty piece of machinery he had there. One of the farm's workers sat in the passenger seat. The skinny teenager hopped out to guide Jake as he did a three-point turn to back the truck up to the tree. Then he cut the ignition and stepped out.

The two of them pulled a chainsaw out of the bed of the truck, and Dayna pointed at the right tree and got out of their way. The manly men could get sticky tree sap all over themselves as they cut it down. They didn't need her help. She hopped in the driver's side of Jake's truck to escape the chill wind.

Within ten minutes, the tree was loaded and tied down. The teenager waved off a ride as he went to help another customer. Jake tugged open the door and leaned his shoulder against it. "You're in my seat."

"This is a very pretty truck." She turned her most endearing smile on him, sliding a reverent hand over the steering wheel. She'd always loved big, shiny trucks, but they were totally impractical in a city like LA. So she'd always had a sensible sedan. Because she was usually sensible. Except in the last twenty-four hours. She squashed that thought—it wouldn't help to remind herself that everything she'd done recently was out of character for her.

Jake fished his keys out of his pocket. A grin that she could only describe as pure evil curled his lips. He dangled the key ring from one finger in front of her. "You wanna drive it, sweetheart?"

Lust wound through her at just the thought of controlling the big red monster. "Yes."

"It'll cost you. A kiss."

She arched an eyebrow at him, letting a mocking smile curve her mouth. "Maybe I don't want to drive it that much."

"Yeah, you do." He set the keys to jingling, taunting her. When she didn't budge, he tucked the key ring back into his pocket and plucked a batch of something green off the dashboard, twirling the stem between his fingers. "Because you need a little extra incentive . . . they just so happened to have been selling mistletoe at the farm's entrance."

She wrinkled her nose at him. "Jake—"

"Come on, it's a Christmas tradition. Don't be a Scrooge." He held the mistletoe over her head, his smile tempting her, inviting her to give in. That's what Jake was—pure, sinful temptation.

She wanted to give in to that temptation. To him. Everything inside her swirled in chaotic dances of lust and longing. Betrayed by her own body. The desires she'd usually suppressed with Nathan wouldn't be still for Jake. She wasn't the one-night-stand kind of girl; she certainly wasn't Jake's kind of girl. She was a nice girl—always had been, always would be. Jake was naughty. Wanting him was . . . It was stupid. It was dangerous. It was irresistible.

She reached for him.

Curving her fingers around his wrist, she tugged down the hand holding the mistletoe and turned in the seat to face him. With gentle pressure, she pulled him forward until her breasts pressed against his chest. He watched her quietly, letting her direct this. He must have known she needed to take this first, totally sober step on her own. The man seemed to know her better than she knew herself sometimes. It was a disturbing thought. One she'd examine later.

Lifting her free hand, she slipped her fingers around his neck. His soft, short hair slid like silk against her palm, making her shiver. She pulled him down until she could feel the warmth of his breath on her skin. She licked her lips, and his pupils dilated as he followed the motion. He swallowed hard, his Adam's apple bobbing.

And then she did it.

Pressing her lips to his, she tilted her head to increase the contact. His goatee prickled against her skin. Electricity coursed through her body, and pure heat followed in its wake. It was better than she remembered. She flicked her tongue out, tracing the seam of his lips, probing for entrance. He groaned and opened his mouth. His hands tightened on her hips for a moment, yanking her flush against his body.

She wrapped her legs tight around his trim waist, moaning when he thrust against her through their jeans. The friction was enough to send her nerve endings screaming but not enough to fulfill her. Her sex dampened with utter want, her muscles fisting on nothingness each time his cock rubbed against her clit. The hard movements of his body were an exquisite contrast to the slow, worshipful way he kissed. Both actions made her blood rush through her veins, made her heart pound and her breathing speed to desperate little pants.

He broke away, dropping his sweaty forehead against hers. "If we don't stop, I'm going to fuck you right here, right now."

"Okay." The chilly wind was like being wrapped in ice, while Jake's fiery heat branded her everywhere they touched. She shuddered, fisted her fingers in his hair, and lifted his head up for another kiss.

The sound he made was halfway between a groan and a chuckle as he unhooked her legs from around his waist and stepped back. Her body screeched in protest, and she clenched her fingers to keep from reaching for him. She could see his erection straining against the fly of his pants. She wanted him inside her, thrusting hard.

"Stop looking at me like that. My control's hanging by a thread here." He dropped his key ring into her lap, tossed the crushed mistletoe to the snowy ground, and walked around to the passenger side.

Scooting into position, she closed the driver's door and clipped in her seatbelt. Jake hauled himself into the passenger seat. Sweat gleamed on his forehead, and he still breathed roughly. He adjusted the heater vents to point away from him, sliding out of his down vest and dropping it on the floorboard. It left him in just a long-sleeved, waffle-patterned undershirt. He pushed up the sleeves and braced an elbow next to the window. She tilted her chin toward him. "I didn't say no."

"Sweetheart, I really want to get naked with you again, and stopping now means you might not stop later. You'd have been embarrassed if we got caught with our pants down in a Christmas tree farm, and you wouldn't have let me talk you into sleeping with me again. Imagine the gossip about *that* if you didn't like the idea of getting drunk in public last night."

That made her grin. "Self-preservation of your sex life?"

A crack of laughter sounded from him, and he shifted in his seat to get more comfortable. She could still see the clear outline of his erection, and her hands itched to reach out and stroke him. She jerked her gaze away as he spoke. "Yeah. My sex life, your dignity. It's a win-win."

That was actually . . . thoughtful of him. She'd never expected the big, bad Jake Taylor to give a damn about what mattered to her long enough to put her wants above his. It was startling. There was a lot about him that she hadn't noticed before. She cautioned herself not to examine anything too closely. That was a dangerous road to let her mind wander down. Anything that happened between them was temporary. Nothing could come of this, but her body burned with a fire only he could put out. Maybe she should let him. Just once more. Her mind rebelled at the thought. No. No way in hell. It was something her mother would do, which meant Dayna wouldn't. Her hormones had other ideas, cajoling with her rational side. Maybe he wasn't the kind of guy for her, and she wasn't staying long enough to find out what else they might share besides animalistic chemistry, so what could it hurt to try it one more time? Yes. No. Yes. No. She didn't know. She always knew what she was doing and when she was doing it. She always had an organized list. She *always* had a plan. But not this time. Not with Jake.

Oh, God. She was in so much trouble.

5

Night had fallen by the time they pulled up in Rainbow's gravel driveway. Jake could see her shadow moving behind the curtains in her windows. He watched Dayna lean forward and look up at the sky through the truck's windshield. He frowned and followed her gaze. A million stars twinkled between the scattered clouds in the dark winter sky. It looked the same as it always did.

He pulled in a deep breath, trying to ignore the spicy rose scent of Dayna that permeated the cab of his truck. The heater was cranked too high, and the interior of the truck was warm and seemed to intensify the smell. He rubbed his knuckles under his goatee, slanting a glance at Dayna. She'd been silent the whole drive back. He could almost hear the wheels in her head churning, and he wasn't sure if that was a good sign or a bad sign. He sighed. It was one of the things he liked about her: someone as tightly wound as she was should be predictable, but she wasn't. Every now and then she let go of that inner control freak and surprised the shit out of him. She met his gaze, but he couldn't read her expression. He nodded toward the house. "You should go in. I'll be in with the tree in a minute."

"It's cold out there." She let her head fall back on the headrest, rolling it to face him. Desire shimmered in her pretty eyes. Her hair slid against her jaw, curving around her face.

He clenched his fingers to stop from slipping them into the silky locks, reminding himself that anyone could see through the windows of his truck. It might not bother him, but it did her. "Dayna . . ."

She laid a hand on his thigh, and every muscle in his body tensed, going on alert. His cock went rock hard in an instant. "What are you doing?"

"Being naughty." A siren's smile curled the corners of her full lips. "That's what you wanted, isn't it?"

He shouldn't reach for her. There was time enough to strip her bare without using the cab of his truck like teenagers. "This isn't exactly what I meant."

"Oh, I think this is exactly what you meant." Her knuckles feathered against his fly, and he damn near came in his jeans. Holy shit, the woman was enough to kill him. He wanted more.

His resistance fled. If she wanted this, right here, right now, then he wasn't going to stop her again—once in a day was about the extent of his gallantry. He slid his gaze over her, wondering how many times he could make her come before Rainbow noticed they were out here. "Hoped. I hoped for this, but this wasn't the whole point of me thinking you should loosen up, and you know it."

"I might loosen up. This once." She left the truck running but scooted out from under the wheel until her thigh pressed to his. She laid a hand on his shoulder, using it for leverage as she twisted around to straddle his lap. "Hey, you."

A rough chuckle rumbled out of his chest. Her warm breath

kissed his lips, and he searched her face. "This once? So, a little more temporary insanity, huh?"

"You have a problem with that?" She unzipped her jacket, wriggling out of it. It pressed her breasts against his chest, and he pinched his eyes closed. Damn, that was good. The friction was amazing.

"Nope. No problem." His eyes opened, watching the dim starlight dance over her face. His chest tightened, a knot of emotion he didn't even want to try to untangle twisting inside him. She was so beautiful. He cupped his palm around her cheek, running his thumb over her cheekbone. "Come here."

Her wide hazel eyes were a little too serious. He wanted to see her smile, but the moment intensified. He shook his head, trying to grin and lighten the moment, but couldn't. She leaned forward, tilting her head until she brushed her lips over his. The flavor of her filled his mouth as he stroked his tongue between her lips. She made a little noise in the back of her throat, her fingers sliding into his hair to fist tight. Her hips surged against his, and his hands dropped to her waist, curving around to cup her ass through her jeans. He pulled her closer, grinding his pelvis into hers. Fire exploded in his veins, shooting straight to his cock.

She broke the kiss, throwing her head back to gasp for breath. He opened his mouth on her exposed neck, biting and sucking little kisses down her throat. She giggled, shivered, and pulled away. "Your goatee tickles."

That sweet sound made him smile, made his chest tighten again.

"Oh, yeah?" He jerked her closer and rubbed his chin over her collarbone.

She squealed, laughing. "Jake!"

"You should laugh more often. I like it." He flicked his tongue against the curve of her neck, inhaling her unique scent. "Life's too short to be so serious."

"Says the man who's almost never serious." Her laughter had stopped and turned into a moan when he took the opportunity to close his hand over her breast, kneading the soft flesh.

He lifted his head, wanting to see the desire glaze her eyes. But their panting breath had overpowered the heater and fogged the windows, diffusing most of the light. His thumb zeroed in on her nipple, chafing it until it stabbed into his palm. "I seriously want to get in your panties right now."

She nodded in quick little jerks. Her fingers clenched in his shirt, tugging it up and over his head. He returned the favor, stripping off her top. Nudging her bra strap out of the way, he kissed his way down her chest until her breast slid free of the cup. His mouth closed over her tight little nipple, sucking the taut peak, batting it with his tongue. Her fingertips slid down his chest, her nails flicking hard over his own nipples.

He released her breast, and her hands slid down, down until she cupped his dick through his jeans. Her nimble fingers opened his pants until she was touching his overheated flesh. A groan ripped from deep inside him. "Jesus Christ."

"Now, Jake. I want you now." She didn't have to tell him twice. He wrestled her out of her pants, jerking open her zipper to shove the denim down her thighs while she stroked his hard cock. He cursed when he struggled with her shoes, but finally he had her legs free.

He grabbed her wrist, pulling her hand away from him. "Much more of that, and I'm not even going to make it inside you."

"You have quick recovery time, if I recall." She grinned, her white teeth flashing. Her fingers moved back to his chest, twisting his nipples hard.

"*Fuck.*"

Her smile widened. "That's what I'm trying to do here, in case you hadn't noticed."

"I noticed. I notice everything about you." Now, why had

he said that? He shook his head. The woman made him lose his mind. He stroked his hands up her back, flicking open the clasp on her bra, and finally, *finally* she was naked in his arms. God, yes.

"I love the way you touch me. I love the feel of your hands on my skin." She twisted in his embrace, rubbing her breasts against his chest. This. This was what turned him on about her. All that buttoned-up control until he had her in his arms. Then it burned away until she was pure greedy woman, shameless and wild. He loved that he could do this to her. He wanted to be the only one who ever did. She was all his. At least for tonight.

"That's good, sweetheart. I like touching you. I want to put my hands all over you." His hand slid around to cup her ass, pushing between the cheeks until his fingers swirled around her anus. Her breath caught, shock flashing in her gaze. He grinned. "You liked it when I fucked you here, didn't you, Dayna?"

"Yes," she breathed.

"Me, too."

Arching her back, she pressed against his probing finger until the tip slipped inside her ass. A little smile tugged at the corners of his lips. He pushed in a bit farther, stroking within her. Reaching between them to grasp his hard cock, she did some stroking of her own. He groaned, his hips thrusting into her touch.

"Condom," she gasped.

"Yeah." His free hand reached for his wallet, fumbling with the leather folds until he came up with a little foil square. He ripped it open with his teeth, and she grabbed it from him, unrolling it down the length of his dick. Sliding the head against her slick lips, she bit her bottom lip.

"Jake." She met his gaze, watching his face as she filled herself with him. Her smooth, wet muscles squeezed around him.

He shuddered, a muscle ticking in his jaw as he clenched it tight. He pushed his finger deeper into her ass until he could rub the head of his cock through the thin wall that separated the two.

Her head fell back, and she panted.

When she clamped her muscles around him, he saw her grin as he froze beneath her. His breath hissed out. "You're trying to kill me, aren't you?"

A husky laugh filled the cab of the truck. "It's a nice way to die, don't you think?"

"I'm not complaining." Hell, no. He was enjoying the ride like any man with half a brain would. The sexiest, smartest woman he knew was in his arms, and he intended to keep her there for as long as he could. Until she left. His gut clenched at that thought, but he tamped down on the feeling and focused on her.

"Good." The seat squeaked underneath them as they moved together, as she fucked him senseless.

"Sweetheart, you have no idea how good." He laughed because, damn, it was so amazing he didn't want it to ever end. He was walking a dangerous edge, but he couldn't seem to stop himself. He'd always had a thing for danger.

He was a risk taker. Over the years, he'd done every stupid stunt to gamble with his life. But this was more terrifying than all those stunts combined. This could lose him everything if it blew up in his face—his best friend, the people he considered family. Everything that really mattered to him. Was it worth it? For a fling with his friend's sister? No. But this didn't feel like a fling. It felt like . . . more. And if that wasn't the scariest part of the whole damn thing, he'd didn't know what was. His chest tightened until it threatened to choke him.

His lungs bellowed for breath, and he got a stranglehold on his thoughts. Best not to think about this. Especially not now. Shutting down his mind, he let his body take over. Thrusting his finger farther into her ass, he lifted his hips to shove his cock deeper inside her sleek pussy. She moaned, and the sound was the most erotic thing he'd ever heard. He watched her face, watched her eyelids droop and her focus turn inward.

He worked his finger and dick inside her in tandem and knew by her heavy breathing that she was close to orgasm. Her inner muscles flexed spasmodically around his cock, pushing him further and further until he had to fight his own orgasm. Pressing his free hand to the middle of her back, he arched her torso until he could dip forward to suck one of her pert nipples into his mouth. She screamed, twisting and sobbing as she worked herself faster and faster on his cock. "Jake! *Jake!*"

Her pussy convulsed around his dick, locking so tight that he couldn't have stopped himself from coming if a gun were pressed to his temple. His hips lifted until her knees left the seat, and he pounded inside her, a rough sound erupting from his throat. His eyes slammed closed, his muscles jerking as every feeling and sensation was ripped out of him. He came hard, her pussy milking him until he thought he would die.

No risk, no thrill, no other woman had ever taken him so high in his life. He never wanted to come down, never wanted to let go of this. Her. Ever.

The scent of roasting turkey and sweet potatoes twined with the spicy smell of the pine boughs, wreaths, and Christmas tree that decorated Rainbow's cabin. Dayna's mouth watered, and a smile curved her lips.

Christmas Day.

After the last few days of chaos and confusing emotions, it was comforting to have a moment where everything was in its place, just as it had been since they had moved in with her aunt. Rainbow stood at the kitchen stove stirring a pot of something that smelled delicious; she glanced over her shoulder, her hazel eyes twinkling. Rainbow looked like an older version of Dayna, her dark hair piled on top of her head, but she was as colorful as her name in a flamboyant caftan and snow boots.

Dayna let her smile widen, propping her shoulder against the kitchen windowsill to look out at the snow-covered yard. Toby and Sam had stayed the night, and her nephew had torn through all his gifts with boyish enthusiasm. The tree he'd picked out had twinkled with hundreds of colored lights, strewn with popcorn strings and homemade ornaments. All of it had delighted her nephew. There really was nothing like experiencing the holidays through a child's eyes.

The sound of Jake's deep laugh drifted across the yard. She watched her brother and nephew gang up on Jake in a snowball fight. White powder flew through the air, and the men played at the boy's level so he thought he was winning. His giggle was infectious.

"Cute as a button, that kid." Rainbow's voice sounded from behind her as the older woman wrapped her arms around Dayna and propped her chin on Dayna's shoulder.

Their heads leaned together, and Dayna let a deep sigh ease out. "He looks like Sam at that age."

"Mmmmhmmm." Her aunt squeezed her tighter. "You're troubled, honey. Do you want to talk about it?"

Did she mean Nathan or Jake? With Rainbow, you never knew. The woman saw too much. Whether she was as psychic as she believed or because she never missed a single detail, Dayna didn't know, but she also didn't know how to put into words everything that was going through her mind. "Not yet. I'm just . . . not ready."

"I'm here when you are." Rainbow kissed her cheek and let her go, wandering into the living room to leave Dayna to her muddled thoughts.

Every phone in the house trilled, making Dayna jolt. She heard Rainbow pick up the cordless phone and speak quietly, so Dayna returned to watching the scene outside. Jake scooped up Toby and spun him in a circle, falling back against a snow-bank. It made her smile. He really was great with her nephew. So many different sides to one man, so many things she'd never noticed. Things that attracted her even when she knew they shouldn't. Her smile faded, and she shook her head.

Things with Jake confused her. How had he done this to her in such a short span of time? A week ago there was no way she would have had sex in some guy's truck, let alone in her aunt's driveway. She hadn't even done things like that as a teenager. Thankfully, no one could have seen them. Their breath had made the windows fog as the heat inside met the cold outside air. But at that moment, she wouldn't have cared if anyone could see. A frisson of heat went through her at the memories. The way Jake touched her—rough and reverent at once—she'd never experienced it before. It felt so right when she knew it was wrong. Getting tangled up in random flings with her brother's best friend was not part of her plan.

Yet she couldn't deny she had loved every minute of it. Every stroke, every kiss, every sobbing breath.

Rainbow called from the other room. "Dayna, your mom's on the phone!"

Dayna closed her eyes, shutting out the lovely scene before her and the even lovelier memories as reality came crashing in. She didn't think she could deal with any more turmoil, and her mother was always high drama. Padding lightly on slippered feet, she crossed to the living room doorway. She whispered, "I really don't want to talk to her."

"It's Christmas." Disappointment filled Rainbow's eyes. Dayna knew her aunt wished things were better between her mother and her, but they were too different. If her mother could just maintain a little control over herself, if she could put someone else before her own wants, then maybe ... But it would never happen.

Dayna's insides twisted tight, and the same love and anger and resignation she always felt whenever she dealt with her mother crowded in to try to overwhelm her. She didn't think she could handle it today. Everything that was happening with Jake had her so confused she didn't know what to do. Sighing, she met Rainbow's gaze and knew she couldn't disappoint the older woman. She took the phone. "Hello?"

"Hi, baby." A babble of conversation in the background made it difficult to hear her mother's voice. Dayna pressed the receiver tighter to her ear and stuck a finger in her other ear to try to catch what her mom said next. "How's Nathan? I'm so sorry I couldn't stay to really meet him, but he looked like just the kind of man I always knew you'd end up with. I'm sure we'll have plenty of time to get to know each other next time you come visit."

Dayna's breath left her lungs in a rush as the havoc of the last few days punched her in the stomach. She couldn't do it. She couldn't tell her mother the truth. That she wasn't marrying the man she was supposed to end up with, that she was sleeping with a man she never should have touched. A flush of guilty pleasure burned her cheeks. The flashing lights of the Christmas tree blurred before her eyes. Clearing her throat, she turned the conversation on her mother and kept her voice light and teasing. "So, are you going to marry this new guy you ran away with?"

"Oh, no. Not him. It's just a little fun. Temporary insanity." Her musical laugh rippled through the phone. "I'm having a great time, going a little crazy. Merry Christmas, baby. I hope you're having as wonderful a holiday as I am."

A little fun. A little crazy. Temporary insanity. Dayna's words. Jake's words. They echoed inside her like a death knell.

Her mouth felt dry, her hands shaking. "I'm glad you're having a good time. Merry Christmas."

Someone called her mother's name in the background. She laughed again. "Okay, honey. I have to go. Merry Christmas! Happy New Year! Love you!"

The line went dead before Dayna could respond. She pushed the button that would turn off the phone and dropped it on the couch. Wrapping her arms around herself, she bent over at the waist and tried to catch her breath.

"Dayna!" Alarm sounded in Rainbow's voice. Her hand settled against the back of Dayna's neck, sending tingles racing down her limbs. "What's wrong?"

"What am I doing?" But she knew. God help her. "I'm turning into *her*."

The world tilted under her feet, and she felt nauseous. She'd thrown one man away and hooked up with another in a matter of hours. It wasn't like her. She didn't go through men like toilet paper—her mother did. She didn't do wild and crazy affairs—that was her mother's territory. The most important person in her mother's life was herself. And who was Dayna thinking about nonstop? Herself—what her body wanted now, not the important parts of her future. This had gotten out of hand, and she needed to stop it right now. She got a tight grip on the emotions she'd struggled to control for days, caging them into a tiny corner of her heart. Straightening, she forced air into her lungs, forced her mind and body to settle.

She shook her head, meeting her aunt's concerned gaze steadily. "I can't become her. That's not me, and I never want it to be."

Rainbow sighed, catching Dayna's face between her palms. "Oh, lamb. You can't control the people you love. You can't hold on so tight. Your mom has to be free. You can't worry about what she is—you just have to love her and live your life the best way you can."

Dayna's lips pressed together, and she swallowed. "You're a

free spirit, too, Rainbow. That doesn't make you irresponsible and selfish."

"We both know this isn't about your mother—she's been this way your whole life. You accepted it a long time ago." Rainbow's smile was soft and sympathetic. "No, this is about *you*."

Dayna's gaze dropped for a moment. "I don't know what you're talking about."

"It doesn't take a psychic to know what Jake dropping you off the morning after you got here means *or* what an extra half hour in a fogged-up truck means." A gentle, wise smile curved her lips. Then she gripped Dayna's jaw tighter, the smile falling away as her face settled into serious lines. "I'm happy for you, honey. I've always known this would happen someday, but you need to hear what I'm saying right now. I know that going from Nathan to Jake so fast scares you, that being in the middle of this thing with Jake before you even knew what you were getting into makes you feel like the world is spinning out of control, but *love* isn't about control—not of yourself and not of the man you're in love with. It's just love. That's all. You love him, or you don't, you have to let yourself go and fall sometimes. Trust that he'll catch you. He's a good man."

Dayna tightened her arms around herself, feeling like she was going to explode out of her skin. Her aunt's words made something snap inside her head, and she wanted to clamp her hands over her ears and scream. No. A thousand times no. This wasn't happening. It wasn't true. *No.* She shook her head so hard her short hair flew, whipping into her eyes. Her vision blurred, her breath speeding until she thought she'd pass out. She backed away from her aunt, slamming into the arm of the couch in her haste to escape. "I am *not* in love with Jake. And he certainly isn't in love with me. That's crazy. We're—we're nothing alike."

Her aunt's eyebrows contracted, and she tilted her head as though she hadn't understood what Dayna said. "Why do you need to be alike? You have more than enough calm and rational. You need someone who'll remind you to stop and smell the roses. He needs someone who'll give him roots, keep his feet on the ground. You *fit.* You balance each other. That's more important than being alike."

Something so sweet it was terrifying bloomed in her chest, but she shut it down. She forced a smile to her lips. "I hope you didn't have a vision about this, Aunt Rainbow, because I'd hate to prove you wrong." She popped a quick kiss on her aunt's cheek. "I'm going to go take a shower and get dressed. Then I'll be down to help you with dinner."

Rainbow sighed loudly. "You always were a stubborn child."

Dayna paused as she reached the stairs, her hand clenched on the railing. "I'm not a child anymore, Rainbow. I have to decide what's right for me. Jake isn't. We'd make each other crazy."

"There's nothing wrong with crazy, honey. I've been there for years." Rainbow hummed to herself, the sound of her steps fading into the kitchen. Dayna shook her head, snorted a laugh, and jogged up the staircase.

When she reached her room, she gathered some clothes and the new pair of earrings Toby had picked out for her—little reindeer wearing Santa hats. She walked across the hall and nudged the door closed with her foot. Stripping quickly, she tossed her pajamas on the closed toilet seat. Someone knocked on the door. "I'm taking a shower. Use the downstairs bathroom."

She was reaching for the lock when the door pushed open, and Jake stepped in. She fell back, grabbing a towel to cover herself. He lifted an eyebrow. "It's a little late for that, don't you think, sweetheart?"

It was. He'd seen everything she had to offer and then some.

She held on to the towel anyway, Rainbow's words flashing through her mind. It seemed scarier now that someone had used the *L* word. It was dangerous, unpredictable. Something she couldn't plan for. Her nerves jangled, and her fingers tightened on the towel. The soft terry cloth stimulated her sensitized skin. Just having Jake this close made her body heat, her nipples bead to hard points of need. "Wh—what are you doing in here?"

"I'll give you one guess." His gaze slid down her body, lingering on her bare legs. She had to clench them together as moisture flooded her sex. Fire streaked through her veins, and he hadn't even touched her. Yet.

He took a step toward her. She skittered back until her calves hit the side of the bathtub. When he reached out to catch her, she twisted away and hopped into the tub. "Jake, this is a bad idea."

"Maybe. Do it anyway." He just stepped into the tub with her, pressing her against the tile wall. He closed in until his chest brushed the tips of her breasts. His brilliant green eyes were more serious than she'd ever seen them. He searched her face, lifting his fingertips to brush them over her lips.

She swallowed, her lids dropping to half mast. "We're in the bathtub."

"You know, I noticed that." He smiled, the intense moment seeming to pass. "You said you needed to take a shower. Care to share?"

"Bad. Idea."

"And I thought nice girls like you were good at sharing." He grinned, stepping back a little. Relief made a sigh whistle from her throat. But he just bent over and unlaced his work boots. Toeing them and his socks off, he picked them up to toss them outside the tub. Reaching over his shoulder, he grabbed a fistful of his shirt and pulled it off. Light blond hair sprinkled his heavy pecs, stretching from one flat, brown nipple to the other. Black tattoos wound up his muscular arms, curving around to his back. The light gleamed on the ridges of his abs. She swallowed, her hands balling to stop herself from touching him. His long fingers popped the button on his jeans, and the rasp of his zipper sliding down sent shivers along her spine. Her body froze, arrested, as she watched every inch of that hard, muscular form come into view.

The pants eased down his legs until he stepped out of them. He pulled a condom out of the back pocket before they joined the growing heap of his clothes on the bathroom floor. Her gaze stayed glue on the rigid arc of his cock. She licked her lips, and it jerked. She looked at Jake's face and saw the way the skin had tightened over his sharp cheekbones, the flush of desire running under his skin, the lust that hardened his green eyes. He tore open the foil packet and sheathed himself quickly. Then he voiced a guttural demand. "Drop the towel, Dayna."

She obeyed, letting it fall away from her body. "I am so weak. I shouldn't be doing this, and I can't make myself stop."

"Me neither." He reached out a single finger, tracing a line along her collarbone.

Swallowing, she let her head rest against the shower wall. "This isn't just fun anymore."

"Yeah." That finger slid down until he circled her nipple. Pleasure zinged straight to her core, making her pussy throb and clench.

She licked suddenly dry lips. "Then what is it?"

"I don't know, sweetheart." He shook his head, still stroking her breast in that slow, maddening way. "I just know I want you."

"I'm leaving after New Year's." She said it because she needed to remind herself, but he winced at the word *leaving*.

"I know." His Adam's apple bobbed as he swallowed, struggled to regain his usual levity. It didn't come. He reached out one hand to flip on the shower knobs, blocking the spray until hot water flowed out. Within moments they were both soaked, and the hot beads of moisture made the moment even more sexual.

Her gaze locked with his—that sweet, terrifying something forming a huge, golden bubble inside her. She couldn't look away, couldn't dismiss the emotion, couldn't dismiss him the way she had every other man she'd ever been with. They'd all been the same: the same as her. Just like Rainbow said. Not Jake—Jake was different. She wanted to deny it, to run away, to escape everything she felt, to regain some internal balance. Withdrawing into herself, she tried to keep her emotions contained. She was usually so good at it, but this week had her unraveling at the seams.

Cupping her shoulders, he turned her around to face the wall, and he nudged her thighs apart with his knee. He captured both wrists with one hand, stretched them over her head, and pinned them against the tiles. Startled, she jerked at her hands but couldn't free herself. His body crowded her against the wall, and she couldn't move at all. It was even more constricting than when he'd pinned her legs down. A flutter of panic went through her at the lack of control. "Jake, I—"

His free hand parted the globes of her ass, and he entered her pussy from behind in one hard push. Her breath caught as a hundred sensations ricocheted through her at once: the heat, stretch, and intense pleasure of him deep inside her; the water running over her wherever they didn't touch, sealing them together where they did. A shiver ran through her, and her nipples hardened painfully, stabbing into the unyielding tiles. His lips played over the side of her neck, kissing his way up until he sucked her earlobe into his mouth.

"Dayna, I love . . ." Her muscles froze as her whole existence hung on how he ended the sentence. ". . . I love the feel of you. You're so tight and wet."

Her hormones reacted to his words, slicking her pussy with

even more moisture, making her wetter than she'd ever been in her life. But her heart stumbled, and she refused to believe that she might be disappointed. She just needed him to let her loose, not to hold her so tightly.

Twisting her wrists, she tried to get free again, but it was a futile gesture. He had her right where he wanted her, and there wasn't a thing she could do about it—except enjoy herself. Her pussy throbbed around his cock at just the thought. She shouldn't like the loss of control, and her mind protested it, but it was drowned out by the needs of her body. And every inch of her reacted to his nearness. She had no idea what she was doing with him, where this was going except to a dead end. It was crazy. She yanked at her hands again, her sex burning with an intensity she'd never experienced before. It wasn't . . . She shouldn't . . .

He rolled his pelvis against her, changing the angle of his thrusts. The thoughts, the fears, the uncertainties—they all slid away until there was nothing but Jake's hands and Jake's mouth and Jake's hard, thrusting cock. He could so easily become the center of her world. If she let him—if he even wanted her to. A sob caught in her throat. Her body wanted one thing, and her mind wanted another. It was going to rip her apart. Tilting her head back against his shoulder, she let a tear run down her cheek to mingle with the shower water.

He slid his tongue down her exposed throat, his goatee rasping her sensitive flesh until he bit down lightly on the sensitive spot where her shoulder met her neck. The world spun round and round until there was only this moment she had with him. She clenched her pussy around his dick with each hot push inside her.

"Damn, sweetheart," he groaned. "That is so good, so fucking amazing."

Sucking in a breath, she pushed her ass back against him

harder. The tears fell faster, but a smile curved her lips. "Will you shut up and make me come already?"

He just laughed and did exactly what she wanted him to. Cupping her hip in his free palm, he pulled her deeper into his rocking thrusts, powering into her in short, hard jabs. His other hand tightened around her wrists, holding her still. Her body burned hotter than she'd ever imagined possible *because* he held her down. She moaned, and it echoed in the bathroom.

Her eyes popped wide, and she bit her lip to muffle her next whimper. Her sex closed around him, milking his cock.

"Jesus Christ, Dayna." Reaching around her, he moved his fingers over her hardened clit. He ground his hips against her, plunging faster and faster inside her. Their skin slapped together, the sound loud and undeniable in the closed-in shower. He froze behind her, his pelvis slamming forward in quick thrusts as he came. He groaned, "Dayna. My Dayna."

She sobbed, pulling at her hands weakly, but it was too late, she was already exploding in his arms. Pleasure sucked her down into a whirlpool so deep she thought she'd drown. Her pussy fisted tight, spasming as her orgasm went on longer than she thought possible. Fire and ice tingles raced over her skin, and she shuddered with the low sobs that tore from her throat. She couldn't stop them, couldn't stop the pleasure, couldn't stop the pain as every emotion she'd tried to keep under wraps for so long was dragged out of her.

"Shhh. Shhh. It's all right, sweetheart. I have you. It's all right. Shhh." He'd released her wrists, holding her tight in his embrace. The tears coursing down her cheeks slowed until only hiccupping little breaths shook her body. He rocked her gently, stroking her wet hair away from her face. She finally relaxed against him, spent and exhausted.

Snagging the soap from the ledge of the tub, he smoothed his palms over her in slow circles. If he lingered over her breasts or between her legs, she wasn't about to complain. She loved having his hands on her and leaned into his touch. When he was finished, he lifted her out of the tub, set her on the counter, and dried her off with her discarded towel. She didn't protest, didn't try to take the towel away to do it herself—she just let herself be pampered. It felt like the most natural thing in the world, and she was too drained to care that it was wrong to think that way.

He pulled away to let her blow-dry her hair, grabbing a towel to dry himself off before he picked up his clothes and re-dressed. In the mirror, she saw him slide a glance in her direction. "Hey, sweetheart?"

"Yeah?" She shut down the drier, running a brush through her hair.

"Are you working on a book deadline right now?" He laid her clothes on the counter, sitting on the toilet seat to pull on his socks and boots.

She shrugged, pulling on her clean clothes. "Aren't I always? They come one right after the other, usually."

"That's what I thought." He stood up, reaching for his dis-carded shirt. "I was thinking you might want to come over to my place, get away from the family for a bit, and do some work. I know I get a little antsy if I'm not letting the creative juices flow for more than a few days."

"Yeah. I love my work." It was odd that they had that in common. She'd never really thought of tattooing as a creative art, but he did draw most of the designs himself—he just used human flesh as his canvas. Which sounded stranger than it really was. She shot him a look and smiled, getting back to his original suggestion. "But I wouldn't get any *work* done at your house with you there. Nice try."

He stole her brush from her and made quick work of slick-ing back his hair. "Then it's a good thing I'm going to be working part time at the shop for the rest of the week. Five to nine in the evenings."

"That's a little late, isn't it?" But her heart leaped at the thought of losing herself in her writing. As frustrating as it could be to find the right words to describe her characters' emotions and actions, it was also comforting, familiar. She could use the familiar right now just as much as she would love to bury herself in something she loved so much.

Love. Everything seemed to be circling back to that today.

Jake shrugged and then scooped up both their towels and hung them to dry. "It's not really that late for me. I usually work until midnight. Think about when people get tattoos."

"After work." She nodded. That made sense, though it meant he always had to be on a schedule opposing everyone else's. It didn't surprise her—Jake didn't feel the need to be normal like she did. Well, as normal as any writer could be, but she did keep herself on a regular schedule. She liked the structure and order it gave her life.

"Yeah. So, I thought you could use a few hours of peace and quiet to work. When I get off, I can come home, and we can both get off." He made a little growling noise and bent forward to nip the lower slope of her ass cheek.

"Jake!" She squeaked and giggled, spinning to face him.

He grinned at her, his green eyes dancing. "I love it when you laugh."

"You bit my butt!"

"He bit your butt?" Toby and Sam's voices both echoed outside the door. The knob rattled as one of them tried to come in.

Dayna reached out and opened the door, glancing back at Jake. His face had gone completely blank.

The look on Sam's face clearly told them they better know what they were doing.

Did she? She shot the silent Jake another look. Still a stone wall. He obviously hadn't wanted her brother to find out he was shagging her, and that said just about everything she needed to know, didn't it? Jake was never shy about his sex life. He didn't brag, but he didn't hide it either.

Rainbow was wrong. He didn't love her. And she didn't want him to . . . did she?

6

Three days later, Jake was still grinning. He tapped his fingers on the steering wheel as a rock rendition of "Auld Lang Syne" came on the radio in his truck. He didn't even like the song, but his good mood wouldn't quit. Then again, any man who'd had days on end of, hands down, the best sex of his life would be grinning nonstop, too.

He'd been right. When Dayna let herself go, she was phenomenal. Watching her loosen up the last few days had been beyond amazing. He'd loved every minute of it. Three nights of her in his bed, and the longer she was there, the wilder she became.

A little encouragement was all she'd needed, and she was ready, willing, and able to do whatever he wanted, whenever he wanted. She'd really given herself over to this affair.

Then again, Dayna wasn't a woman for half measures. When she was uptight, she was really uptight. Now that she'd given herself permission to relax—if only for the week—she was really throwing herself into it.

He hoped she would take some of that with her when she went back down to the corporate ladder climbers in LA.

His smile faded a bit.

The thought of someone else touching her made his hands clench on the wheel, and he fought back the reaction. He wasn't possessive of her, he was just concerned for her well-being. He wanted her to be happy, and she needed to see that some up-tight asshole who encouraged *her* to be uptight was not going to do that for her. She needed a guy who'd remind her to live a little. Not that he was applying for the job, but he could push her in the right direction.

And if he got to have some of the most intense sex of his life in the process, he wasn't about to complain. His grin returned. It was going to be a damn good day. He'd pick Dayna up, take her back to his house so she could write, drive to work, tattoo for a few hours, and then head home to Dayna.

Home. Dayna. It felt a little too domestic, too comfortable. He swallowed hard and reminded himself for the hundredth time since this had started that she was leaving. It was temporary. Then they'd go back to the way things were before.

He'd known Dayna long enough to know she wasn't the kind of woman to indulge in a little no-strings sex on a long-standing basis. He might have her this week, but he knew it was over as soon as she left town. Then he'd just be her younger brother's best friend again.

The emotion that had fisted in his chest so often lately began a painful burn. He swallowed and shoved it aside. He wasn't his father; he wasn't going to get too attached. He'd had women go from friend to lover to friend again. This was no different, es-pecially considering the whole affair would last only a week.

Forewarned was forearmed. He'd be fine. *They'd* be fine. His lips twisted. At what point he'd gone from thinking of this as a little fun to something he had to worry about later, he didn't know.

He snorted. Something else to worry about later. Right now, he was going to enjoy his time with Dayna. Enjoy this moment. He couldn't deal with the future now, he could just get his fill of her body, her laugh, her smile, her face. A lifetime's worth of enjoyment in one week.

When he turned on to Rainbow's street, he saw the older woman driving in from the opposite direction. She pulled into the driveway, and he parked his truck behind her car. Popping open his door, he stepped out into the slushy powder on the driveway and reminded himself to shovel it and the walkway before Rainbow did it herself. The stubborn woman didn't want to admit that she was getting a little too old to do it all herself. He grinned at her as he shut his door, meeting her at her passenger-side door where she lifted a sleeping Toby out of the car.

Rainbow gave him a narrow-eyed glance. "I'm glad I have you alone for a minute. I've been meaning to talk to you."

"Oh, really?" He fought a wince and let his smile widen into his most charming. There were so many things she might want to have a little chat about, and he couldn't think of one of them he'd enjoy. He had a feeling this one might be about his affair with Dayna, but he wasn't incriminating himself by asking, just in case he was about to get chewed out for something else.

She waved her free hand at him, cuddling Toby's limp body against her chest. "Don't give me that pretty smile, Jacob Taylor. I'm too old to fall for that crap."

"No one is too old, honey." He winked at her.

Then she swatted his shoulder with that same hand. "Be serious, Jake. I want to talk to you about Dayna."

Well, shit. He braced himself for a discussion on anything from dismemberment for messing with her niece to safe sex to *Kama Sutra* position suggestions. You just never knew with Rainbow. "What about Dayna?"

"You've been working on getting her to decompress this

week. I don't want details on your methodology for that"—she paused to offer a wicked, knowing little smile that faded as quickly as it had come—"but I do what to know what your endgame is."

He lifted an eyebrow, uncertain what she was getting at. "There has to be an endgame?"

"Don't be cute. You've known Dayna a long time. You know she doesn't take sex lightly. If she just wanted an orgasm, she would have used a vibrator." She talked over the little choking laugh Jake gave. "I want to know what you think you're doing. Is this just a quick lay or . . . what? I can't believe you would ever hurt Dayna on purpose. Knowing how she is, and knowing how long you've had a yen for her, I'm just not sure how you expect all this to work out."

"I would *never* hurt her." The words jerked out of him, a reflex of pure honesty. He rubbed a hand over his mouth and down his goatee. Confronted with Rainbow's words, with the truth of what he *knew* about Dayna, he had a gut-wrenching moment of pain. She was going to get hurt by this. He'd never wanted that. Shaking his head, he met Rainbow's hazel eyes—eyes so like Dayna's. "I did want her to unwind and not worry so damn much about having everything be perfect. I just . . . wanted to show her what she was missing."

The older woman snorted, patting Toby's back when he stirred a little. "You showed her, all right. Showed her she was missing *you.*"

"Don't *say* that," he snapped. He closed his eyes, that band of emotion tightening around his chest until he couldn't breathe through it. "She's leaving in a few days. Then we'll go back to how it always was."

"Ha. Things with Dayna have always been like a pot waiting to boil over. And now it has. It's not going to go back to how it was, especially considering how deep in denial the two of you have always been about how you really feel about each other."

Her sharp look cut off his protest, and he snapped his mouth shut when she spoke again. "Let me put it to you this way: When was the last time you felt jealous when you were with a woman? When was the last time you *weren't* jealous when Dayna was with another man?"

Swallowing, Jake clenched his fists, anger and too many other dark feelings twisting through him to handle at once. "It doesn't matter how long I've wanted her. It doesn't matter if I was jealous. She'll be gone after New Year's."

And that was the real problem, wasn't it? He was in deeper with her than he'd ever been before, and he knew she was going to be the one leaving, not him. She'd end it, not him. He could end it now, but he didn't want to. He didn't even think he could force himself. Fuck, fuck, *fuck*.

Rainbow sighed. "Honey, I know you think you have to be the one to walk away. I knew your father and your mother, so I understand why you feel that way. But what happens when you find a woman you want to keep?"

"I—" Rainbow's words echoed his thought so clearly, for the first time in his life he actually wondered if she was telling the truth when she said she was psychic. He shook away the asinine thought.

A gust of wind and snow blew a lock of her long, dark gray hair in her face. She swatted it away impatiently. "Ask yourself, when did protecting yourself by always being the one to run become self-destructive? When did it stop being protection and start keeping you from what you wanted?"

"Shit." He sighed. Everything that had been whirling through his head and heart for days came pouring out. "I don't know what the hell I'm doing anymore. It was just supposed to be a little fun—I've done it a hundred times before."

"Oh, Jake. You're an idiot." She patted his shoulder, sympathy in her gaze. Her head gave a little shake. "Dayna was never going to be like all the other girls. She's your soul mate. You've been half in love with her since you were a kid. You just finally fell the rest of the way."

Yes. The band snapped, and all those tumultuous feelings fell into place. It fit. Dayna was different, special. She'd always been special. She'd always been *his*. It had just taken them both this long to reach out and take it. He closed his eyes and swallowed several times, working to make his mouth form the words. "I do love her. Fuck. I fell so fast, I didn't even have time to run."

"Sugar, it's time you stopped running away from being like your daddy. You're nothing like him. And Dayna's nothing like your mother. She's nothing like *her* mother either." She lifted her eyebrows, her expression and tone telling him how much he and Dayna had tried her patience by being dense. "You tell her you love her, you ask her to stay, and she'll never leave you. My girl is a stubborn one—she'll stick it out with you through good times and bad."

Don't leave. Stick it out. Ask her to stay. The breath squeezed out of Jake's chest in harsh puffs, clouding the cold air in front of him. Something so sweet it was almost painful dug roots deep within his soul. No running this time. Ask her to stay. He could. What was to stop him? He'd never know if Dayna wanted to see what else could happen between them if he never said anything.

And he sure as hell wouldn't know if he stood out here freezing his balls off.

"Thanks, Rainbow." He popped a quick kiss on her wrinkled cheek. Wrapping his fingers around her elbow, he helped her up the walkway so she wouldn't slip on the new snow.

Time to face the music.

Nathan was the last person Dayna had expected to show up at the door, but that didn't change the fact that he was sitting on her aunt's couch.

"It looks like you're going somewhere." His dark eyes searched her face, taking in the bag she had slung over her shoulder. "I'll take up only a minute of your time. I'd like to speak with you."

She'd been home alone and had really enjoyed having the house to herself. Rainbow and Toby had run to the store, Sam was working, and Jake was supposed to be there in a few minutes to pick her up and take her to his place to write. She'd packed up her laptop, making sure she had her backup flash drive with her. A wide smile had broken over her face when she'd heard the rumble of a big engine pulling up to the curb in front of the house. Jake.

She was no closer to figuring out what was going on between them, but she'd stopped trying to resist the physical pull Jake had on her. It could wait until she got back to the city, until she sorted everything out with Nathan, until she had some emotional distance on the situation and could make some rational decisions. While she was home, she was doing what Jake had suggested. She was loosening up just a little and enjoying what he was offering her. He didn't mention the future, and neither did she, existing in the unsettled—but highly pleasurable—limbo of *now*.

Anticipation had bubbled within her, making a huge smile curve her lips. Jake. She couldn't wait to see him, to touch him. Slinging her bag over her shoulder, she'd hurried to the front door to meet him on the porch and come face to face with Nathan. Heart jolting, every muscle in her body had gone rigid as she'd fought the screaming need to slam the door shut.

The breath had seized in her lungs. Of all the people in the world she had not wanted to see right then, her ex-fiancé topped the list. Rocking back on her heels, she'd let him in, numbness spreading through her as the shock wore off. She'd glanced over his shoulder, hoping against hope that Jake would show up to save her from this. All she'd seen was a blue SUV parked on the street in front of the house. Nathan's new rental, apparently, but no sign of Jake's big red monster.

Dragging her thoughts back to the present, she forced herself to focus on the man before her. She was going to have to deal with him on her own. "Wh—what are you doing here, Nathan?"

He clasped his hands loosely between his thighs, elbows braced on his knees. "I've been thinking about some of the things you said before I left, and I think we should calmly discuss it, now that our tempers have cooled. I think we behaved rashly. I don't want to throw away a long-term relationship over one visit with your family."

Her stomach twisted into knots so tight she wasn't sure how she kept her lunch down. "My family will always be my family, Nathan. If you can't get along with them—"

"I can. I can make an effort when we're here. Our life is in Los Angeles, but I know I can keep the peace whenever we come visit them." What she wouldn't have given for him to have said those words a week ago, for him to have shown even an ounce of understanding and compassion—traits that came so naturally to Jake, but not to Nathan . . . and not to Dayna either.

Should she tell him about Jake? No. No, that wouldn't be fair. Telling him would only hurt him, and it would be a selfish way to unburden herself of guilt. The problem was, she felt guilty for . . . not feeling guilty. She couldn't bring herself to regret her time with Jake. It had been wonderful.

And yet—and yet looking at Nathan, she remembered why she'd thought he was so perfect for her. She knew what he was thinking, what he was feeling, how he would react because he thought and acted much the same way she did. Not Jake though—as much as she knew about him, he would always be predictably unpredictable. She liked that about Jake. She also liked that she could read Nathan like the back of her hand. It was comforting.

But . . . did she want to be comfortable for the rest of her life? Jake challenged her, made her think, made her grow. Nathan never would. He would always want her to be exactly who and what she was now. Did that mean he accepted her or that he stifled her?

She didn't know.

A bitter little smile twisted her lips. She'd lost count of the number of times in the past week she'd thought, *I don't know*. Well, if she didn't know what she wanted—who she wanted— she'd better not throw away what she might want later.

She pulled in a deep breath. "Nathan, I'm willing to think about giving us a second chance, but I can't say yes right now. I need some time to think."

Nodding slowly, he pushed himself to his feet. Curling his hands over her shoulders, he kept his dark gaze level with hers. "Take all the time you need. I want us to be together, I want to marry you, and I can learn to bend when it comes to your family. I'll do what it takes to keep you."

But could he keep her happy? Could he make her laugh at private jokes and scream in pleasure at night? She wanted him to be able to, wanted him to give her everything Jake did and more. She'd always thought Nathan was the one for her, and if he could match her physically, maybe they'd have a better shot. She'd learned enough about herself lately to know that shoving aside her body's needs didn't make them go away. And when they demanded satisfaction, there was little she could do to quell them. She didn't even want to. She wanted to embrace that part of herself. Could she do that with Nathan?

"I'm staying at the inn on Third Avenue." A thin smile curved his lips. "They had a cancellation."

She snorted a soft laugh. "Figures."

He bent forward to kiss her, and her first instinct was to turn her head and let him kiss her cheek. Instead she threw herself into the kiss, wrapped her arms around his neck, and plunged her tongue into his mouth to encourage him to respond. She needed to know if he could bend for her in this area as well. She could feel his surprise, and his fingertips came up to rest on her back. He tilted his head to deepen their contact, and his erection pressed thick and hard to her lower belly. She willed herself to feel something. Anything.

She didn't.

No, actually, she felt nauseous. She dropped her arms, grabbed his wrists to pull them away, and tried not to heave as her body rebelled against what she was forcing it to do.

Then the front door swung open. She jerked back from Nathan, turning to see Rainbow holding Toby. And Jake. She opened her mouth to . . . what? Explain? Justify herself? Apologize?

It didn't matter what she might have said—the look of stunned, agonized betrayal on Jake's face made the words tangle in her throat. Then his face went blank, his eyes hollow. He took a step back, two, and then turned and walked away.

Shock rolled through Dayna in icy waves, and her body began to shake. Tears welled in her eyes, blurring the image of him climbing into his truck and calmly pulling away from the house.

He never looked back.

And then she knew. She finally knew. Rainbow was right. She was in love with Jake, and she'd ruined everything. The look on his face would be burned into her memory forever. In all the years she'd known him, all the pain and loss and wild insanity she knew he'd been through, she'd never once seen him wear an expression like that before. It made her believe that Rainbow was right about that, too. Jake was in love with her.

Jake, who didn't do forever but didn't believe in infidelity, who'd seen Dayna kissing another man while in the middle of a love affair with him.

Oh, God.

The world closed in around her as realization of how badly she'd mangled things flooded her mouth with a bitter taste.

Fifteen minutes. Things had gone from bright and beautiful to an unspeakable disaster in fifteen short minutes. She managed to haul herself up to her room to lick her wounds and try to do what she did best. Make a plan. Figure things out.

Dayna's knees gave out from under her, and she collapsed on the bed. She couldn't make her mind focus. It gibbered uselessly from one panicked thought to the next.

What was she going to do now? What did she really want, and how was she going to get it? Would Jake ever forgive her? What would she do if he didn't?

She didn't know. She just didn't know anything anymore.

Hours later, Dayna still had tears streaking down her face, curled up on her mattress and sobbing as if the world had ended. Not even Rainbow could lend any comfort, no matter what her visions said.

Something precious had died, and Dayna had lost it before she knew she had it. God help her. She'd been happier in the last few days than she'd been . . . ever. And it was because of Jake. He made her smile, made her laugh, made her relax and not analyze everything to death or worry so much about what other people thought of her. She hadn't even felt the need to write more than a couple of lists in the last week. It was unnerving. It was wonderful.

It was over.

7

Jake didn't sleep. He didn't eat. He just sat in his house, staring out the huge window in his living room overlooking the snow-frosted lake. He'd always loved this view. It was why he'd bought the place. His eyes burned with exhaustion when he forced himself to his feet the next afternoon. Time for work. He had to work. That was all he had left.

It had been almost twenty-four hours since he'd seen the worst nightmare of any man in love.

The woman he loved kissing another man.

Dayna. Nathan.

Even now, the memory had enough power to make Jake's stomach heave. It was just like with his parents. His father loved, his mother left. Another man.

But Jake wasn't his father. And he'd done the one thing his father had never done. The one thing Jake *always* did.

He'd walked away.

Nothing had ever made Jake feel so empty. He should have been jealous, should have punched Nathan for touching her, but he didn't. He couldn't even wrap his mind around anything else but pure, blinding agony. His body had gone numb, but his heart felt as if it had been ripped, beating, from his chest.

The pain just wouldn't quit. From the moment he'd left Dayna, it had eaten him up inside. He suddenly had a hell of a lot more sympathy for his father than he'd ever had before. Sympathy he'd never wanted. He closed his eyes, swallowing.

The only thing keeping him upright was the knowledge that he'd done the right thing for both Dayna and himself by walking away. It didn't matter that it felt like shit; it was the right thing to do.

Walking into the bathroom, he took a quick shower. He didn't let himself look at the bed when he passed it, didn't let himself think about the times he'd made love to Dayna in his room, in his shower. It wouldn't happen again. She'd gone back to Nathan. He shut down that line of thought, hustling to get ready. To get away from his own house.

When he stepped out of the bedroom, his best friend's fist connected with his gut, and he was on his knees before he knew what was coming. His breath rasped in his throat as he fought for breath. Pain echoed through his entire body, but after the night he'd had, it didn't even faze him.

"You know, I'm starting to think giving you a key to my house was a bad idea," Jake wheezed out when he could breathe again. He glanced up, met Sam's furious hazel gaze, and decided to stay right where he was on the floor. "I was trying to do the right thing, man."

Sam's knuckles whitened, and he clenched his fists tighter. His jaw worked for a moment before he spat, "How? By fucking with her life and her mind and then dropping her like she's some skank you picked up in my bar?"

"It's not like that." Jake pulled up his knees, propping an arm across them. His other hand rubbed over his aching abs.

Shit, Sam packed a hell of a punch. Years of bouncing drunks out of a bar had improved his aim, too. He'd never been *that* good in a fight.

"Right, it's not like that." Sam snorted. "It's not as if I didn't know you were sleeping with her, but I thought you would keep her away from that dumbass she was engaged to. But you used her for a little while the way you have every other woman since the day we both started dating and then ditched her when it got too heavy for you. I know how you operate, so, tell me, how else could it possibly be, Jake?"

Letting his head fall back against the doorjamb, Jake closed his eyes. "She deserves everything she wants, Sam. She wants a straight-laced, suit-wearing guy. She should have it." He swallowed, pressing his fingers against his eyelids. God, it hurt so damn bad. Like a thousand pounds of lead weight was sitting on his chest, crushing the breath out of him. "I was so sure I knew what was best for her, what she really needed. I was a stupid, selfish son of a bitch."

He opened his eyes to see a look of mingled surprise, disgust, and pity on the other man's face. "Ah, hell. You're in love with her."

A rusty laugh wrenched out of Jake. "Tell me something I don't know."

Sam's dark eyebrows drew together in a deep frown. "Then why are you pushing her back to him?"

"I'm doing what my dad couldn't do." Tears stung his eyes, and he turned his head, coughing. "I'm letting her go and hoping she gets exactly what she wants. *Because* I love her."

"Damn." Concern edged Sam's voice. Yeah, the man knew everything about Jake—even more that the rest of the Sharps. How he'd grown up, his experiences since, his fears. All of it. "Jake—"

Jake shook his head, sighed, and met the hazel gaze that he

associated as much with Dayna as he did with Sam. He lifted his hands in a placating gesture. "Don't worry about me. I'm not going to bury myself in a bottle. I'll get over it eventually, and I'll move on. If I'm not what she wants—what she needs—then it's best she go now, you know?"

"Yeah." Something flashed in Sam's eyes, some bit of painful wisdom, but it came and went in an instant. "Yeah, I know."

Jake squinted up at him, knowing Sam well enough to realize he shouldn't ask how he understood what Jake was going through with Dayna. "You gonna hit me again if I get up?"

Sam chuckled, holding out his hand. Jake grabbed it and let himself be hauled to his feet. "I'm sorry it didn't work out, brother."

"Me, too." Jake took a breath and realized he *had* done the right thing. He wasn't just saying it over and over, he really meant it. That was the real difference between him and his old man. The woman his father had loved hadn't loved him back, had wanted someone else, and his dad hadn't been able to accept it, to heal, to get on with his life. Jake would.

He knew it was going to hurt like hell for a long, long time, but he also knew it was best. If she didn't want him now, they'd be setting themselves up for a whole lot more pain down the road. And the thought of her getting hurt because of him . . . He couldn't handle that. *That* would kill him. A shaky breath slid out. Yeah, he'd done the right thing, and eventually he and Dayna would both be okay, a little wiser, knowing themselves a little better, but . . . okay.

He could live with that.

Dayna walked into Jake's shop an hour before closing. The low buzz of a tattoo gun filled the air. A gray-haired woman lay on her side on a black table facing the far wall. She had her sweatshirt pulled up to reveal her ribs, which was what Jake bent over with a look of concentration. He didn't so much as glance toward the door when a chime sounded to announce her entrance. "Be with you in a bit."

Just seeing him settled something deep inside her. Yes. This was what she really wanted. She'd already made her choice and sent Nathan back to LA. He might want to debate with her about it in his very lawyerly way, and he might not understand that they'd never be good for each other, but she hoped he would understand someday. Now she just had to convince Jake they could work things out between them. If he was even willing to listen. She knew how he felt about any kind of unfaithfulness, and anxiety twisted inside her. Would he be less forgiving of a woman he was in love with? Would he be able to understand how scared she'd been, how torn and confused?

Her heart thumped hard in her chest, and she spun to face the wall. She pulled in a slow breath and forced herself to focus on something else. Panicking wouldn't help. A funky-looking Christmas tree made out of sheet metal stood against the wall, and behind it the wall was decorated with sample tattoos—more were available in photo albums sitting on a table. She let her gaze move over the wall, knowing most of the artwork was Jake's. It was beautiful. The colors and lines and attention to detail made a statement all its own about how talented he was. She'd seen some of his work over the years, his sketches and his tattoos, but this showed her so clearly how huge a part of his life it was. Just like her writing. The pieces fell into place so easily, so neatly. No matter how it appeared on the surface, the two of them fit.

Dayna cast a quick glance at him over her shoulder, and her heart squeezed. He was such a gorgeous man—wicked and kind in equal measures. Just what she wanted forever. She squared her shoulders and lifted her chin. It might have taken her far too long to figure it out, but now that she had, she wasn't letting him walk away again. Ever.

His deep rumble of a voice soothed the woman he was working on when she flinched away from him a bit. "Almost done. Hang in there for another few minutes while I finish the shading."

She snorted. "I gave birth to five boys, Jacob. You want to talk about pain, I'll tell you about pain."

"Yes, ma'am." He chuckled, never pausing in the sure movements of his hands. "You're gonna have to show this off to your students."

Dayna's mouth dropped open when she realized Jake was tattooing her eighth-grade math teacher, Mrs. Simpson. Then she grinned. Figures he would be able to corrupt her, too. *Way to go, Jake.* She took off her coat, set it on a chair, slid her hands in her pockets, and waited.

Jake sat back and set down his gun, grinning at Mrs. Simpson. "All right, that should do it." He reached behind him and grabbed a small hand mirror. "Take a look."

Rolling so she could sit up, Mrs. Simpson twisted to see the tattoo. Her eyes widened, and she touched the mirror and what it reflected reverently. "Oh, I love it."

"That's what I like to hear." He bandaged the area and ran through aftercare procedures as he helped her to her feet.

She righted her clothing, a smile wreathing her wrinkled features. "I've always wanted to get one of these, but my husband wouldn't have liked it. Now that he's gone . . . well, it doesn't really matter what anyone but me thinks, does it?"

"Not a bit." He smiled back, cupping her elbow to steady her on her feet. "I'm glad you like it. You call me or come back in if you run into any problems or have any questions."

"I will." She tucked a wad of cash into his hand, kissed his cheek, and picked up her purse, still wearing that wide, delighted grin.

"Thank you, ma'am." His big body froze when he finally glanced up at Dayna. Some emotion flashed in his eyes, but he masked it. Walking to the door, he held it open for Mrs. Simpson. "Good night."

He shut the door and locked it, flipping off the light to the neon sign that said OPEN. Then he moved to his table, wiped it down with disinfectant, started cleaning up the tattooing equipment, and stripped off the rubber gloves he wore. His voice was flat and emotionless. "What can I do for you, Dayna? I figured you'd be hanging out with your family . . . and your fiancé."

"Well, you were wrong." She pulled her hands out of her pockets and crossed her arms protectively in front of her.

He shot her an icy glance. "Wouldn't be the first time."

"I came to get a tattoo." Swallowing, she tried to smile as she met his green gaze. She'd deliberately picked his shop to have this conversation because she knew he might try to shut her out. So she'd come here for business, and he'd have to listen while he worked. She'd prove on as many levels as she could that she wanted him and he wanted her. Once he'd walked away from a woman, she'd never known him to take one back. She had planned for that, she was prepared, but if there was one thing she'd learned this week it was that the heart didn't follow the guidelines of any plan.

"A tattoo? You?" He gave a short laugh. "Yeah, right."

Uncrossing her arms, she strode forward to sit on his black table. She arched a brow, lifted her shoulder in a nonchalant shrug, and made her grin widen to the most wicked she could muster. "Even nice girls go naughty, Jake. Isn't that what you wanted?"

His chin dropped to his chest, and he closed his eyes. "Dayna—"

"So I want the family tattoo," she continued as if he hadn't spoken. Even if things didn't work out between them—and please, God, let things work out between them—she still wanted this indelible reminder of how much she loved and accepted her crazy, off-the-wall family. Just as much as they loved and accepted her with all her flaws and foibles. The first real smile since she'd walked in curved her lips. "I'd like the tattoo on my left hip. Can you do that?"

He met her gaze, deadly serious, with none of the good humor she was used to. "It's permanent, what I do. You can't take it back."

"That's what I'm hoping." Lifting her hand, she touched him for the first time and stroked her fingertips down his cheek.

He flinched but didn't pull away. His skin went ghostly pale, but his expression was cool and composed. She fidgeted under his scrutiny, tucking her hair behind her ears and then twisting her fingers together in her lap. "So should I lie down for this?"

"You don't have to do this."

"Yeah, I do. I want to. It's important to me." She stilled, meeting his gaze and letting all the certainty she had about her feelings for him, her determination to run him to ground if she had to, show on her face. She knew what she wanted, and she always went after what she wanted. That wasn't about to change now, especially not for something this critical.

His brows drew together, but he nodded. "Let me prep a few things and we can get started."

Rising, he went into a back room, and she heard running water and then the whirring of what sounded like a copy machine. When he came back out, he carried a sheet of tissue paper with the family design on it. He finished breaking down the tattoo gun he'd used on Mrs. Simpson and replaced the ends with new ones. He set up pools of black and white ink in a little tray and snapped on a new pair of gloves. "You'll need to pull your pants down enough for me to work, and I need to clean the area first."

"I bet you say that to all the girls." She grinned and popped the button on her jeans, watching his chest expand in a deep breath as his green eyes locked on the movements of her hands unzipping her pants. His mouth worked, but no sound came out, and a flush raced up his lean cheeks. Good, at least he was still affected by her. It made this all a little less scary and gave her *something* to use in her campaign. She worked the left side of her pants down to bare her hip, trepidation and excitement rolling through her. She motioned to an area high on her hip. "I'd like it to be right here."

"Like that?" He held the paper design up to the place she'd indicated, and even that very professional touch made her heart trip.

"Yes, that's perfect," her voice erupted in a breathless whisper.

She shivered when the cool liquid disinfectant stroked over her skin. He took the paper with the design and transferred it onto her skin. Then he pointed to a full-length mirror mounted on one wall. "Go look and make sure that's exactly how you want it. I can change it, if not."

Pushing away from the table, she went and stared for a moment. A grin bloomed on her face. This was it, a break from her old, perfect self who never would have considered marking herself permanently. A new beginning. A new Dayna. Still her, but more certain of what she wanted. Happier. She wanted to share that with Jake. "That's just right."

He motioned with his hand for her to lie on her side on the table, so she scooted around until she could obey. She curled her arm under her head, watching him while he prepared. A frisson went up her spine as the tattoo gun buzzed a few times while he dipped the needles into the ink. "I'm going to do a test line so you can see how this feels. If it hurts too much, I can stop there."

"So, what—I'd just have a line on me, and that's it?" She made a face at him. "Has anyone ever stopped after the one line?"

"Once or twice." His hand settled just above where her tattoo would be, and then the tone of the buzzing changed as the needles hit her skin.

Her muscles clenched as a sharp sensation somewhere between a pinch and a burn seared her flesh. Air hissed through her teeth. He lifted away from her, and she wriggled herself to settle against the table more comfortably. It hurt, but it wasn't intolerable. "I'm okay. Keep going."

His voice again took on that low rumble she liked so well. "You're sure?"

"Totally sure." Shifting her shoulders, she tried to relax as he continued tattooing her. She breathed slowly, tingles rippling through her limbs in waves. The pain was still there, but distant. She closed her eyes and focused on each sensation. The needles on her skin, the heat of Jake's hand through his glove. The almost sensual movement of his fingers that contrasted with the burn of the tattoo.

Opening her eyes, she watched him work. The only time she'd ever seen such an intense expression on his face was during sex. The thought raised goose bumps on her arms and tightened her nipples. No matter how painful the tattooing was, she'd probably have to be dead not to react to his touch. Maybe if she was lucky, he'd kiss it and make it better later. A small grin quirked her lips but faded when his gaze flicked up to look at her while he changed the nozzle on the gun. He'd joked and teased with Mrs. Simpson but hadn't said a word to her. She spoke softly, "Are you just not going to talk to me?"

A muscle ticked in his jaw. "So when are you and Nathan headed back down to LA?"

"I'm not going back. Not to Nathan and not to LA."

The buzzing stopped for a second, and he swallowed. He pulled in a big breath, let it ease out, and then resumed his work. Whatever expression had flashed over his face was gone before she could discern what it meant. The cool facade was firmly in place. He cleared his throat. "Good."

"I'm glad you think so."

He made a soft sound in the back of his throat. "I need to say something to you so we can . . . so we can be okay again. Just listen."

She nodded, desperately wanting to ask what he meant by "okay again." Did he just want to be friends again, or did he want to be okay moving into a deeper relationship? What did it mean—what did *he* want? Loving her didn't mean he wanted to be with her. Her belly knotted tight.

"I've been an ass." He kept his voice low, his hands still moving over her hip. "I didn't think about how what we've been doing would hurt you. I just thought about how wrong that guy was for you, how he couldn't give you what you need. I wanted to show you that being the nice girl, being this perfect person all the time, wasn't what life is all about. But I didn't stop to think about how much it would mess things up for you. I just want you to be happy, Dayna. That's all I ever wanted. I just . . . wanted you to see that working to be perfect all the time wasn't how to find happiness." He drew a breath but snapped his mouth shut on whatever else he might have said. The buzzing stopped abruptly, and he stood. He looked anywhere but at her as he set the gun aside, peeled off his gloves, and tossed them toward a garbage can. "Okay, I'm done. You can go look at—"

"I love you." Gingerly leveraging herself up onto her hands and knees, she moved until she was on her feet in front of him. He backed toward the low counter that held the cash register, something close to panic in his gaze. Her heart clenched, but she wouldn't let him run away from this. When he could go no farther, she cupped his face in her palms. "I love you so much, Jake. I'm sorry it took me so long to figure it out, and I'm sorry you saw me with Nathan yesterday. It was stupid, and I hated him touching me. I don't . . . I don't want anyone but *you* touching me ever again. I know I'm an anal-retentive pain in the ass most of the time, and you don't do the forever thing with anyone, but I . . ." Her voice trailed off, but he didn't say anything. He just stared at her, his face pale. She dropped her hands. Tears welled in her eyes, and she blinked rapidly to keep them from falling. A wobbly smile was the best she could manage. "No one will ever love you like I do. Plus, I come with great in-laws."

He didn't laugh at her weak joke. His face remained serious, and his throat worked for a moment before he spoke in a harsh rasp, "Are you sure you can handle me? I'm no picnic either, sweetheart."

"Yes." Her heart leaped at his words. Was it possible she was getting through to him? Could things *actually* work out? Hope so sweet it was painful churned inside her. God, she loved him so much. Swallowing hard, she slanted him a rueful grin. "I made a list about why I should be with you."

He chuckled, the sound rusty. "Show me."

Tilting her head, she lifted an eyebrow. "How do you know I have it with me?"

His hand came up to cup her cheek, the look of reverence mingled with a teasing humor in his eyes that she'd come to need so much. He stroked his thumb over her cheekbone. "Because I know you. Show me the list."

"It's in my back pocket." She just waited, knowing he'd pull it out himself without asking her. He didn't disappoint. His fingers dipped into her jeans and curled around the curve of her buttock. She arched her ass into the contact, loving the automatic heat his touch created.

Slowly, oh, so slowly, he pulled his hand out of her pocket. He unfolded the piece of paper and read it aloud. "One, I love Jake. Two, Jake understands me better than I understand myself. Three, I love Jake. Four, Jake loves my family, and they love him even more. Five, I love Jake. Six, Jake and I laugh together. Seven, being with Jake makes me a better, happier person. Eight, I love Jake. Nine, Jake makes me scream in bed."

The look he gave her when he repeated the last item on her list made her pulse race. Fire flooded her body, dampening her pussy. He'd turned her into a wanton, sexual being, and she craved him. It had been more than a day since he'd made her come, and it was too long to wait. She licked her lips, staring at his mouth. He shuddered, dropped the list beside the register, bracketed her waist with his hands, lifted her up, and set her on the countertop. Closing his eyes, he leaned his forehead against hers. "Dayna, I—"

She kissed him, unable to stop herself. His arms wrapped tight around her, plastering her body to his. The contact made her moan. She clamped her legs around his waist. The counter was just the right height to let his erection rub against her clit. And he was fully erect. She squirmed, needing to get closer. "I want you inside me."

"Sweetheart, I've been hard from the moment I started tattooing you." He kissed her every few words—soft, drugging kisses that made her body burn and throb. "It's never been a sexual experience for me, but, damn . . . it was with you."

Everything with him was an erotic experience. He could read her the phonebook, and it would get her hot. Her tongue tangled with his, his goatee a sensual scrape against her lips and chin. She slid her palms under his T-shirt, letting her fingertips brush against the rough silk of his torso. He jerked his shirt over his head, dropping it on the counter beside her. His hands tugged at the hem of her top, baring her to his gaze. His eyes burned an incandescent green when he saw she wasn't wearing a bra. Cupping her breasts, he chafed her nipples with his thumbs before he dipped forward to suck one of them deep into his mouth. A soft, keening sob erupted from her throat, pleasure slicing through her like a blade. Her fingernails dug into his scalp as she clutched him closer. "Please, Jake. *Please.*"

A low, rough whisper answered her plea, "Lift your ass."

Leaning back on her hands, she raised her hips so he could slide her unfastened pants down. He took her panties with her jeans, yanking her shoes and socks off, too. Desperate want pounded through her, made her muscles shake. "Now yours. I want to see you naked."

He obeyed, shucking his pants and boots in one swift motion. When he straightened, his cock stood in a hard arc against his lower belly. Her sex clenched, wetness slicking the lips of her pussy. She held out her arms for him, needing him more than she needed air. She craved the feel of him moving within her and the knowledge that he was so deep inside her she couldn't tell where he ended and where she began.

Grasping his cock, he guided himself until the flared crest rubbed against her dampness. A lopsided grin quirked his lips as he filled her slowly. "You left something off your list."

"What?" She moaned, not really listening to what he was saying. Her heart nearly stopped, every emotion that streaked through her lying still as her body, mind, and soul recognized the deep connection with this one man. This was what she'd been looking for. This was real perfection. And then he began thrusting within her, and the world whipped into light speed. Stars exploded behind her eyes, tingles racing over her skin.

"That I love you back." He changed the angle of his thrusts, grinding against her clit with each push.

"I know," she gasped. Her head fell back on her neck, and her sex contracted. She was so close she could feel the orgasm shimmering just beyond her reach. Yes, yes, *yes.*

"*You know?*" He stopped and leaned back, scowling down at her. "What the hell kind of response is that?"

She couldn't hold back a laugh or a strangled moan as her

body clamored in protest. Her hips arched a bit, taking him as deep as possible, but still he wouldn't move. "Rainbow told me so. She had a vision that we'll have two kids and a dog."

"I like kids." His eyes remained narrowed, but his cock was hard and throbbing inside her. His chest heaved as he panted, and streaks of sweat ran down his skin.

"Me, too." She flexed her inner muscles around him until he groaned. Her heart pounded, the sound rushing in her ears. Heat roared through her, and flames licked at her flesh. "Let's make one right now."

That was the moment the realization hit both of them. He wasn't wearing a condom. His pupils dilated until only a thin ring of green showed. His hands clamped over her knees, holding her in place as he began thrusting again. Hard. "No arguments here."

They moved together, their gazes locked, racing each other toward orgasm. He came inside of her, hot fluids filling her. A sob tore from her throat as she exploded into a million pieces. Her pussy clenched around his cock over and over until she screamed, tears slipping down her cheeks. He bent to suck her nipple into his mouth again, rolling the other one with his fingers. Aftershocks of orgasm slammed into her, and she choked as her body spasmed on his semihard cock. "Jake, I love you. *Jake.*"

She felt his smile against her skin as he released her nipple. Satisfaction gleamed in his gaze as he looked down at her. His breathing slowed, and so did her heart rate as they came down off the high of orgasm. His hands cupped her hips loosely, brushing over her new tattoo. She hissed as pain echoed through the area, and her back arched reflexively. He dropped his hands. "Shit. I'm sorry, Dayna."

"It's fine." She slid a reassuring hand down his arm.

He shook his head. "I need to dress it. Hold on."

"I'm really fine. It didn't hurt that badly." He pulled away, his dick slipping from her body. She moaned an objection. "You're just going to leave a naked, willing woman all alone? That's so wrong."

Not that she'd complain about the view. His muscular ass flexed with each step. He glanced at her over his shoulder. "Sorry, sweetheart. It could get infected if we leave it. I don't take risks with you. Or with my work."

She slid off the counter and met him in the middle of the room. He smoothed ointment and a white bandage over the tattoo and then kissed the skin just above it. God, she loved him. It would kill her to have to watch him walk away from her ever again. "Jake."

"Yeah?" He pulled her into his embrace, running his fingertips up and down her naked back. She looped her arms around his neck, and he smiled down at her.

"I know we're not perfect, we disagree on just about everything, and we've always argued as much as we've laughed together. I doubt that will ever change." Unlike with Nathan, who'd just wanted to reason or rationalize. She liked Jake's upfront approach better.

He shrugged. "That's how compromise happens, sweetheart. The bottom line is I'd rather argue with you than make love with any other woman."

"I know what you mean." And that was probably the nicest thing anyone had ever said to her. Tears sprang up in her eyes, one of them escaping to slide down her cheek. "Promise me . . . promise me no matter how bad we fight that you'll never walk away from me again. I think I've finally realized that we're not our parents, and we don't have to end up like them. We can make different choices, and I choose you. I'm always going to choose you." She blinked away another tear to lock her gaze with his. "I swear I'll always stick it out with you if you swear to stick it out with me."

"Deal." His voice was rough with emotion, and she thought

his eyes had gone a little misty. He swooped down for another soul-stealing kiss that had her rising up on tiptoe to get closer and made her cling to his shoulders and moan. They were both panting when he pulled away. "I choose you, too, and I'm not budging. I love you, sweetheart."

"Good, because I'd hate to have to hunt you down." She lightly raked her nails over the tattoos on his skin. "It would really suck, and I would make you pay if you put me through the trouble."

His beautiful, blinding smile flashed as he laughed down at her. "This was, without a doubt, the best holiday ever."

"It certainly had its moments." She reached between them to stroke his cock back to full attention, giving him a look wicked enough to send all the blood rushing right where she wanted it. "Looks like I really will end up on the naughty list next year."

The amazing, wonderful part was she really couldn't think of anywhere she'd rather be. Jake loved her no matter what, and she was free to be herself with him in a way she'd never allowed herself before. Naughty or nice, she just wanted to be right here with him for every holiday season for the rest of her life. He'd given her the best Christmas gift ever.

His heart.

Nativity Island

Lorie O'Clare

1

——————

"What do you mean, engine trouble?" Mercedes Porter leaned forward, wrinkling her nose as she stared where one of the crew members pointed. "But you can fix it, right? I mean, three weeks with all of you has been a blast, but I need to get home in time to do my Christmas shopping."

"We're docking at a nearby island in about an hour." Captain Huraldo, an older man who'd been full of tales of the sea during the past weeks Mercedes and her team had been studying marine life, didn't usually look this stressed. "If we can make repairs there, we should be able to return to the mainland soon."

"Soon," Mercedes grumbled, following her team members out of the engine room. "This doesn't sound good."

"I'm sure they'll have it fixed in no time." Hyde, one of Mercedes's lab partners, glanced over his shoulder at the crew members.

Mercedes didn't like the way they huddled together, arguing in hushed whispers. As she headed toward her cabin, a sinking feeling she didn't like made her stomach hurt. "I think I'll pack a few things."

"Might want to pack more than a few," Hyde said, scowling and then leaving her, his flip-flops slapping on the stairs as he hurried downstairs to his cabin.

An hour later Mercedes walked along a sandy path with her crew, scowling at the zero bars on her cell phone. She glanced up as they approached a row of thatched huts, complete with what looked like straw roofs.

"Is there even electricity on this island?" one of her crew members immediately complained.

The comment instigated a spew of protests. Mercedes barely heard them. They passed a wooden sign with the words SEA SIDE RESORT burned into it, and, beyond that, she watched a man walking from the other direction. He appeared to be coming from the beach, his bronze, bare chest noticeably well built, even from this distance.

"Scenery isn't that bad." Trudy Montrose, a biologist from the mainland, nudged Mercedes with her elbow, giving her a knowing wink as she, too, admired the half-naked man who ignored them.

And he had to be intentionally doing so. They were a noticeable group, lugging suitcases and complaining loudly as they approached the hut labeled OFFICE with a similar burned wooden sign. The man disappeared around the back side, taking the few seconds of pleasure from Mercedes. Shoving her way into the office with the others, she fought for space in the stuffy, dimly lit cabin.

"Plenty of rooms for everyone," a woman announced in her singsong accent.

After being shown to her room, Mercedes relaxed at the edge of her bed, facing her TV but staring out the sliding glass doors at the view outside. She'd loved the ocean since she was a child dreaming of exploring the world. During her more rebellious years she imagined being a pirate, taking what she wanted while ruling the dangerous and wild sea.

The aqua-green water faded into shades of dark turquoise as she stared at the calm ocean. The white beach with its border of palm trees nearer the resort could have been right off a post-card. Maybe enjoying a fine meal and then hopefully being on their way by morning, at the latest, wouldn't be such a terrible interruption in their schedule. She pulled her attention toward her laptop, deciding she might pull off some of her Christmas shopping online.

There weren't a lot of gifts to buy. Something for her grand-parents in Seattle and parents in Sacramento. There was her sis-ter and her brother-in-law and their kids. No doubt her family would descend on her sister's home for Christmas. Porsche was the happy homemaker, the one who made their parents proud, landing the perfect husband and producing perfect grandchil-dren. Mercedes was the explorer, the one who couldn't stay in any one place long enough to get a date, let alone start a rela-tionship. Her grandmother always asked what was she running from. Mercedes gave up trying to explain herself years ago and just stayed away. There wasn't a man for her anyway; no one would tolerate her work or her love for the sea. And she wouldn't tolerate settling down so she could be around a man and where he worked.

Sighing, she opened her laptop and pulled out pen and paper, deciding to make a list to help get her shopping underway. "You're going to have to priority mail, if not overnight, every-thing to get it there on time," she reminded herself, noting that she had less than a week until Christmas. When was the last time she'd actually done her Christmas shopping in a mall, fighting crowds and struggling with lots of bags and boxes to hurry home and wrap everything? "And pay to have everything wrapped," she added, jotting down the reminder on the corner of her notepad.

After writing names of who to shop for—plus the names of everyone on her team—she checked her bank balance and then headed to her favorite online stores. Two more hours slipped by before she realized she hadn't heard a word from the ship's crew or captain.

Can't be a good sign, she thought. Her team would need answers, as would she. Staying at this resort indefinitely wasn't part of the schedule. With more than half her shopping done, she stood and stretched. She needed a shower and clean clothes and then some exploring and answers.

She thought of the man she'd seen while checking in and pictured the small island they were on being filled with such gorgeous creatures. A hot, invigorating shower—and images of gorgeous men at her beck and call, surrounding her and eager to take care of her every need—had her skin tingling as she adjusted the spaghetti straps on her mini dress while staring at herself in the mirror.

"Feast your eyes on this, cabana boy," she purred, shifting and turning as she ran her hands down her ass and decided that, for thirty-two years old, she still had what it took to turn heads—slim, with not too much rear but enough to give her figure some shape. "And you aren't sagging either," she added, cupping her breasts in her hands while continuing to stare in the mirror. "Maybe you aren't a showstopper, but you aren't doing that bad."

Mercedes never did much with her hair. She fingered her natural curls until they lay the way she wanted them, with the damp strands brushing her shoulders. Then, deciding on a bit of makeup, just in case there was any truth to her fantasy, she grabbed her purse and headed outside. The sunset was breathtaking, although she was disappointed when she discovered there was no formal dining area.

"Have you heard?" Trudy asked, appearing to have also

showered and cleaned up a little as she hurried to join Mercedes at the edge of the beach.

"Heard what?" Mercedes cringed, staring at the mixed drink Trudy sipped and wondering where she'd gotten it. She was ready for bad news, knowing their ship was worse off than they'd originally been led to believe and knowing she'd now need to make other arrangements to get herself and her crew home. "Just break it to me quickly."

"You know the book *Give Them What They Want*?" Trudy asked, sidling up next to Mercedes and lowering her voice conspiratorially. "We think Jeremy Fall is here." She wagged her eyebrows and hummed delightfully. "You know the book, right?"

"I just ordered it for my sister for a Christmas present." She wouldn't add that she'd gazed at the cover longer than she should. Jeremy Fall, who was on the cover of his *New York Times* best seller had written the perfect book about how a man should treat a lady. He was every woman's dream, and rumors were Jeremy Fall was really a woman, and the cover was simply a model, making for perfect drool material. Everyone said there was no way any man could have such perfect insight into the mind of a woman. "But Jeremy Fall isn't really a man." Mercedes didn't add that she'd tried reading the book and hadn't been able to get into it. Everyone loved the book, and sharing her opposite opinion only started arguments she didn't want.

"Then the model on the cover is here," Trudy said stubbornly. "The man we saw when we first arrived—he was on the beach a few minutes ago." She turned around, holding her hand over her eyes as she squinted and frowned at the beach behind them. "I don't see him now. But I'm serious. If that man I just saw isn't him, he's his twin."

"Any word on the ship?" Mercedes asked. She really didn't have time to drool over some stranger.

"None. I figured you would tell me. How long are we going to be here?" Trudy continued scanning the beach. "I guess he's gone now."

"I need to find out our status," Mercedes said. "There's no restaurant, is there?"

"You're kidding, right?" Trudy held her hands out, her pale, thin body almost glowing against the incredible sunset. "There are these huts, and that's it. I'm not sure if there is even a town on this island."

"Oh, no," Mercedes groaned. "It can't be that bad." She forced a laugh. But Trudy's skeptical look wasn't reassuring.

In fact, it was worse than bad. The ship wasn't going anywhere until after Christmas. They were stuck, as close to shipwrecked as they could be on an island that indeed didn't have anything resembling a town. It was a village at best, with more huts, a gas station, a few cars, and no restaurants. Mercedes's phone had a decent signal in her room, but nowhere else. After spending more than an hour placing calls to get her team home—arranging for a charter plane to take them to New Zealand, where they would then be able to arrange for flights to the U.S.—she found a guide to take her and the captain around the island. Although the beauty on the island could almost make a person forget their worries, there were no tools or supplies they could use to fix the ship.

"Do you want me to book you and your crew on the charter plane as well?" Mercedes asked Captain Huraldo as they walked away from the small village toward the beach and his ship.

"You take care of your crew, and I'll take care of mine." Captain Huraldo was gruff but nice in his own way. "And again, I'm very sorry. I'll stay with the ship if you need to keep your equipment running on board."

"That would be great." Mercedes finished her phone call and confirmed a charter plane would be there to fly all of them to New Zealand first thing in the morning. "I'd hate for three weeks of research and our marine life samples we've gathered to go to waste. I'll probably arrange to ship most of them back with my crew."

"Whatever works." Captain Huraldo took off his hat and ran his leathered fingers over his almost shaved head. He looked exactly how a captain of a small ship should look, in Mercedes's opinion. When he squinted, his tanned, smooth skin created perfect crow's-feet on either side of his green eyes. "I didn't have plans for Christmas, anyway."

Mercedes thought of her own situation. Her family didn't expect her to be there for Christmas. It had crossed her mind to try making it to her sister's, but it seemed more work than it was worth. Sending gifts was enough. "No family?" she asked.

"None I'm close with. The sea is my family."

Mercedes nodded. "I understand."

She headed back to the huts, deciding that being stuck on an island named Nativity Island was rather appropriate for Christmas. There were worse places she could be. The sun settled on the horizon, creating a radiant glow across the ocean. Magnificent shades of reds and oranges mixed with the radiant blue, stealing her breath. It was the most incredible sunset she'd ever seen—she hated heading back to her room, where she'd e-mail everyone and tell them of the scheduled charter plane that would take them all to the mainland in the morning. Slowing her pace a few moments to take in such a glorious sight was certainly worth it. As if the sun knew it had an audience, it seemed to suspend just under the horizon, holding position while unimaginable streaks of color raced across the sky and over the ocean.

It took some effort to pull herself from the view, but Mercedes turned toward her cabin. The man she saw when she arrived stood in front of the cabin next to hers. That door was open, and he stood just outside, not wearing a shirt. The first thing she noticed was the dark sprinkle of hair that stretched across his bare, tanned chest. He was muscular and tall. Sandy, dark blond hair, and a brooding expression added to his mysterious appearance.

Mercedes squinted, realizing she stood there, staring, without moving. But the man wasn't moving either. They were staring at each other, both of them still. Her mouth went dry.

Crap. He was the epitome of perfection. From that breathtaking bare chest to the loose-fitting khaki pants and loafers, he reminded her of Tom Selleck on *Magnum, P.I.* My God, he was too much man and standing a short distance from her.

Not moving. Staring at her. As she was him.

2

_____

Jeremy Faulkner turned from the woman staring at him when the owner of Sea Side Resort walked out of his room. "That is the lady I told you about," she said, sounding proud and also looking at the woman. "She is quite pretty, isn't she? Maybe you should invite her to dinner with you. I could bring more food," she offered, rocking up on her heels.

Jeremy glanced up as the woman he'd watched turned from him, hurrying down the path away from the cabins. "I'm not interested in company. How long are all these people going to be here?" It was easier to growl at Francis. She left him alone faster that way.

"They are leaving in the morning." Francis visibly sulked as she walked away, muttering something about not being able to enjoy romance.

"Welcome to the club," he grumbled after her, closing his cabin door loudly behind him and stalking his food, which had been left on the tray on the table by the sliding glass doors, just as he liked it. Francis had made his bed while in the room; a fresh scent, some kind of air freshener, made the room smell like flowers.

With a two-week deadline breathing down his neck, he didn't have time for romance. And that was exactly what he'd been imagining while drooling over that hot little piece standing outside at the edge of the beach. He was a leg man, which was what had grabbed his attention when he'd spotted her heading in from the beach. But she had everything else, too—a narrow waist and breasts he bet were more than a handful, perfect to bury his head in and enjoy their soft, full roundness. He'd caught a glimpse of her firm ass and the way that sundress she wore had hugged it perfectly when she'd turned from him.

God! He now sported a nice hard-on, which wouldn't make working during the late-night hours any easier. Maybe a cool shower before eating his dinner, and then he would settle into his work. He needed to concentrate, remain focused. It was the entire reason he was here. Once his book was turned in to his editor, he would then make time to find a woman or two. All of which these days needed to be kept on the hush-hush, as his editor loved to repeatedly remind him.

His first book, *Give Them What They Want*, had soared to the top of all the best-seller lists as soon as it had hit the shelves. He was an overnight legend—the perfect man. And the only way to uphold that image was to keep a very, very low profile. The moment any woman talked to him and learned he was an old-fashioned guy at heart, he'd be exposed as a fraud. His second book would never sell.

After writing about how men should treat women, Jeremy Fall had become an overnight icon. Jeremy Faulkner, on the other hand, never got laid, was a terrible hermit, and hid behind curtains to watch gorgeous women.

"Maybe you should go invite her to eat with you," he grumbled, spotting her traipsing along the beach as he stared out his sliding glass doors.

She pulled off her sandals and started running toward him.

He needed to back out of view. But, damnit, the view she offered, breasts bouncing as she bounded toward him, kept him locked in place. What he wouldn't do to make them bounce while she was riding his cock. He was harder than stone staring at her as she neared the cabins.

Her hair was dark and curly, not quite black, but more than brown. As she neared he saw highlights he'd bet were natural—dark auburn shades streaked through her silky-looking hair. With her tanned skin he figured whatever she did for a living, she was outside a fair bit.

She damn near slid to a stop, also sliding out of his view. Jeremy edged closer to his window. Apparently, she didn't see him. Her attention was focused on opening the sliding glass doors to the cabin next to him.

"Well, hello, neighbor," he growled, his cock throbbing so hard the cold shower was now imperative.

He heard the glass door slide open and then closed. She was gone, yet right next door. Damn shame she'd be gone in the morning.

"No! Not a damn shame," he grumbled, sporting his hard-on as he almost limped to his bathroom. "You wouldn't get a damn thing done with a hot vixen like that living next door to you."

Wasn't that what chapter twelve in *Give Them What They Want* was all about? Women hated Peeping Toms and stalkers. They wanted a forward man, someone not ashamed to come out and say they appreciated what they saw and wanted to learn more. Jeremy couldn't count how many e-mails he received on that chapter alone. Women adored him, loved him. As long as they never knew the true him.

Nativity Island had its advantages. Waking up early and enjoying the sunrise with some of the best coffee he'd enjoyed in a long time was one of them. Francis was nowhere around, as Jeremy helped himself to a cup of hot brew in the resort office. He stepped outside, not missing Francis's early morning chatter. With everyone leaving, including the distracting dark-haired beauty he'd fantasized about last night while jacking off in the shower, he could almost imagine himself the only man on the island. Exactly what he needed to meet his deadline.

"And there she goes," he murmured, watching a group of people boarding a charter plane. Blowing on his coffee, he kept an eye on the woman as a small group hovered around the plane with their luggage.

Today she wore shorts that showed off her ass as nicely as the dress she'd worn last night. Her hair looked thick and streamed down to the middle of her back. When she turned slightly, hugging another woman, and then the man next to her, the view was just as exquisite. She was tall but not too tall, maybe five-six or so. The way she held herself, with an air of confidence and elegance she didn't flaunt, made her stand out in the group. Anyone would notice her. He liked her sultry moves. They weren't pretentious yet were distracting to the point that he willed her to get on the plane. She held him captive, standing there with the heat of his coffee steaming in his face.

Jeremy watched the small group board the plane until all of them were finally out of view. "Damn," he muttered under his breath. "I hate to say good riddance, but, darling, you are one hell of a distraction." More than likely she was headed home to be with her family—a doting husband who couldn't wait to see her, possibly even children who'd missed her desperately.

Everyone his age was married with children. Jeremy didn't regret holding on to his bachelorhood. In fact, with the success of his first book, it was more of a blessing than ever. His editor made him swear never to settle down and marry.

Jeremy chuckled to himself, turning toward his cabin, ready to get busy writing. "Like that will ever be a problem." The last thing he wanted was to be chained to some woman. "Well, maybe not chained," he muttered under his breath. His book in progress, *Take What You Need*, described the perfect female. She knew how to treat a man—and now he had an image of what she looked like. Perfect motivation to get his book done. Giving the woman in his book a face would make it even easier to write how a woman would treat a man in an ideal relationship.

When he reached his cabin door, he couldn't stop himself from turning around. The plane revved up for departure. Jeremy damn near dropped his coffee when the woman got off the plane, waving good-bye to those on board as she hurried away from the portable staircase. Her hair blew around her face, and she arched her back, reaching and pulling the long, thick, dark strands into a ponytail behind her head as she watched the plane prepare for departure.

"Son of a bitch," he snarled, his insides tightening with unwanted anticipation as he forced himself to quit gawking and hurried inside. "Why the hell isn't she leaving?"

Jeremy paced his cabin, waiting to hear her enter hers next door. When she didn't, he opted to open the window next to his front door and slid the glass door open in the back of his cabin. He wanted to know where she was, what she was doing, and why the hell she was still on his island. Forcing himself to sit at the desk along the wall by the sliding glass doors, he opened his file and read what he'd written yesterday. Then, making a page break, he titled his next chapter *Always Keeping Her Man Informed*. The words started pouring out of him.

More than an hour passed, and he was in need of more coffee. Stretching, he stood and heard her footsteps before she entered her cabin. Jeremy slid to a stop when she stopped at his front door and knocked.

"Oh, hi," she said through his open window, her voice a soft, sultry whisper.

He hadn't given her a voice in his mind and now decided that her husky tone—breathless yet calm and subdued—fit her perfectly.

"Are you lost?"

She flinched, staring at him through the window. He was being a jerk. A big-time, miserable ass. But, damnit, he'd made her his fantasy woman, and talking to her would ruin everything. Not to mention, that her seeking him out was too damn hot. His insides prickled, heat surging through his body as he reached for the doorknob and then opened his door.

"Hardly," she told him. "The island isn't big enough to get lost. I'm told you and I are the only ones here. You've been watching me. I've been watching you." She shrugged, her long, silky hair falling over her shoulder. "It appears we're going to be neighbors for a while. I thought I'd introduce myself." She extended her hand. "I'm Mercedes Porter."

Her hand was warm, her flesh soft and smooth, and her fingers delicate in his larger hand. "Jeremy Faulkner," he told her, hesitating only for a moment while deciding if he should tell her his real name or not.

"You aren't by any chance an author, are you?"

"No," he said without giving it a thought.

Mercedes blushed, pulling her hand from his. She was beyond beautiful, especially now that she'd put herself in an awkward position. It gave him the upper hand, one he decided to use before losing it.

"Why are you here?" he asked, knowing he still sounded gruff and annoyed. This was his island, though, his paradise and safe, reclusive corner of the world where he could live in his fantasies while creating what he hoped would be his next best seller.

"I just sent my crew home for the holidays." She lifted her shoulder, her hair parting over her slender, tanned features. "But it's best I remain here because all our work is on the ship, and it wouldn't exactly be right for me to make the captain take responsibility for it."

He didn't have a clue what she was talking about. "How long are you here?"

"It sounds like until after Christmas." She nibbled her lower lip and shifted from one foot to the other as her thick black lashes fluttered over incredibly blue eyes. "I'm sure we'll see each other occasionally because we're the only ones here, so I just wanted to say hi."

She started edging away from him, her gaze dropping to her hands as though she suddenly couldn't wait to get away from him. He should let her go and make her think what she was obviously concluding at the moment—that he was a terrible grouch. But something inside wasn't ready for her to leave.

"Occasionally?" he asked, stepping out of his cabin and moving in on her.

Mercedes looked up at him, her mouth puckering into a perfectly shaped, small circle. Her lips were full, naturally red, and moist. "I said that because you didn't seem pleased that I took time to say hello."

"I wasn't."

Her lips parted. He'd taken her off guard, and although her calm, confident air didn't sway, he noticed she seemed hesitant about how to respond. She watched him, searching his face, those incredible baby blues checking him out. The heat from her gaze showed interest, curiosity, and possibly the slightest bit of trepidation.

He liked keeping her guessing. "But because you did say hello, you can accompany me for more coffee."

"I don't drink coffee."

"I do." He placed his hand on her back, encouraging her to walk alongside him. Her hair was soft as silk, full and thick as it brushed over the back of his hand. "Do you not celebrate Christmas?"

"Of course." She glanced his way warily, and then her gaze traveled down his body. "Don't you?"

His editor had taken his Christmas list, agreeing to make arrangements for everyone on it to receive their gift from him so he wouldn't be bothered while meeting his deadline. "Born and raised Catholic. Francis tells me they'll have a midnight mass in the village on Christmas Eve."

"I'm not Catholic."

"What are you?"

She shrugged. "I guess I'm not anything." It was hot as hell the way she nibbled her lower lip when trying to decide what to say to him. "Maybe it's the scientist in me. Or maybe work just takes up so much of my time I don't think about religion."

"What kind of scientist are you?"

"Marine biologist. Although I have a degree in oceanography. Anything to do with the ocean fascinates me."

"Why is that?"

Her voice was breathy, and when she continued, staring at the sea while explaining, he saw that what he'd originally viewed as a look of confidence was in fact one of incredible intelligence. Beauty and brains. Maybe that would be the title of his next chapter.

"I think maybe because no matter how much I learn about it, it is and always will be filled with mystery. There's no way in a lifetime I can exhaust all there is to know about her." Her laughter was melodic, but she paused, stepping to the side and out of reach of his hand when they arrived at the office. "I'm sure that sounds ridiculous."

Francis grinned her toothy grin as she walked around the front desk with a coffeepot in hand—as though she'd seen them coming and waited on him. Which more than likely was the truth. Her knowing grin was more than annoying, and if Jeremy had had any sense, he would have avoided this moment.

He predicted Francis's words before they were out of her mouth.

"I knew you two would like each other," she announced, her accent thicker than usual. "Tonight I will make a special dinner for you both. Whose cabin will you be eating in?"

"Oh, um . . ." Mercedes began, her hair falling around her face when she looked down at her clasped hands.

Jeremy studied her for only a moment, focusing on the cleavage pressing above the top of her low-cut tank top. He had no problem imagining where having dinner with Mercedes might lead. Maybe spending time with her would be advantageous instead of detrimental. Already he had the title for his next chapter. She might very well be an inspiration to his writing.

"It would only be proper to have dinner at the lady's cabin," he said, catching Mercedes's surprised look. "A gentleman is never forward or assumptive in suggesting a woman come to his place."

"Perfect!" Francis clapped her hands together, preventing Mercedes from saying whatever it was she had opened her mouth to say. Instead of speaking, she licked her lips, shifting her attention to Francis, who continued speaking. "I will prepare a romantic dinner for two. At seven when the sun sets. And to make the lady at home, I will serve it outside the back of her cabin. Not to worry at all. I will have a table set up, and it will be a meal for lovers."

"I'm not sure . . ."

"That is most gracious of you, Francis," Jeremy said, interrupting Mercedes before she could back out. Then, holding his full coffee cup up in a silent salute, he nodded to Mercedes. "I'll leave you two ladies to iron out the details and will see you at seven."

"Wait—" Mercedes began.

For the first time since arriving on the island, Jeremy was grateful that Francis was so talkative. As he turned away from the ladies, he saw the older lady wrap her bony fingers around Mercedes's tanned arm as she started discussing the menu options. Mercedes was trapped. And he was free to write his next chapter.

Jeremy kept his window open, as well as the sliding glass door. The breeze was perfect, the temperature proof of paradise. At five that evening, he closed his laptop, cleared his notes from the desk, and then showered. If the evening went the way he planned, they would never be in his cabin. Just to be safe, though, he removed all indication of his writing. Thankfully, he'd been wise not to share with Francis who he really was. As talkative as the older woman was, it would be the first thing she'd tell Mercedes. He stripped, stepped into the hot shower, and then let it soak his back while imagining Mercedes preparing for their date as well.

Would she shower or take a hot bath? Would she soak in scented soap, creating a fragrance that would linger on her skin and make her cabin smell just like her? He pictured her shaving, taking her time while suds streamed down her soft curves. His cock started throbbing as he imagined how soft her breasts were. He prayed she shaved her pussy. There was nothing hotter than smooth, silky flesh between a woman's legs.

"Crap," he growled, grabbing his dick and feeling the pressure build as his balls tightened, growing heavier by the moment. He didn't want to masturbate again. He wanted to sink deep inside Mercedes's heat and feel her wrapped around him. He wanted to fuck her until she cried out his name. More than anything, he wanted to see her body glistening with sweat, in the throes of passion, while he rode her hard and gave her everything he had.

Jeremy pressed his free hand against the shower wall, maintaining his balance as need hit him harder than it had in ages. He had to get a grip on himself. The last thing Mercedes, or anyone, would ever find out was that he wasn't the perfect gentleman, the perfect bachelor with insight and understanding into the woman's mind. The truth would destroy his career. He was a pervert, craving a lady who would submit to him and desire hard, rough sex as much as he did.

3

Mercedes twisted in front of the mirror after trying on yet another dress. She had only three dresses, some shorts and tops, and a few pairs of jeans. It wasn't as if there was a huge selection to choose from for her date.

"Date. Hell," she groaned, moving closer to the mirror and inspecting the makeup she'd applied. "How did I get myself into this?"

If it wasn't for the way her flesh had tingled while Jeremy Faulkner had watched her say good-bye to her team, she wouldn't have gathered the nerve to introduce herself. At the time, it had seemed a smart move. He was distracting the hell out of her, and she figured if she met him—showed herself he was just some man and wasn't that big a deal—she would get him out of her system.

"Talk about a plan backfiring," she grumbled, frowning at her reflection and then down at the makeup on her bathroom counter. "Now you're a nervous wreck, and why? He's forward and too good-looking for his own good."

Mercedes sighed, picking up her lipstick but then dropping

it. She moved quickly to catch it before it rolled off the counter. There wasn't any reason to primp further. A man like Jeremy would notice the work she went to in order to impress him and would probably use it against her somehow. She hated feeling so grossly out of her league.

She walked out of her bathroom and spotted two young boys placing a table outside her sliding glass doors. Francis was with them, speaking softly but quickly as she instructed the boys. They spread a tablecloth over the table and arranged candles and place settings and then disappeared, hurrying out of view, more than likely to return with dinner.

Mercedes plopped down on the edge of her bed, staring at her laptop, which was still open to the Web site for the author Jeremy Fall. He was a dead ringer for Jeremy Faulkner.

"Like hell you aren't an author," she said, wondering why he would lie about it. Although, in truth, he was probably alone on this island because he was tired of people hanging all over him. Especially women. "And I prance up to his door to introduce myself."

But he was the one who had dragged her with him to get his coffee. He had encouraged the conversation when she would have backed off after their initial introductions. Her first impression was that he didn't want to be bothered. He'd told her as much.

"Then he traps me into a dinner date." She shifted on the edge of the bed, pressing her legs together while willing the pressure inside her to subside.

Squirming around simply made her wetter. Mercedes stood as the boys returned pushing a silver cart loaded down with covered platters. A feast had arrived. And she'd be surprised if she could eat a bite.

"It's almost seven. Might as well get this over with." She couldn't remember ever being so nervous about a date. Hell, when had she last gone on a date?

There was a reason why she didn't date, she reminded herself, planting a pleasant smile on her face and stepping outside.

"If you aren't the vision of beauty?" Francis swooned, clapping her hands together and then snapping at one of the boys to pull Mercedes's chair out for her. "There is no better place for romance than Nativity Island," she added, gripping Mercedes's bare shoulders and giving them a harsh squeeze.

Jeremy stepped out from his cabin, pausing before closing the door and staring at her. The immediate sensation that a hungry predator was staking out his territory and contemplating his best method of attack sent Mercedes's heart pounding out of control. His gaze dropped to her chest, and she wondered if opting for her strapless dress had been such a good idea. She didn't want to send any false messages.

"What a handsome couple the two of you are," Francis said, her singsong accent hitting a high pitch that bordered on annoying. "Now hurry, you two," she snapped, swatting one of the boys on the back of the head.

The child didn't acknowledge her but continued placing food on the table, his gaze lowered and his expression bordering on annoyance. Within seconds, though, the two boys had laid out a feast suited for at least ten people.

"You ring this bell and we come running." Francis picked up a small bell and held it in front of Jeremy's face as though it was something to be proud of.

"You've set a perfect table," Jeremy told Francis, his deep baritone obviously affecting her because she finally quit moving and clasped her hands to her chest. Jeremy offered her an easy smile, taking the bell out of her hands and placing it next to his plate. He eased into his chair, his button-down shirt undone at the top and revealing dark, curly chest hair over bronze skin. "I can't imagine there is anything we'll need, but I'll let you know."

Francis beamed, her adoration for Jeremy obvious when she

smiled a moment longer than she needed. Her expression changed quickly though when she snapped at the boys, who immediately took off running. She then turned and followed them without another word.

"I sure hope you're hungry." Jeremy focused on the wine, pulling the cork and reaching for Mercedes's glass.

"I doubt I could put a dent in all the food here."

He chuckled but didn't say anything, instead appearing intent on his task. Maybe he was as nervous as she was. Francis had turned the simple invitation into something elaborate. If Mercedes was better at small talk, she would try making him comfortable. She wasn't, though. She was a scientist. It was easier to dissect his nature by watching Jeremy than to learn about him by talking to him.

And, no, it wasn't because she didn't care about his mind. "Do you normally eat like this here?" she asked, lifting her wineglass and breathing in the fruity fragrance while watching his long fingers slide over the moist, smooth glass as he put down the bottle.

"Not once." Jeremy lifted his glass, holding it up for a toast. "To the beginning of what will hopefully be a pleasant evening."

She tapped her glass against his and then sipped. The cold, sweet wine slid down her throat easily, and she took another swallow. "Pleasant," she murmured, lifting her gaze when he looked at her. "That could cover a broad area."

"Then maybe I should say I'm leaving the evening open for whatever might happen."

"What is it you think might happen?" Mercedes had never been accused of not being forward. Which was probably why she sucked at relationships. Her insides churned as she lowered her attention once again to his muscular chest. If he had worn his shirt unbuttoned just far enough to torture her on purpose, she was in trouble. Although it hung loosely on his torso, his shoulders were broad, and she imagined muscles rippled under the cotton fabric.

He reached for her plate without asking and began scooping portions of the food onto it for her. "At the least, we'll part ways very stuffed."

His smile was irresistible. Mercedes leaned back, searching her mind for a safe conversation topic that would keep her mind off undressing him. Instead of returning his grin, she sipped again at her wine and then put the glass down. It had been too long since she'd drunk alcohol, and if she had much more, he would have the advantage.

"Tell me about yourself, Jeremy Faulkner," she said.

He lifted her plate toward her but then held it in midair, looking at her as if she'd just asked something forbidden. "There isn't much to tell. I was looking forward to hearing about what you were studying while out on the ocean. It sounded fascinating."

The fact that he didn't want to talk about himself made her itch to press further and learn more about him. "We were studying plant and marine life off the coast."

"And all your work is still on that ship?"

"Well, not all of it," she said, dipping into her food and tasting it. She hummed her approval. "This lobster is incredible."

Jeremy brought a good-sized bite of the lobster meat to his mouth. She watched him chew and swallow, wondering if anything he did would turn her off. Too much sex appeal radiated toward her—the way roped muscle flexed in his arm, how his fingers wrapped around his fork. His dark blond hair was tousled, windblown, and long enough to run her fingers through. It would be silky yet thick. It tapered past his ears and curled against his neck at a perfect length.

"Yes, it is," he said, his hooded gaze making it difficult to know where he stared. "I'm glad you're enjoying it."

"Are you?" She searched his face, willing him to give her his attention. When he did, she felt herself once again being drawn by dark gray eyes that appeared to smolder with knowledge of things to come that evening. Knowledge she wasn't sure she'd be better off knowing. "Is that why you invited me to have dinner with you?"

"So you'd enjoy yourself? Partially," he admitted, lowering his attention once again so long, dark lashes prevented her from seeing where his focus lay. "And partially so I would enjoy myself."

"I see." She slid more food onto her fork but then considered what he'd just said. "Did you know when you came here you'd be alone on this island?" Maybe he was lonely.

"Yup. I was assured I would be."

That blew the excited-to-have-company theory out of the water. "Why do you want to be alone?"

"It's easier to work," he said, eating more lobster and then putting his fork on his plate as he reached for his wine. "I'd much rather have a beer. How about you? Anything else you want with your food?" He rang the bell before allowing her to answer.

"Everything is perfect," Mercedes offered, realizing she was anxious to ask more questions. He was sitting across from her, eating with her, and she didn't know a thing about him. While they dined, she had the right to learn what she could about him before they parted ways. "What is your work?" she asked when he put the bell down.

One of the boys raced around the side of the cabin, almost sliding to a stop and somehow managing not to topple into the table.

Jeremy told the boy to bring beer and watched the child run across the yard. Then turned his brooding eyes her direction.

"What is your work?" she asked again when he simply stared at her.

There was something interesting, if not slightly disturbing, about how his gray eyes, with hints of blue, darkened the longer he studied her. It was as if he had decided something while searching her face. She wasn't sure she liked being analyzed without being allowed the opportunity to explain or verify whatever it was he thought he saw in her.

"There are many ways I could answer that question," Jeremy began slowly.

"Oh, really?"

He continued studying her, his gaze moving over her face as though memorizing every feature. The young boy didn't run to the table when he returned but instead walked, tall and proud, holding two bottles. He held one out to Jeremy, as if handing him a treasure, and then stuffed the other one in the container of ice along with the wine bottle on the table next to them.

"I guess there can't be any harm in your knowing," Jeremy mused, looking at the ice surrounding the beer and wine bottle after the boy left.

"In my knowing what?" she asked, watching when he opened his beer and then tilted it back. His Adam's apple rose and fell as he drank. A man's neck wasn't a part of the body she ever gave a lot of thought to, but his was perfect—not too long or short, and tan as his arms.

"What I do for a living."

"Is it a secret?"

"More than you know." He downed almost half the beer and then returned to his food. The silence grew between them, but waiting it out worked in her favor. "I do research—similar to what you do."

"You study the ocean?" She didn't like that he appeared so perfect in her eyes. She forced her attention back to her food—though she wasn't sure she could eat much more. But she needed a distraction, or, better yet, she needed to learn something about him that didn't appeal to her. Staying on this island for a couple weeks with Mr. Perfect would be her undoing and only result in regret after she left.

"The ocean and other things as well. This island, the way people live, and what stimulates them to do what they do."

"Sounds like an interesting job," Mercedes said, not having a clue what he meant. "So you do research then? For a particular company?"

"Yes." Jeremy had put away almost all the food on his plate and leaned back, nursing his beer while searching Mercedes's face again. "So, let me guess, you're from California?"

"No," she said, shaking her head at his blatant effort to change the subject again. "Where are you from?"

"Originally Nebraska, although I spent time in New York before coming here." He studied her through those thick lashes of his, once again making it hard to know exactly where he focused.

"That's quite a change in cultures."

"More than you know. But you, you're a West Coast girl."

"How can you tell?"

"Your actions," he said, tilting his head slightly. His sandy hair waved around his face, and a single strand moved over his forehead. He didn't move it. "So if not California, then north? Washington state?"

"I have family in Seattle," she admitted. "I've moved from one ship to the next this past year, spent some time in laboratories, so I really don't have a permanent home right now."

"A rolling stone," he mused.

"I don't really think of myself like that." Mercedes wasn't a drifter. Her feet were firmly on the ground, but her work kept her moving around.

"So, being on this island was completely accidental."

"If it weren't for our ship having engine trouble, I'd be in New Zealand right now with my crew, probably waiting at the airport."

"I hope you don't regret being here too much." He didn't smile or give any physical indication he was glad she was here, other than his tone.

Mercedes hated it when she couldn't read a person that well. Usually she credited herself with decent insight into a person's nature after she spent a bit of time with them. Jeremy's comments seemed intentionally vague to her, as though he was trying to keep up the conversation without saying anything of importance. She wasn't sure why he intrigued her when she should have been annoyed. Everything she shared with him was up front and honest.

"I don't usually regret my actions," she offered.

Jeremy raised one eyebrow, which made her heart pick up its pace. When he slid his chair back, stood, and then extended his hand, she couldn't get the notion out of her head that she'd just offered a challenge—which he'd readily accepted.

"Let's take an after-dinner stroll." He took her hand from where it rested on the table, not waiting for her to offer it, and brought her to her feet.

"I'm so full I don't know how far I can walk," she admitted, feeling his warm, strong fingers wrap around her smaller hand as he guided her from the table. "We were served an incredible meal."

"I'll make sure Francis knows you approved," he said, his voice lowering to a soft growl as he escorted her across the lawn toward the beach.

They walked in silence for a few minutes, the warm sand clinging to the sides of her heels through her sandals. Jeremy stood several inches taller than she, and his arm brushed against hers more than once as they held hands. She was acutely aware of how solid he felt, how silently he moved in spite of being at least six feet tall. And although he didn't speak, the way he held her hand, moved with her as if they'd taken many walks together, and kept his stride in tune with hers told her so much about him.

He had intentionally avoided sharing with her what he did for a living, but she believed he spent a lot of time learning about people by watching them. He matched her step, kept his hold on her hand firm but not constricting, and avoided patches in the sand not conducive to her sandals. Jeremy was observant, and it made her skin prickle thinking about what he might be learning from her as they walked in silence.

"Do you like to hike?" he asked, pausing and letting go of her hand.

"Hike?" She rubbed her hands together and then was almost surprised when she looked up and noticed the rocky cliffs in front of them. She hadn't noticed that they'd approached the end of the beach, which wasn't a good sign. Being that lost in thought meant she wasn't remaining alert to her surroundings. Regardless of how Jeremy appeared the gentleman, they were now very much alone, and it was growing dark. "I'm not really dressed for it."

"Good point." He turned to face her, his gaze dropping down her body. "Tomorrow we'll come back this way, and you can wear shoes to hike. That is, if you like the idea of exerting a bit of energy."

"Looks more like rock climbing to me," she said, managing to laugh as if the thought didn't bother her. She couldn't remember the last time she'd spent time walking like this, let alone breaking a sweat by doing something like hiking up a rocky incline.

"It isn't as bad as it looks. And the view from up there is worth the hike."

Mercedes jerked when he touched the side of her face, stroking a strand of hair behind her shoulder. "There are so many different shades to your hair," he mused, his voice lowering to a provocative tone that sent chills rushing over her flesh. "Are you nervous?"

"I wasn't." She hugged herself, stepping backward but then looking down when the ground appeared uneven.

"Why are you now?" His soft baritone caressed her soul, creating a heat inside her that spread too fast, stealing her breath. He touched her again, his knuckles grazing her cheekbone.

"I barely know you, and suddenly we're very alone."

Jeremy laughed, but even his amusement was raspy, deep, compelling and dangerous at the same time. "That's why we're spending time together, to get to know each other."

"The more time I spend with you, the less I seem to know," she informed him, lifting her face to stare at his. "You really haven't told me a thing about you."

"I guess I find myself boring. There isn't a lot to tell. But I have learned that discovering what a person is about often isn't done through a question-and-answer session."

"How is it done then?"

"You're the scientist. You should know that answer already."

"I should?" His eyes were an even deeper gray at that moment, adding to the dark, compelling way he watched her as he spoke. "Why don't you tell me how it is done?"

"I can't do that. That's my point." His knuckles moved down her face, and he lifted her hair from her neck and gripped her shoulder. With the slightest tug he brought her closer and then used his thumb to tilt her head. "You learn more about a person through experience."

Mercedes didn't close her eyes when he lowered his face, coming closer while his lashes hooded his eyes. But she didn't need to watch to know his intentions. Although everything inside her told her to step away from the kiss, when his lips brushed over hers, sensations washed over her so quickly she couldn't move.

"This is a perfect example," he whispered.

If Mercedes's brain hadn't seized up as her body had, there would have been a perfect, snide remark to throw out. But when he finished speaking, his mouth found hers again, his lips moist and warm and tasting of beer and lobster. She tilted her head slightly, but it was enough invitation. Jeremy moved his hand behind her neck, holding her in place, and eased his tongue inside her.

The moment she opened up to him, he growled, and his grip tightened. He grabbed her hip with his free hand, his fingers pressing into her flesh. There was something about the slight aggression, his primal growl, and his lack of hesitation that turned her on a hell of a lot more than it should have. In spite of his intentional sidestepping around their conversation all evening, she was very aware of his intelligence. His suave manner—the air of sophistication about him even in his casual attire—showed her Jeremy came from a secure, stable background.

Mercedes liked a man who was classy, who appeared to be successful and wealthy. She wasn't a gold digger. Hell, who had time for those games? But that *GQ* nature in a man was one hell of a turn-on. Yet when he showed his aggression, growling and suddenly releasing an air of primal, demanding male domination, her insides soared with uncontrollable need. Raw, hardcore lust swelled inside her, and the thought of grabbing him, matching his sudden feral nature, made her even hotter.

As if Jeremy had read her thoughts, his hand tangled in her hair, forcing her head back farther, and he impaled her mouth. Mercedes opened to him, wanting all he offered, and managed to move her hands between them before he could press her body against his. His tongue twirled around hers, the primitive, age-old dance of discovery truly exactly what he had claimed it would be. As she pressed her palms against his hard, muscular chest, she was aware of everything about him.

He'd just claimed that conversation wasn't always the best way to learn another person's nature. In that moment Mercedes learned a lot more about Jeremy than she'd learned all evening. Not only was he possibly the best damn kisser she'd ever known, his sex appeal radiated off the charts. At the same time, self-discovery came into play as well. She never would have guessed herself the kind of lady who would willingly fuck a man she didn't know. But more than anything, she wanted him inside her—now.

4

_____

Jeremy dragged his hand down Mercedes's back, his fingers gliding through her thick, silky dark hair. When he moved his hand up her side, gripping her dress and yanking it up, her breath caught. The slight gasp let him know he'd exposed her ass and encouraged him further.

Mercedes was quite possibly the sexiest woman he'd ever laid eyes on. He'd thought as much when he'd first seen her. Ever since then, he'd imagined what she would taste like, how she would feel in his arms, her body pressed against his. None of his fantasies about her came close to the hot, sultry creature who arched into him. The way she tasted, how her body stretched like a cat—not to mention the total submission that had exploded inside her the moment he'd instigated the kiss—were hotter than his wildest thoughts about her had been.

"Have you ever made love outside before?" he whispered into her mouth, his voice raw with the need that pulsed through him.

"No."

He didn't allow her time to offer more information or suggest they not have sex. Lifting her dress farther, he reached around and cupped her ass.

God! She wore a thong!

If that wasn't proof she had planned on allowing him to find out what was under her dress, he didn't know women as well as he thought. His brain rationalized this as he stretched his fingers over her smooth curves, opening her round buttocks and then moving lower until he felt heat scorch his fingertips.

"You're hot as hell. Fucking outside appeals to you."

"I don't know," she murmured but didn't fight him when he began a trail of kisses down her neck.

Mercedes's head fell back, the arch of her neck as appealing as the moisture that pooled between her legs. He moved his hand, needing better access to explore, and damn near exploded in his pants when he stroked smooth, damp flesh. Her pussy was shaved and already wet.

His cock throbbed and grew inside his jeans, demanding freedom. Jeremy's fingers shook as he forced himself not to lift Mercedes and bend her over the nearest rock. He couldn't wait to be inside her. Very little of his brain wished to think rationally. A thick fog of lust descended upon him, making it even harder to plot his way through this without simply demanding she put out now and fuck him.

But maintaining patience, making sure she didn't balk, would be worth the torture he endured while continuing to explore her hot, perfect body.

"Do you realize how wet you are?" he asked, tasting her skin and feeling the solid beat of her heart against his lips when he pressed his mouth to the curve of her neck. He eased his fingers inside her while moving his other hand up her body until he gripped her shoulder.

"Yes," she moaned, her hair draping over her shoulder.

The swell of her breasts threatened to spill over her strapless dress. It would take nothing to free them, watch her nipples harden and pucker in the cool night air. Mercedes's breathing turned almost to pants as he fingered her. He enjoyed how her dress kept her breasts confined, pushed together and offering a view to die for. It was too perfect to ruin by yanking it off.

"Have you been this wet all evening?"

Mercedes's long lashes fluttered over blue eyes. Her gaze was glassy, glazed over with a sensuality and erotic stare that showed how turned on she was. Her lips were parted, and he watched her face, the way her eyes cleared slightly, as though contemplating how to answer had sobered her slightly from the thick, needy state of desire in which she'd been trapped.

"I admit there was a curiosity," she whispered, speaking so softly he might have missed her admission if he hadn't been inches from her, drowning in those deep pools of sensual blue. "Obviously, it's mutual."

She surprised him when she moved her hand down his chest and stroked the length of his shaft through his jeans with her fingernails. Mercedes sucked in her lower lip, never taking her attention from his as she moved her fingers delicately over him. The slight touch was enough to send his body temperature to dangerous levels. Jeremy gritted his teeth, staring into her smoldering gaze and watching a level of confidence simmer inside her when she saw how her actions affected him.

"Have you been this hard all evening?" she purred, daring to taunt him while making him grow even harder and thicker in his jeans.

"I think you know the answer to that one already, my dear," he growled, his voice darker, deeper.

Mercedes's eyes opened wider. He loved her naturally submissive nature, although watching her grow confident, trying to take him on and fighting to be assertive, was just as fucking hot.

"If you're going to touch me like that, you're going to release me and do it right," he told her.

Mercedes swallowed and then dropped her attention to his cock. Knowing that she watched his face while she undid his pants forced all the blood in his body straight to his groin. It seemed to take her forever to unzip his zipper and then even longer when she pushed his pants down.

When his cock sprang free, Jeremy swore he started floating. The sensation that his feet had left the ground made him light-headed for a moment, as though the beer he had drunk had been too much for him. Yet the moment Mercedes wrapped her fingers around his cock, Jeremy stabilized himself quickly. There was no way she'd end this evening with her curious touch. He clamped his teeth down so hard he bit his lip, but the sharp, eye-watering pain helped keep him steady. More than anything, he needed to enjoy the moments while she stroked him, took her time fingering his shaft and learning him.

"How are we going to do this?" she asked, her hair streaming over her bare shoulder. She watched herself continue to stroke him. "I mean, I really don't want to lie in the sand."

"You're not going to." It was perfect timing when he grabbed her, turning her around. "Put your hands on that rock," he instructed, pressing her forward slightly.

Mercedes supported herself against the flat, dark rock at the base of the cliffs and bent over in front of him. Her exposed ass glowed against the moonlight, which was just enough light to allow him to see the most glorious rear end he'd laid eyes on in as long as he could remember.

Soon he would have her in her bed, possibly even later tonight. But he didn't need to ask to know she didn't want to wait another second. Mercedes needed to be fucked as desperately as he needed to be inside her. She kept her legs straight but parted them just enough to show off the sweet curve of her ass and barely offer a view of her shaved, soaked pussy.

Jeremy rubbed her smooth bottom, loving how her dress was wrinkled around her waist and her long, slender legs were spread. She tried looking over her shoulder at him and appeared ready to say something, but Jeremy gripped her hips, positioned himself, and then thrust deep inside her.

The fire that ransacked his soul, burning and clutching his cock, driving him in deeper, spread throughout his body in a matter of moments.

"Holy shit," he hissed. "You're absolutely perfect, sweetheart."

"Oh, God!" she cried out, arching her back and moaning loudly as she shifted just enough to allow him to fill her completely. "Yes, oh, hell yes."

He would love to sing her praises, stroke her lovingly while saying all the words he was an expert at putting on paper. But the voice of the famous author eluded him as he fucked her, building momentum and unable to do anything other than enjoy the many tiny muscles that vibrated against him and held him deep inside her.

It was all he could do to focus and watch his cock disappear inside her, only to pull out almost all the way before impaling her again. Thick, white cream coated his shaft, the imagery beyond perfect. Mercedes was hot, incredibly tight and wet. Although he couldn't swear to it, the way she cried out, exploding again and again as he fucked her harder and faster, led him to believe sex wasn't something she got on a daily basis.

When he thrust even harder, her arms gave out, and she collapsed over the rock, crying out his name. It was the most beautiful sound. Mercedes was perfect, beyond perfect. And that she would howl his name as her orgasm swept through her was enough to push him to the edge.

"I'm going to pull out," he told her, not wanting to but somehow able to hold on to a small part of sanity as his balls tightened painfully and the pressure became unbearable.

"Jeremy!" she cried again, neither confirming nor denying his actions.

Her come coated his cock, and he was hot and sticky when he grabbed his shaft, retreating from her scorching heat and then releasing everything he had over her bare, creamy, smooth ass. As he came, her cries tearing deep into his soul, the mess he created over her rear end made him come even harder. His entire world nearly toppled over, leaving him almost too drained to even straighten and dress, let alone make sure Mercedes was alright.

"We're going to do that again," he breathed, his voice raspy as if it had been him howling in the throes of ecstasy instead of her.

Mercedes struggled to look over her shoulder, shaking her ass and teasing him as she puckered her lips. "I'm ready when you are."

In a less secure world, Jeremy would have believed that her final comment after they'd finished fucking on the beach implied that he hadn't satisfied her. If it weren't for the way she'd willingly collapsed against him, letting him hold her for a long time with neither of them speaking, he might have thought that. But he'd seen how hard she'd come. Her legs had visibly trembled when she waited for him to clean her before helping her straighten her dress. And when they returned to the cabin, holding hands, her quiet, contemplative mood only told him she had digested the new level their relationship had reached and how quickly it had moved to that point.

The table and all the food were gone when they returned to her cabin. Jeremy stood silently at her sliding glass door when she entered and moved to the nearest lamp.

"Well, that's thoughtful," Mercedes said when she stared at the bottle of wine and several beers now on the table in her room, submerged in fresh ice. "It looks as if we're being offered a nightcap."

Her hair was tousled as she fingered the chilled bottle. Her strapless dress was crooked, pressing her breasts together and creating a deep ravine of cleavage. Jeremy knew the longer he stood there watching her the more he would want her. And he already craved burying himself in that hot pussy again.

Mercedes didn't say anything but instead ran her finger along the length of the damp wine bottle. Finally she shot Jeremy a furtive glance. No way would she send him away.

"I'll tell you what," he said, his voice gruff and raw. "Tonight was perfect. We're going to see each other again. We're the only ones on the island."

"Other than Francis and the villagers," she offered, her smile suddenly shy.

"I want to end this evening with the memories we've just created." He suddenly felt a twisted knot in his gut, feeling like a schmuck for using a line straight out of his book. It was the how-to-get-out-of-an-awkward-evening line, and he didn't want to get out of anything. But he didn't want her sending him away either. He cleared the distance between them and lowered his mouth to hers. "I will see you tomorrow."

The kiss was tender, erotic, and got him so fucking hard it was all he could do to turn and walk away from her. Even as he stripped out of his clothes and collapsed on his bed in his cabin, her smell was still on him; his fingers tingled, aching to touch her again. Tomorrow couldn't come fast enough. He would wake up and write for a while, making a show of not stalking her first thing, and then he would hunt her down. Jeremy drifted off to sleep, refusing to allow his mind to travel to places he didn't want to go. It was no use wondering why he longed to pursue Mercedes. It was physical. He didn't need to be the sex therapist his books implied he was to know lust was a strong and powerful emotion.

Although, by noon the next day, he still struggled with the chapter he'd been working on since the day before. Entering into the mind of the callous female jaded from so many men didn't sit well with him today the way it usually did. Mercedes might be that voice. Her brooding stare the night before when she'd stood in her dimly lit cabin, her face flushed and hair in a disarray from good, hard sex, wasn't the image he wanted planted in his mind. He didn't want her leery of him. Yet she was, and there wasn't anyone to blame but himself. From the beginning of their night, he'd been evasive, misleading her and definitely not honest. More than anything right now, he wanted her to know the real him. But telling her who he was would probably piss her off.

Jeremy Fall would never bend a woman over a rock on the beach and fuck her just to get *his* rocks off. Jeremy Fall would have asked her what would please her, taken the time to learn her body so he knew where to touch her, how to caress her, because her orgasm meant more than his.

"Jeremy Fall, you're a prick," he grumbled, pushing away from his laptop and standing to stretch. Fall was an annoyance to all men, making them have to work harder and fight to understand the intricate minds of women. What sucked worse than anything was that he didn't have a clue how women thought. He'd faked it and pulled it off—big-time. But could he continue faking it and pull it off with Mercedes?

After showering, Jeremy headed to the office for fresh coffee. It didn't bother him that Francis wasn't around. One glance at Mercedes's cabin through the open curtains, and it was obvious Mercedes wasn't around either. He looked toward the ocean, and then walked in that direction before thinking it through. It wasn't until he'd come to the grove of trees that he saw the large yacht and the long dock that reached out to it. His footsteps echoed against the wooden planks, the ocean lapping under the boardwalk, filling the air with the fresh smell of salt. Nursing his coffee, he slowed when he reached the ship. There wasn't anyone visible.

"Hello?" he called out, wondering how the captain of the

ship would react to him boarding. He obviously was not a thief, or trouble, to anyone who took the time to look at him.

An older gentleman appeared around the corner from the stern at the same time Jeremy stepped onto the ship.

"May I help you?" he asked. His closely shaved head looked as tanned as the rest of his body.

"I'm looking for Mercedes."

The older man studied him with shrewd green eyes. "Does she know you?"

"Yes. I'm Jeremy Faulkner. We had dinner last night."

The man didn't say anything, but he took in Jeremy a moment longer, his dark expression not revealing whether he cared who Jeremy might be. Then, turning, he disappeared, leaving Jeremy standing where he was. He had half a mind to follow the old man. He wanted to see Mercedes in her own environment, working with her marine life. Hesitating for only a moment, Jeremy headed after the man, finding the staircase that led into the belly of the ship.

"Mercedes, there is a man who wants you," the man announced.

Mercedes turned, studying the older man with a frown before looking past him to Jeremy. "Hi, there," she said, her voice turning breathy.

She wasn't upset to see him. He straightened when the man turned around; Jeremy no longer cared if the guy seemed a bit put out that Jeremy had followed him instead of waiting for a formal introduction.

"It's okay, captain," Mercedes offered, touching the man's arm. "Thank you."

The captain grumbled something about being just outside and gave Jeremy a warning look as he walked past, leaving the two of them alone in a small, well-lit room.

"This is where you work?" Jeremy felt like he'd just seriously scored, seeing approval in her eyes. On top of that, he was witnessing her in action as she turned to a computer and scattered notes on a desk she'd been standing in front of when the captain announced him.

"It has been for the past couple months," she said. Mercedes wore blue shorts today that hugged her perfect ass. He loved short shorts on a woman, especially when she had the hips and long toned legs to show off. The tank top she wore with no bra gave her a youthful look and made for a mouthwatering view, even from her back side. Her hair was pulled back at her nape in a barrette. The dark brown strands fell in waves over each other, curling at the middle of her back. "Are you just waking up?" she asked, glancing over her shoulder and meeting his gaze only for a moment.

"No. I've been online most of the morning."

"Research, huh?" She started typing when he leaned on the counter next to her. Her lips pressed into a thin line, and she shot him a furtive glance. Jeremy might not be the man he claimed, but that didn't mean he didn't have good insight into women. Mercedes obviously didn't believe him. He'd spent the first hour, after answering e-mails and checking a few of his favorite blogs, reading several reports on the chemical makeup of men and women.

"Actually, yes." He relaxed against the tall counter, picking up a ballpoint pen and glancing at notes scribbled on a legal pad—a formula of sorts that appeared completely Greek to him. Mercedes was the epitome of sex appeal and intelligence. He doubted he could compete. What he might lack in brain smarts, he could make up for in smooth talk and his persuasive nature—again, behavior he dogged in his book. "In fact, let's do a little experiment."

"An experiment?" Mercedes stopped typing and shifted, matching his pose as she, too, leaned against the tall counter. "I've been running experiments all morning with little luck.

Unless yours offers a strong probability of a favorable outcome, I doubt I'm interested."

She didn't look stressed or worn out from the work she claimed had annoyed her all morning. The corner of her mouth twitched, and he guessed she hid a smile. Either that or she contemplated what a favorable outcome might be from experimenting with him. As he studied her face for a moment, color washed over her cheeks until she looked down at her notepad. He liked pushing her. Maybe he'd take this experiment one step further and see how long it would be until he got her to submit.

"Then we'll conduct two experiments." He put down the pen and covered her hand with his. She returned her attention to his face while sucking in a breath. He loved how her nipples grew hard and poked against her tank top. "Here's the first one. Look at this equation on your legal pad and tell me what you see."

Mercedes groaned. "I see that it's wrong."

He couldn't help laughing. "I see a threat."

She yanked her hand out from underneath his and clutched both her hands to her chest, as if he'd just burned her. Her blue eyes were bright as she stared at him, her lips barely parted.

"Are you saying intelligent women threaten you?" she whispered, the flush in her cheeks disappearing as she paled noticeably.

"Actually, no. But I'll admit when I walked up to the counter and stood beside you, it was the first thing I noticed. I don't have a clue what it means, so it presented a challenge to me."

"Well, if you think I'm going to act like a stupid twit while we're on this island together, just to entertain you, think again, mister."

"I doubt you would be able to pull it off if you tried," he said dryly. "And I told you this was an experiment. Are you ready for the second one?"

She stared at him warily, pursing her lips. It was all he could do not to lean in and kiss her. As it was, he moved a loose strand behind her ear that had escaped her hair clasp. Mercedes lowered her gaze, her long, dark lashes fluttering over her pretty eyes. When she sucked in a sharp breath, his cock stirred in his pants. It was a damn good thing he'd opted for loose-fitting khaki pants today instead of jeans, or he'd be giving her a show right now that wouldn't do either of them any good at the moment.

"Okay," he continued when she didn't say anything. Brushing his fingers under her chin, he turned her attention back to his face. "Here is the second experiment. When you look at me, what do you see?"

Mercedes smiled, her eyes darkening until they glowed like sapphires. "Is this a two-way experiment?"

"Yes."

"Then you go first."

"Okay." He remembered the doubt in her voice when he'd told her he'd spent the morning doing research. Already she questioned the validity of who he said he was. The explanation behind this experiment had been the premise for the chapter he'd been writing since yesterday. For the results to be accurate and measurable, all participants needed to be incredibly honest. "When I look at you I see a challenge."

Her expression didn't change. She was ready with her response and answered so quickly he doubted she'd given herself time to allow his comment to register before speaking her mind. "When I look at you, I see a threat."

5

_____

"A threat?" Jeremy demanded, his eyes the shade of a stormy sky.

"A challenge?" Mercedes narrowed her gaze on him, hating how the longer she stared at him, the harder her heart beat. He was a threat to her mind, her heart, her body—hell, to every aspect of her life. "Sounds like we'd both be better off parting ways right now."

"You think?" He didn't move.

Not that she wanted him to. Her experiments weren't cooperating, because she couldn't think straight. Ever since she'd woken up, all that had been on her mind was Jeremy. She'd wondered where he was, what he was doing. But mostly she'd worried he didn't want to see her again today.

"Challenges and threats don't sound too appealing," she said, a mixture of desire and trepidation making for an odd sensation in her belly. Jeremy looked incredible this morning, or was it afternoon already? And the way he'd followed Captain Huraldo down here, as if he'd known what he wanted and didn't hesitate in taking it . . .

Despite the fact that she didn't want him to leave, already her mind had worked up more of an argument as to why they were incompatible. Her defenses were in place, prepared to state a case to relieve both of them from pursuing something that would inevitably lead to at least one of them getting hurt.

"I'm up to the challenge of making you see I'm not a threat," he growled, grabbing her arm and yanking her to him.

Mercedes almost tripped over her feet, collapsing against his hard chest and slapping her palm against it to stabilize herself. "Oh, well," she began, but when she tilted her head to look into his eyes, he cleared the distance and captured her mouth with his.

His kiss was hot, greedy, demanding and had her losing her footing all over again. His hands moved over her back, bringing her closer to him while he took his time devouring her mouth.

Mercedes wasn't sure she'd ever met a man who could kiss like Jeremy. He made the simple act seem primal, rough and needy. No one ever would have made her believe a man who bordered on being chauvinistic could make her so hot and swollen with need.

It took more effort than she thought she had to simply turn her head. When she did, she was gasping for breath.

"Tell me how I threaten you," he whispered, his mouth finding her earlobe and sucking it; then he scraped the bit of flesh with his teeth until chills rushed over her feverish skin.

"You're doing it right now." The last thing she wanted to do was push him away. It felt so good wrapped in his arms with his tall, strong warm body pressed against hers. "This isn't a vacation for me."

"Nor me," he breathed, his baritone rumbling through her brain. "But Christmas is right around the corner. Because we're here together, maybe we can be each other's Christmas presents to brighten the holiday."

"Be each other's what?" She shook her head, finding the

strength to stretch her fingers across roped muscle and do her best to push. "How are we supposed to be each other's presents? You don't take presents back."

He allowed her to move but then gripped her arms, making her face him. "You tell me I'm a threat, but in truth you're not sure you trust me."

Her heart started pounding. She'd been told more than a few times in her life that she wasn't that easy to read. If he guessed she didn't trust him, Mercedes would bet good money it was because he knew he held out on the truth about himself. Although she'd yet to figure out why he was so evasive when it came to talking about himself, Mercedes loved a good challenge.

"My gift to you will be showing you I'm not a threat," he added.

"And you want me not to be a challenge?" She seriously doubted a man like Jeremy would enjoy a woman he couldn't hunt and conquer.

His grin bordered on dangerous. Mercedes's mouth went dry, and then suddenly she worried she'd start drooling. She really liked how his eyes changed color with his moods. As she watched, they turned a bright gray, radiant and intense as he gazed down at her.

"The point of the experiment is to show that men and women see the exact same situation through very different eyes."

"Isn't that old news?" It was on the tip of her tongue to ask why he did research on men and women. Of course, if he were Jeremy Fall, it would be obvious why he did. He'd denied being a writer already, and something told her cornering him on his lie wouldn't be pretty.

Reminding herself he had lied, or at least she thought maybe he had, sobered her a bit, and she lowered her attention to his chest. The tank top he wore today, along with his brown khaki shorts, made him appear a man without a care. In the couple of days she'd known him, though, Jeremy was without question filled with cares and concerns. Whatever it was he did for a living, it was on his mind a lot. That brooding stare he blessed her with too often was the look of a man very preoccupied with something. Mercedes wasn't conceited enough to think it was her.

"Just because we know something doesn't mean we completely understand the whys of it." He nodded toward her work. "Isn't that what you're doing here? You're researching something that more than likely many people know about, yet you're trying to learn more to understand it better."

She ached to demand he tell her more about this research he was doing and why he was doing it. But then, what was the point? They were here for a couple weeks, and then it would be over. Once she returned home, she wouldn't see him again. Nodding, she returned her attention to his unwavering gaze.

"So what is the gift I'm supposed to give you?" she asked.

"I can't tell you what to get me for Christmas. You have to decide that." He pulled her closer, kissing her forehead and then brushing his lips over her cheek. "I do know I'm going to enjoy the hell out of convincing you I'm not a threat."

Jeremy's mouth found hers just as Captain Huraldo cleared his throat in the doorway. Mercedes jumped back, her heart exploding in her chest, making it hard to catch her breath. In spite of herself, she laughed, shaking her head at the captain, who was not smiling.

"I feel like a schoolgirl busted when her parents walked in," she said, still grinning and at the same time grateful when Jeremy didn't hold on to her as she stepped out of his arms and walked over to the captain. "Captain Huraldo, this is Jeremy Faulkner."

The men grunted, nodding but not smiling. Captain Huraldo scowled when he gave her a quick once-over. "I'm heading out on the charter plane here in a couple hours. Hopefully, I'll be bringing back parts and a mechanic or two to help fix my ship."

"Is there a chance we'll have it up and running in a few days then?" she asked, knowing it would disappoint Jeremy if she left soon, but also knowing the more time she spent with him, the harder it would be to leave him.

"Don't count on it," he grumbled, glaring at Jeremy and then leaving them without a good-bye.

Mercedes turned in time to see the hard look on Jeremy's face. "You really should research why the level of testosterone quadruples when two males confront each other," she said.

"It only happens when both are interested in the same woman," he offered easily without looking at her but continuing to stare at the doorway.

"Captain Huraldo doesn't want me." As she spoke, Jeremy's words sunk in until they registered.

"But he knows I do want you." There was a hard edge in his voice, his dominating, aggressive nature coming out in full force as he slowly approached her. "Men are protective by nature. You're on his ship, and he's keeping an eye on you."

She shook her head slightly, willing the intensity in the air to lighten. There wasn't any way Jeremy was implying that he was instigating a relationship between the two of them. When he said he wanted her, he meant sexually. Which was obvious. She could feel the sexual tension making her skin tingle even when his hands weren't on her.

"More material for you to research," she said, waving her hand through the air between them. "Why do men feel a need to protect women? If anything, we're more protective, while men are the players."

"Do you think I'm playing?" His expression was focused, intense. A strand of hair fell over his forehead, and sandy-colored waves bordered his face. He definitely looked like a sex god, an international playboy, yet his gray eyes pierced her with a serious intensity that caused her heart to race in her chest.

"I think you're serious about what you want," she answered carefully, managing to pull her gaze from his and return to her work.

Jeremy gripped her arm and spun her back around so fast her hair flew in her face. She brushed it out of the way, but not before he slammed her body against his. His fingers tangled in her hair behind her head, causing her barrette to slide loose. He captured her mouth, pressing his tongue past her lips and impaling her with a fierce hunger that attacked her senses in more than one way.

Mercedes's legs were suddenly like wet noodles. It was a damn good thing he was holding her up. She didn't know a man could do what Jeremy did with just a kiss; he didn't just kiss her with his mouth but with his entire body. The way he grabbed the back of her hair—tilted her head exactly how he wanted it, pressed his body against hers, and held her pinned with one muscular arm—made the act more of a union.

His lips felt soft and full and moved over hers with the grace and skill of a master. He didn't hesitate gliding his tongue between her lips, opening her for him and then delving into her heat. As she opened her mouth, leaning her head to the side farther and then moving her tongue around his, Jeremy growled into her mouth.

His approval of her actions fed a fire she didn't know had been smoldering until that moment. Already her equilibrium was shot to hell as the room seemed to tilt and then turn. Her legs were weak. Her heart thudded so hard in her chest blood rushed through her veins, sounding like a steam engine in her brain. And while her body did the complete freak-out, his was touching her everywhere. Corded muscle stretched down his leg, which he moved between hers. His thigh was harder than steel, and when he pressed against her pussy, she damn near passed out from the need that surged out of control inside her.

"Does that feel like I'm playing?" he growled, keeping his mouth over hers and tugging harder on her hair.

Mercedes didn't fight him, and her head fell back. She opened her eyes, his face a blur for a moment. He was so strong, so confident, and so incredibly determined she see things the way he did. She didn't see any problem appeasing him on this. "No, it doesn't," she whispered.

"Good. I'm not." As quickly as he'd swept her off her feet, Jeremy straightened her and let her go.

Her lips tingled, and her heart still raced when she pressed damp palms against her shirt. She looked down at her hard nipples as she straightened her clothes.

"How long will you be working?" Jeremy asked, moving behind her and lifting her hair from her shoulders. He unsnapped her barrette and gathered her hair, clasping it so it was secure at her nape.

"I planned on being here most of the day." Only because she couldn't stand pacing her cabin wondering what Jeremy was doing or if he'd seek her out today. Now that she knew, going over the work they'd done over the past few weeks had lost its appeal.

"Then I'll see you this evening." He turned her around and tapped his finger to her nose, then walked out of the room and up the stairs.

Mercedes drooled over his hard ass and his bare, muscular legs. He hadn't suggested what they might do tonight, although their options on the island were limited. She opened her mouth to call after him, ask what he had in mind. Snapping her mouth shut before the words spilled out, she stood there until she couldn't see him any longer, and then she focused on her computer screen.

It wasn't Captain Huraldo's business what she did with her

time. More than likely he was within earshot, and if she did make a scene—yell for Jeremy—it would be invitation enough for the captain to seek her out afterward and give her his two cents about the entire matter. Mercedes didn't need a father breathing over her shoulder. If she wanted to have a fling while stuck on this island over Christmas, that was her business.

Above and beyond keeping her affairs private, Mercedes didn't want Jeremy thinking she was anxious. He was so damned dominating, a trait she normally would claim not to like in a man, but somehow it worked with Jeremy. Leaning against her counter, she tapped the space bar on her keyboard, clearing her screen, and moved the cursor to the search bar.

"Jeremy Fall," she said aloud as she typed and leaned her chin on her fist while she waited for her page options to load. The Internet was slow as hell, worse here on the ship than it was in her cabin. And it was bad there. "Maybe you aren't a writer."

She'd bought *Give Them What They Want* when it had first hit the best-seller list. Everyone was talking about it, and the joke at the time was that any man interested in seeing a woman was required to read that book first. The book described how a man should treat a woman, breaking it down from the first date to when a couple had been married for thirty years. Although Mercedes had skimmed a lot of it and not finished the rest, finding it too good to be true and almost a bit superfluous for her taste, she remembered the tone of the writing. Jeremy Fall was a gentleman to a fault. He strongly believed a woman should be honored and adored. He stressed repeatedly in the book that animalistic behavior such as hair pulling or bossing a woman around, throwing her around, even in the throes of sex, was immature and insulting. The only time a man should treat a woman like that was if she requested it, and even then he should follow her instruction and not treat her like a sex toy.

Jeremy Faulkner obviously hadn't read that book.

"And maybe that's why you never finished reading it," she mused, clicking on the link that took her to the official Web site for Jeremy Fall.

She'd never realized it before, but the man described in that book wasn't the man for her. Jeremy's strong nature—the way her scalp tingled from where he'd pulled her hair—and his aggressive manner—sweeping her off her feet with a mere kiss—got her so damn hot she was soaked and horny as hell now.

It wasn't as if she'd given serious thought to what type of man would be her soul mate. But looking back now, it made sense to her. *Give Them What They Want* had had everyone talking. Mercedes had tried to read it so she could be part of the conversations. She'd never told anyone the book hadn't done anything for her though it seemed to have an effect on everyone else. And she hadn't thought about why it didn't appeal to her. If she *had* thought about it, she wouldn't have made that conclusion at the time anyway. It had taken meeting Jeremy, experiencing how he treated her, and feeling her insides swell and burn alive in reaction to him to realize her "type" of man.

"You like it rough, baby," she said, grinning and sighing as she shifted, rubbing her thighs together and willing the throbbing to go away.

Jeremy Fall's Web site opened, and the cover of his book appeared on the page. Mercedes squinted, staring hard at the man on the cover. Maybe they looked alike. One of the links on top of the page said ABOUT JEREMY. She hadn't thought to read about the author when she'd looked at his Web site before. She knew a bit more about Jeremy now. It was time to compare notes.

It took forever for the new page to load. Mercedes groaned, afraid she'd locked up her computer. Walking away from the computer, anything to make it cooperate, she glanced at her legal pad and the pen lying on top.

"Do I threaten you?" she asked, picking up the pen and clicking it as she stared at the equation she'd been struggling with throughout the morning. It was an equation that had been passed around through e-mails among her crew and some of the teams working back off the coast of California. Supposedly, the problem was solvable, but it appeared not to be. It was a math trick, a brain tease. "Are you intimidated by an intelligent woman?"

Jeremy hadn't acted too intimidated when he'd damn near made her come by kissing her.

Mercedes dropped her pen on the pad, making a very unladylike sound as she glared at the equation. She wasn't all that smart. She couldn't figure out the problem.

Glancing over at her screen, she moved to her computer when she noticed the page had loaded.

"Do you have everything you need?" Captain Huraldo's booming voice made her jump. "I didn't mean to startle you," he added.

Mercedes closed the Web site and clasped her hands behind her back, facing the captain with her back to the computer. "Are you heading out now?"

"In about half an hour."

"It won't take me that long to gather what I need."

"I'll help you take what you need to your cabin. I'm sorry you can't work here while I'm gone." He'd apologized repeatedly after telling Mercedes he would lock down his ship while he was gone getting more parts and whoever he could find to help fix his ship.

"I completely understand," she said, waving him off and then stacking her notes and notepads next to the computer. Jeremy showing up had made her completely forget that the captain leaving this afternoon meant she needed to leave, too. He'd allowed her to work here until he had to go, but now she needed to wrap up what she could and relocate to her cabin for the next few days. "And thank you. I won't take anything other than my notes. I can work more on my projects here once you return."

"A lot of people do take Christmas off and don't work," he teased. He was back to his jovial self. Although he often appeared gruff to her crew, Mercedes knew the older guy had a heart of gold. She really liked him but was grateful that he didn't take advantage of their friendship and lecture or advise her concerning Jeremy.

Captain Huraldo walked her to her cabin, insisting on carrying her notebooks, although she could have easily carried them herself. Then, giving her a fatherly hug, he grumbled something about being safe and then stalked away from her, heading to the landing pad.

Mercedes didn't see Jeremy anywhere while she arranged her cabin so she could work. Even after a shower and applying a bit of makeup—just in case she saw him through her windows or the open sliding glass doors—there wasn't any sight of him. More than likely he was doing exactly what she was doing: working in his cabin. Which meant he was right next door.

Her insides fluttered, and again she imagined what they might do this evening. Booting up her laptop, she stretched, staring at herself in the large mirror over the low dresser along the wall next to her desk. Her shirt lifted, revealing her belly, which looked flat and taut as she clasped her hands and reached for the ceiling. Still damp, her hair looked almost black, which offset her creamy white skin. Men probably liked women with nice tans, shorter than she was, and blond.

"Well, that's three strikes against you," she grumbled, dropping her hands and then reaching down and touching her toes.

No matter what she did—walk, shower, change clothes, or stretch—the tingly anticipation swelling inside her continued to distract her. And no matter what Jeremy might have in mind for the evening, she was pretty sure it would include sex. A man didn't kiss a woman the way he'd kissed her earlier without wanting to fuck her.

"Crap," she groaned, plopping down in the chair in front of her laptop and opening her search engine. Without giving it too much thought, once again she typed in Jeremy Fall's Web site. It didn't take as long to load this time. Clicking on the ABOUT JEREMY link, she rubbed her palms up and down her legs while waiting for the page to appear. "Jeremy Fall, age thirty-five, never married, and a Capricorn," she read.

Mercedes leaned back, glancing toward the open glass door when a breeze hurried into the cabin. A mixture of sweet aromas from flowers in bloom nearby and salt from the ocean made for a pleasant combination. Glancing back at the screen, something toward the bottom of the page caught her attention.

"You're kidding me," she grunted, reading the remainder of the blurb about Jeremy Fall a second time. The last paragraph glared at her, her stomach tightening as she read it aloud a third time. "Jeremy is currently working on his second book, *Take What You Need*, which is scheduled for release next summer. Although he won't even tell his editor his exact whereabouts, it is reported that Jeremy is cloistered on a small island in the South Pacific."

Her heart thumped uncomfortably against her rib cage when she found another link to a gallery. A handful of pictures showed Jeremy Fall at several book signings. She swallowed the lump in her throat and stared at Jeremy . . . Faulkner.

"Why did you lie to me?" she whispered.

6

Jeremy double-checked his source, copying and pasting the paragraphs he would use as a reference in the section he was explaining. It had been a lot easier to get lost in his writing after knowing where Mercedes was and confirming he'd see her this evening. He'd licked the taste of her off his lips, though it did cross his mind more than once to go find her and kiss her senseless again.

He looked up at the sound of someone outside the glass doors. Mercedes's pensive expression didn't sway him. She was beautiful, sensual, intelligent, with the perfect amount of hesitation wrapped up among it all.

"Hi, there," he said, standing and moving to the screen, remembering at the last minute that he couldn't let her inside with his work opened up on his computer. Easing the screen back, he stepped outside and closed it behind him. "What's up?"

"Would you come with me, please, for a minute?" she asked, her soft voice enticing yet serious.

He'd follow her anywhere she wanted to go and fell in pace

behind her without commenting. They didn't walk far. She stopped at her cabin in front of her closed screen door.

Jeremy reached over her head, pulling the screen open for her. "Is everything okay?"

"Well, I'm not sure. That really depends on you." She faced him, searching his face, her blue eyes glassy. "I was curious about what you said earlier today and last night, about the research you do."

"What about it?" Her hair was damp, and she smelled of shampoo and something musky, possibly perfume. He liked the makeup she'd applied, eyeliner on her lower lids adding to the fullness of her pretty eyes. They were dark, like sapphires, when she studied his face. He reached for a strand of her hair, but she walked farther into her room. "Is there something wrong?" he asked and then saw her computer screen. "Shit," he hissed under his breath.

Mercedes collapsed on the edge of her bed, also focusing on her computer for a long moment before letting out a loud breath. "Why did you lie to me?" she asked.

It crossed his mind to play out his story. It would be tricky, but he could convince her he really wasn't Jeremy Fall. There wasn't any way she could prove him right or wrong, shy of the pictures on her screen that really looked like him. He should have been more adamant about keeping pictures of him off that damn Web site.

Jeremy shifted his attention from the computer to Mercedes. He'd allowed the silence between them to go on too long. She sucked in a breath, straightening and pressing her hands into her lap. Her eyes turned a shade he hadn't seen before, a dull, dark shade of blue, the shade of a deadly sky before a torrential storm erupted.

"I asked you if you were a writer, and you told me you weren't." Her voice was soft as she spoke slowly, taking her time uttering each word.

"You're right." There was only one way to handle this situation. The hell with his books, with the solid, confident advice he offered in them. The damn things might as well be fiction, along with all the documented charts and test studies used to back what was in them. His gut told him how to handle Mercedes. And waiting until she demanded to know what she needed to hear would cause him to lose the upper hand. He wouldn't relinquish control of the situation by having her throw out accusations and presumptions to him. "I didn't want you to know."

Mercedes's eyes grew wide when she shot her attention to his face. "You didn't want me to know?"

"No."

"So you lied to me?" Her expression begged for his response to be something she could stomach. Mercedes was a good woman, hot as hell, and incredibly intelligent. She would get kinky and creative, exploring sexual avenues she hadn't been down before, but only if she trusted him. Her imploring expression was enough to let him know she ached to have him set the matter straight so she could continue enjoying her time with him.

"No," he told her without hesitating.

Mercedes lifted one eyebrow and then looked pointedly at the computer. "I asked if you were a writer, and you told me no. Exactly how is that not lying?"

"I told you I did research. Granted, it's a matter of wording, and if you require a guilty plea, you may have one in my being evasive." He wondered what had compelled her to pull up his Web site. Glancing around her room, he didn't see any books. Other than a couple notebooks and her laptop and cell phone, there weren't any items in her room indicating she'd been doing anything in here other than working. "I didn't want the conversation being about me or my writing."

"Did you think I would be some obsessed fan?" she asked incredulously.

If her question wasn't sarcastic, it should have been. One look at her face told him the answer. "I would prefer if you weren't," he said flatly.

"I was never able to finish reading it, and it wasn't until earlier today that I realized why. But none of that matters now. I think you should leave, Jeremy. Forget about this evening." She almost jumped off the bed, hugging herself and refusing to look at his face but instead pressing her lips together and focusing on something behind him. "Please leave."

Studying her for a moment, it was easy to see that if he pushed her, she'd be an emotional wreck in no time. Mercedes was pissed, feeling she'd been wronged but determined to show him she wouldn't tolerate deception at any level.

"Is that what you want?" he asked, fighting the urge to yank her into his arms and kiss her until she forgot she was mad at him. Fighting over something as petty as his writing wasn't worth it. As much money as that fucking book made him, it had been equally one hell of a big headache.

Her eyes were bright with her outrage when she snapped her attention to him. "I don't lie," she hissed. "And I don't hedge around a situation either. I'm not afraid to say things how they are."

Her words sliced deeper than he wanted to admit. But if he said anything else, it would only make things worse. Whether either of them liked it or not, they were on this island together for the next couple weeks, and they were neighbors. Jeremy didn't say anything else. He left her cabin, closing her glass door behind him as he did. And maybe he imagined it, but he swore he heard her crying when he left her.

It took another lie to get him through the evening. And as hard as he tried convincing himself that after two days there was no way any woman could get under his skin enough to matter all that much to him, he didn't believe himself. Even the next morning, after traipsing to the office and downing one cup of coffee before refilling his cup and heading back to his cabin, he couldn't convince himself he didn't care he'd upset Mercedes.

There were several more chapters needed before the first draft of his book was done. He was on schedule, although as tightly wound as he was this morning, sitting down and working sounded like an impossible feat. Heading toward his cabin, sipping at his coffee, he stared at the sky past the cliffs he'd planned hiking with Mercedes at some point—dark clouds loomed above them, looking as dark and dangerous as Mercedes's eyes when she'd kicked him out of her cabin.

It was going to storm. With only a few days until Christmas, it was only appropriate they receive some bad weather. Maybe he'd head into the village and learn what they planned on doing to celebrate the holiday. Jeremy had stopped in front of Mercedes's door before he realized his actions.

"Good morning, Mr. Jeremy," Francis sang out from behind him. "You've missed the pretty lady this morning. Do you know she's named after a car?" She grinned, her uneven teeth with large gaps between the ones in the front adding to her eccentric, unique appearance. She tugged on the loose-fitting flower-print shirt she wore. "I told her it wasn't the right day to go today, but who listens to Francis?"

"To go where?" he demanded, frowning at her closed cabin door. "She's not here?"

"Oh, she will be back. I promise." Francis cackled when she laughed. It fit her nature, although it bordered on irritating, especially when she wasn't making a hell of a lot of sense.

"Where did she go?" Jeremy demanded.

Francis's expression sobered, and her lips almost disappeared when she pressed them together.

"What?" He fought the urge to grab and give her a firm shake until her wits settled back where they belonged. "Francis." He sighed. "Is something wrong?"

"Not with me," she said, straightening to her full five feet at the most and puffing out her flat chest. "You are the one who is wrong," she snapped, her accent thickening. Francis pointed a bony finger at him. "Miss Mercedes is a good woman, a kind woman. And I don't have to tell you she is a beautiful woman. She likes you a lot, and you blew it."

Apparently Mercedes had unloaded on Francis. Now he would have to endure Francis unloading on him. Thunder rumbled in the distance, and it seemed to grow darker as they stood in front of Mercedes's cabin.

"Do you know when she'll be back?" he asked, seeing how fruitless it would be defending himself. Francis had already convicted him of his crime.

"Not soon enough." Francis turned her attention to the sky, squinting and then holding her hand up. "It will be a bad storm and be here too soon for Mercedes to return."

"Then I'll go get her," he said. "If you'll tell me where she is."

"She told me not to tell you."

Jeremy sucked in a sharp breath, feeling the humidity in the air as the moisture filled his mouth. "If you don't tell me, Mercedes will be stuck in this storm."

"And if I do tell you, both of you will be stuck in this storm," she announced, rocking up on her toes as if she'd just solved some riddle.

"Please, Francis. I can't make amends with Mercedes if you don't tell me where she went. And I know you want her safe in her cabin. It is going to be a bad storm."

Francis chewed her fingernail, pondering his words for a moment. Then, sighing, she waved her hand toward the cliffs. "She went hiking early this morning. Maybe she will be back soon on her own."

Thunder rumbled again, but this time lightning shot across the sky behind him, racing over the ocean before disappearing in the heavy, low, dark clouds.

"She's hiking up in those cliffs?" he asked, gulping down his coffee and then handing the almost empty cup to Francis. "You should have a fresh pot of coffee ready when we get back. I'm going to go get her."

Jeremy didn't wait for Francis to respond but sprinted across the yard, not stopping until he reached the base of the cliffs. Large drops plopped on his arms and back when he started climbing. The rocks were slippery and sharp in spots. He reached the path that wound up into the cliffs to where he'd wanted to take Mercedes. Holding his hand over his eyes, he squinted against the rain and searched around him.

"Mercedes!" he yelled, and his voice echoed around him.

"Jeremy?"

Thunder shook the ground beneath his feet, and the hair on his arms stood on end as lightning sizzled through the air. As if that were the introduction needed, rain started pelting his body. His shirt was soaked instantly, and a cold wind whipped around him, pushing him to the side.

"Where are you?" he yelled, worrying that the wind pushed his words right back into his mouth.

"Jeremy?" she called again, her voice faint against the roar of the rain.

He stepped around a large rock, trying to get to a spot where he could better see his surroundings. There was no way to tell which direction Mercedes called from. This wasn't the first storm he'd seen since arriving on Nativity Island, but it was definitely the worst. Suddenly he couldn't see, and his next step was on uneven ground. He damn near fell on his ass.

"Jeremy!" Cold, wet hands wrapped around his arm and pulled him to the side.

He squinted against the storm, staring at Mercedes. Her long hair was soaked and stuck to her bare shoulders and back.

"What are you doing here?" she demanded, continuing to pull him farther into the rocks.

"I came out here to get you," he told her. "This storm is going to get dangerous, and it's not safe out here alone."

Thunder erupted around them, simultaneously releasing lightning. It rained so hard he could barely see her, even though she kept a firm grip on his arm.

"Come on!" she yelled, encouraging him farther around the rocks.

"Where are we going?"

Instead of answering, she pulled him around a large black rock. It wasn't exactly a cave, but she moved them under a ledge, and suddenly he could see again.

"Why are you here?" she demanded again, letting go of him and shoving her soaked hair over her shoulders.

Jeremy studied the glass wall of rain that streamed at dangerous speeds over the edge of the ledge in front of them. He was able to stand without ducking, but even pressing against the rock wall behind them, there wasn't more than three feet of space.

"I came out here to get you," he told her, shifting his attention and noticing how her shirt clung to her ripe, full breasts before she hugged herself.

"You didn't have to come out in the rain just to find me." She was shivering as she stared at the steady flow of rain.

"It wasn't raining when I left," he admitted.

She shot him a furtive look. And, he had to admit, she looked like a drowned rat. The cutest, sexiest, most adorable drowned rat he'd ever seen.

"Don't look at me like that," she grumbled. She shoved her tennis shoe into the rocky ground, her wet hair falling over her shoulder as she looked down.

"Like what?" He fisted his hands at his sides, all too aware of his clothes clinging to him, soaked and hanging wrong. At the same time, he again noticed that Mercedes's clothes also clung to her, which showed off her entire body and all her delectable curves.

"Like you're hungry," she mumbled, still not looking at him.

Something about her, even knowing she was mad at him, made it impossible to keep his hands off her. Her complaint translated in his mind that she still wanted him but didn't like the foundation they'd created by his lying.

He gripped her chin, forcing her to look at him. Her pretty blue eyes glowed, and her lashes clumped together with droplets of rain. "Do you want me to lie to you again?" he asked.

She didn't hesitate. "No."

He rubbed his thumb across the length of her jaw, enjoying her thick lashes fluttering over her eyes. "I *am* hungry. And you already know that. Do you think I'd stand under a ledge in a tropical storm with just anyone?"

She made a snorting sound and tried pulling her face from his grip. He let her go but then tangled his fingers in her wet hair.

"I don't know what to think about you," she admitted. "Why did you lie about being an author? You had to have known there was a decent chance of me recognizing you."

He would tell her the truth. There wasn't any way of knowing what might or might not happen once they left this island, but Jeremy didn't care.

"I didn't want you to see how much of a hypocrite I am," he admitted and willed her to look at him.

7

Mercedes stood under the hot shower, watching the water stream off her hair. She stared at her toes, wondering if they'd look better if she took off the pink polish and painted them red. She had only two colors with her—pink and red—and at the moment she didn't know if she was in the mood for either.

It was Christmas Eve, three days since she'd been caught in the rainstorm with Jeremy, and three days since she'd spent serious time with him. She needed to see him. Hell, she wanted to see him. She'd listened to him, understanding immediately why he'd lied and admitting to herself it made perfect sense. Jeremy wasn't the man in his book—although she couldn't help thinking if he wrote from his heart it would sell better than the book he'd already written. But she wasn't the writer and honestly didn't know anything about the publishing world.

But she wouldn't forgive him. As she'd told him when they'd run through the rain back to the cabins and stood outside her door dripping wet, how would she know if he ever lied to her again. Even if they were just a two-week fling, she wouldn't have a brief affair with a man she couldn't trust.

Remembering how his eyes had darkened when she'd mentioned them having just a two-week affair still stopped her heart when she pulled up the vision in her head.

How could he want more? she asked herself, her thoughts going insane as she straightened and moved so the water streamed down her back.

God, she was stupid for even thinking about this. There wasn't room in her life for a relationship. And a long-distance relationship would really suck. Not that she really ever stayed anywhere that long. She went where the grant money was, carrying out her research with whatever company or organization would take her on. Regardless, her work was her life. She was happy. Why stir up the waters and complicate things?

As the water turned cold, she shut off the shower and reached for her towel. It was hard to believe it was Christmas Eve. Normal people would be waiting for family to show up, filling their homes with the smell of rich food cooking and shaking gifts under the tree while waiting with baited breath for the moment to arrive when the presents could be opened.

It wasn't the first Christmas she hadn't been around family; there wasn't any reason to feel melancholy about it this year. Mercedes didn't mind easing into a sundress instead of bundling up in pants and sweaters—the cold weather never had been her thing. Opting for one of her strapless mini dresses, she pulled the zipper up under her arm and then shifted in front of the mirror, admiring her figure. Once again Jeremy's face, his eyes dark and predatory, appeared in her mind.

"You're going to see him." She stared at her reflection, knowing she wasn't asking herself a question.

In the past few days she hadn't done any work—she'd barely left her cabin. If she had, the chances of running into Jeremy would be too great. Maybe she was intelligent. Maybe playing math games and challenging her mind appealed to her. Maybe she was the classic geek. But that didn't mean she would have the strength to stay out of his arms despite knowing he could so easily break her heart.

"Just don't let that happen." She gave herself a firm nod, reminding herself for the hundredth time—as she'd argued over the right thing to do—that no one could hurt her unless she allowed it. "Don't pass up the hot sex. Let it go at that. Everyone leaves happy."

It would be her Christmas present to herself. Fucking Jeremy. One hell of a gift.

After taking her time applying makeup and then brushing out her hair until it glowed and curled at the ends, she slipped into sandals and stepped outside her cabin for the first time in days. The bright sun immediately blinded her. Turning her back to the sun, she faced Jeremy's cabin.

"Decide to join the living?" he asked, leaning in his doorway with a cup of coffee.

"I figured I couldn't stay in there forever." She offered him a small smile he didn't return. His dark, brooding stare wasn't readable and sent chills rushing over her flesh, even though it was warm outside. "And it *is* Christmas Eve and all," she added, suddenly wondering if she'd spent days mulling over something that wasn't even an option.

"Where are you going?" he asked, his demanding tone the same as always.

She could get really accustomed to having a man in her life who cared so much he always wanted to know what she was doing and where she was.

"I thought about seeing what was going on in the village," she said, saying the first thing that came to her mind.

He let silence pass between them, not letting go of her gaze and watching her with a hard, aggressive look that made her feel as though he might leap without a moment's notice.

"And that's the only reason you're out of your cabin—to go to the village?"

"Do I need another reason?"

Jeremy pushed away from the door frame, still holding his coffee as he moved in on her slowly. "Tell me something, Mercedes."

"Okay," she said, swearing she felt tiny hairs prickle to attention down her spine.

"Is this honesty thing you demand a two-way street?"

"What?" she gasped. "I have never lied to you!"

"You're looking that hot to go into a village?" he demanded.

He stood so close she had to tilt her head to see his face. That hardened expression didn't change. If she didn't know better she'd swear he was pissed that she looked nice. She focused on his mouth, how his lips were pressed together into a thin line, and let his words sink in.

"What do you mean a two-way street?" she asked.

"Just what I said. You look beautiful," he added, his tone dropping to a husky growl.

"Thank you," she whispered.

"I know you're just as beautiful when you don't go to all this effort." He raised his hand between them and brushed his fingers over the top of her strapless dress.

Mercedes hissed in a breath, her breasts swelling and aching as he brushed his finger over the exposed cleavage.

"Yet today you're absolutely stunning. Did you prepare yourself for villagers you don't know?"

"No," she uttered, the one word barely audible.

"Who are you trying to impress?" he demanded.

"You."

Jeremy turned and walked away from her, entering his cabin but leaving the door open. Telling him the truth was so easy, yet if her reward was him storming away from her, she wasn't sure she could handle it. No matter how much she'd argued with herself over the past few days that she could seek him out and make him her lover without getting her feelings tangled up, she'd failed to do that within minutes of him seeing her.

Mercedes stepped forward, approaching his open doorway as if it might be a trap of sorts. She rubbed her hands down her hips, feeling how damp her palms were when she fisted them and tried to get her heart to quit pounding so hard.

"Crap!" she screeched when Jeremy suddenly appeared in the doorway, storming back out as quickly as he'd stormed in. He no longer held his coffee cup, and he lifted her, yanking her into his arms, and then backed into his cabin. "Jeremy!" she yelled.

Mercedes slid down roped muscle, her heart pounding so hard she could barely breathe. Digging her fingers into his shoulders, fighting to hold on and to get her world to quit spinning, she felt her breasts smash against his rock-hard chest. She stared into his smoldering gray eyes, seeing the intensity of his unadulterated lust. But there was something else, something predatory and raw that made her insides quicken as she lost herself in those incredible eyes.

"Tell me you want me," he growled.

The swelling in her womb throbbed between her legs and burned her insides alive. She opened her mouth to answer, worrying it was too dry to utter the words. "The past few days . . ." she began.

"Tell me you want me," he repeated, barely moving his mouth when he stressed each word.

"I want you," she whispered.

"I'm not perfect," he told her. "But there is a possibility I'm perfect for you."

She couldn't help grinning.

"This isn't a joking matter." His expression grew even darker, which she was surprised to see was possible. "You're not going to run from me again."

"Jeremy, we're here for two weeks—"

Again she wasn't able to finish her thought. Jeremy pounced on her mouth, moving his hands as he stepped forward until her backside pressed up against the wall. He pinned her there, devouring her mouth with the hunger she'd seen in his eyes the last few times she'd looked at him. Obviously, that hunger hadn't diminished since she'd last seen him. Maybe while she'd been in her cabin battling her demons, he'd been over here doing the same.

One thing was for sure: she wasn't going to make sense out of it while he was kissing her senseless. Mercedes didn't know what it was about the way he kissed that made her lose focus. With her backside pressed against the wall and his hard-packed, muscular body smashed against her front side, she couldn't think about anything other than what he was doing to her body.

A fever rushed over her, boiling her alive and giving her chills at the same time. But more so than that, the need pouring out of him—the raw, untamed, intense desire he released upon her—ransacked her brain until all she could do was hold on and pray he wouldn't make her come so hard she'd pass out.

Jeremy nipped her lip. She cried out and then slid down the wall when he grabbed her arms and started feasting on her neck.

"God—shit, Jeremy," she moaned, the pressure building to a boiling point that would make her mad if he didn't do something about it.

"You're the one who made me wait several days." He found her zipper on the side of the dress and yanked it down.

Her dress slid down her body, exposing her breasts and rendering her naked in seconds, shy of the lacy underwear she'd opted on when she'd dressed. The material tangled around her ankles, but Jeremy didn't give her room to move from between him and the wall. The moment her breasts were free, he cupped them with his large, strong hands and then pinched her already sensitive nipples between his fingers and thumbs.

Mercedes arched her neck, feeling the hard wall behind her

head but not caring. Sparks ignited inside her, and a streak as powerful as a bolt of lightning charged from her oversensitive nipples straight to her pussy.

She shoved her hips against him. "You aren't accustomed to going a few days without sex?" she asked, her voice so husky it didn't sound like her speaking.

"I've gone more than a year without sex," he growled against her throat and then bit the sensitive spot just above her collarbone.

Mercedes jumped, digging her fingers into solid muscle. "Then why are you complaining?"

"That was before I met you."

God, he had the lines. "How did you survive?"

He stepped back so quickly Mercedes staggered forward. "I don't think you understand."

She brushed hair away from her face, trying to catch her breath. It was hard as hell just having a conversation. Her body sizzled with unleashed desire that would make it hard for her to comprehend much of anything at the moment, other than that he'd stopped touching her.

"What don't I understand?"

"I don't want a fling. I don't want to just fuck you and then pretend we don't know each other the next day." He took her hand and pulled her from the wall. Then, gripping her arms, he pushed her forward until she crawled onto his bed. "There's something here between you and me. Something strong enough it's driving you as crazy as it is me. We're going to explore it, and we're not limiting it to a two-week time period."

Mercedes slid her legs underneath her, facing him as she sat in the middle of his neatly made bed. Papers were scattered along the desk and dresser with an open laptop amid it all. Proof of his writing—and being lost somewhere in the South Pacific working on his second book. Jeremy wasn't focused on his work now, though. He stared at her as if she were the only thing around him. Just him and her.

"I didn't get any work done the past few days." Mercedes wasn't sure why she'd made that her response to what he'd just said. Her heart had swelled to the point where it was too large for her rib cage. Blood rushed through her veins so fast the rushing sound in her head drowned out her ability to think about anything else. "And you were right when you saw me leave my cabin. I spent all morning getting ready to come see you."

He'd started unbuttoning his shirt and paused at her admission. Raising his gaze to her face, his incredible gray eyes smoldered with an emotion so strong it stole her breath. "Take off your underwear," he instructed her, glancing at her for only a moment but then returning to his task, making incredibly quick work of getting out of his clothes. "I really like how they look on you and would hate to rip them off you and ruin them so I couldn't see you in them again."

Mercedes slipped out of her underwear and tossed them to the floor in the general direction of her dress. When Jeremy was naked he climbed over her, forcing her to lie down. She ran her fingernails down his chest, relishing the feel of the tight, dark curls that spread over his chest. As he moved between her legs, she lifted them, wrapping her thighs around his hips and pulling him closer. His cock was swollen, thick, and hard and pressed against her entrance as soon as he was on top of her.

Bracing his arms on either side of her, Jeremy stared down, gracing her once again with that smoldering gaze. His expression was pinched, as though he concentrated on something so fiercely it took every bit of his energy to maintain it.

"I have a confession," she whispered, knowing she had been the one who'd demanded that anything between them be built on a foundation of honesty and trust.

"Oh, yeah?" he growled, lowering his mouth to her shoulder and scraping his teeth over her flesh.

She jerked in reaction, breathing in hard while fighting to keep her thoughts about her so she could say what she needed to tell him. "Yes. Like I said earlier, I never did like your book."

He chuckled, not looking up. "I can live with that."

"I didn't like it, because it described a type of man who didn't appeal to me."

Jeremy did raise his attention to her at that, searching her face without saying anything.

She needed to get this out and then take whatever reaction he had. "I never knew this before meeting you. You're bossy, pushy, demanding, and aggressive."

Jeremy didn't say a word, watching her and not touching her, other than with his cock, which continued throbbing against her soaked pussy. Obviously, listing his character defects had done nothing to sway his confidence. He remained hard as steel as he tortured her, the swell of his cock stroking her but not entering her.

"I would have sworn to anyone that a man who tried to dominate me would get a swift kick in the ass and a firm goodbye."

The corner of his jaw twitched. Jeremy's opinion of himself was solid. Obviously, he didn't regret any of his actions with her since meeting her. He would be a handful, testing and trying her patience throughout their time together. Just thinking about taking him on, daring to stand up to the overwhelming male domination that radiated from him, had her thrusting her hips up, eager to feel him inside her.

"Which is why only a strong man would work for you, my dear. Otherwise you'd chase him away."

She hadn't thought about it, but he was right. "And that's why I didn't care for your book. It didn't describe the type of man for me."

"I'm the type of man for you."

"I think you are," she whispered. "The real you."

Jeremy impaled her, giving no warning but filling her with everything he had. Mercedes howled, dragging her fingers down his arm while clenching her legs together and willing him to fuck her.

There wasn't any torture. No longer. He didn't tease or take his time. Jeremy moved in to hard-core lovemaking, riding her hard and giving her everything she needed. His face was a blur, but Mercedes could feel the smoothness of his flesh, the coarse hair that covered it, and his warm, powerful body tensing over hers as he fucked her.

There wasn't any way of knowing how long they'd be together. But, then, couples who'd been together for years couldn't say if they'd make it a lifetime. It was one day at a time, and today Mercedes was willing to give it her all. Jeremy had written a book about the perfect man, but that man wasn't him. And he was perfect—for her. He'd been given credit for helping relationships around the world—though his book didn't do anything for the two of them. If anything, without their own desire to be honest and try and make what had sparked between them work, his book might have torn them apart.

"Mercedes!" he roared, every inch of him tightening while his cock seemed to grow and swell inside her.

The pressure he'd released and built back up now swelled to dangerous levels, robbing her of her breath as she struggled to focus on his face. He brought his mouth to hers, his breath hot and ragged.

"I'm going to come. Come with me, baby," he whispered, sounding hoarse and growling as he slowed the pace, his strokes now torturously meticulous when he moved deep inside her.

She didn't need to tell him what he needed to do to make her come. As he spoke, he gave one final hard thrust, diving deep into her heat and pressing against that spot that sent her over the edge.

Fireworks erupted before her eyes as her world exploded. A dam broke inside her, and with it all reservations of being able to live without this guy. They were off to a good start, she thought, and regardless of their work, they would make whatever it was between them survive. Jeremy was bullheaded enough to see to it. And she was intelligent enough to know how to use his stubbornness to her advantage.

"Merry Christmas," she whispered, curling up alongside him when he pulled out.

"It might just be the best one so far," he muttered, wrapping his arm around her and pulling her closer. "For once, I got the present I wished for."

"What was that?"

"You," he said and noticeably relaxed next to her.

Mercedes placed her hand over his heart, feeling its solid beat, and had to agree with him. "I'm getting what I want for Christmas, too."

"Yes, you are."

She chuckled, loving his self-confidence and making a mental note, as she got incredibly comfortable in his arms, to suggest that his next book use more of his real voice. After all, every woman loved a real man. And now she had hers.

Escaping Christmas

P.J. Mellor

1

Sweat-slicked skin slid against sweat-slicked skin, heartbeat to heartbeat. Their labored breathing filled the silent, darkened bedroom.

Samantha Harrison huffed out a breath and licked her lips, waiting for her heart rate to slow down. Wishing the air conditioning would come on. It had been a hot December, even by Houston standards.

"Hmmm," she purred and stretched when Sean rolled to her side. She absently stroked his bare hip. "That was really great. I mean, *really* great. We may have killed off some brain cells that time."

In response, her boyfriend—and, really, at her age, should she call him that?—grunted. Had he just pushed her hand away? No doubt he was still dealing with aftershocks.

"I'm thirsty," she announced, crawling to the edge of the mattress and sitting up. "Want anything?"

Another grunt.

Biting back a smile, she pulled her discarded tunic over her nudity and padded toward the kitchen. Lights from the half-decorated Christmas tree lent the apartment an intimate glow.

Samantha sighed. She loved Christmas, and this one promised to be the best ever. Remembering how she and Sean had been overcome with lust while attempting to decorate the tree brought a blush to her cheeks.

Wobbly legs took her as far as the kitchen table, where she had to sit down to rest and think about what she should get Sean for Christmas—while she gathered enough strength to make the trek to the refrigerator.

Sean's jacket fell to the floor with a clunk.

Rhetta, Samantha's black Lab, immediately ran over to nuzzle the jacket, her thick tail whipping against Sam's bare leg.

The dog grabbed something off the floor, her butt in the air, tail wagging playfully.

"That better not be Sean's wallet," Sam whispered, leaning toward her playful pet. "He was not happy when you chewed up his last one. Give it to me. Rhetta, release."

Reluctantly, the dog gave up her bounty. Sam looked down at a spit-covered box in her palm. "Uh-oh. What's this?" She grabbed a dish towel and wiped doggy drool off the soft leather. With a guilty glance at the bedroom door, she eased open the lid, its creak sounding loud in the quiet apartment.

Her heart hiccupped and then raced.

"Crap." Breath wheezed in and out of her lungs. A dazzling diamond solitaire reflected the twinkling lights of the tree. She met her dog's curious gaze and whispered, "Rhetta, what am I supposed to do?"

She and Sean had been together for a little more than eleven months, having hooked up at last year's apartment association Christmas party. It would be only natural, now that she thought about it, for him to pop the question at Christmas. But . . . what would she say? True, she was twenty-nine years old. And, as her mother was always quick to point out, Sam's biological clock was ticking. She wasn't against marriage, per se. She just wasn't sure she was ready for it.

At least, not with Sean.

Wait. What was she thinking? If not Sean, then who? Little by little, he'd moved in with her. They got along well, the sex was good . . . when they had it, anyway. He wasn't a troll—they would make decent looking, if not pretty, babies. Assuming they had children.

Her palms began to sweat. Her heart beat a tattoo against her rib cage.

They'd never even discussed marriage, much less having a family. And speaking of family, she'd never even met any of his. She swallowed around the lump threatening to constrict her airway. What was he thinking? They hardly knew each other!

Her heart pounded faster against her breastbone, her breath coming in panicked gasps.

Calm down, calm down. Don't hyperventilate and pass out on the kitchen floor. Think. What are you going to say when he proposes?

Damned if she had a clue.

Noise coming from the direction of the bedroom had her scurrying to replace the box in the jacket pocket.

She'd just strategically draped the jacket in its previous position on the back of the chair when Sean shuffled into the room.

Rhetta grunted, did the equivalent of a doggy eye roll, and went to lie down by the patio door.

"Hey," Samantha said through teeth that wanted to chatter. Eyes still trained on the ring box hidden in the jacket, she got up and sidled over to him, slipping her arms around his narrow waist. "Did you change your mind about a drink?" Hoping to buy time, she nuzzled his neck. Fabric stopped her, mid-nuzzle. "You're dressed."

"Yeah."

Snuggling closer again, she began unbuttoning his shirt.

Maybe she could distract him with sex, despite the fact he had never done a repeat performance in the same night since the first time they'd been together. And speaking of time, she needed more. A girl might get a proposal only once in her life. It was important to formulate exactly the right answer. She had to think of something. Anything.

Sean's hands on her shoulders drew her attention as he set her cold, shivering body away from his heat.

"I need to tell you something."

Here it comes. Don't freak. You should have seen this coming, you've been practically living together for months. Of course he'd want to marry—"What did you say?" She frowned, concentrating to hear through the roar of blood in her ears. She must have misunderstood. He couldn't have said what she thought she'd heard.

"I said I've met someone." He looked everywhere but in her eyes. Did that mean anything? "I think she's the one, Sam. And I want to ask her to marry me." He reached for his coat and took out the now hated box.

This can't be happening. She blindly groped for a chair and sat before her legs refused to support her weight. A fist of nausea sucker punched her stomach and then pummeled her heart.

Oblivious, Sean flipped open the box, the ring sparkling obscenely. "I'm not sure how to ask her or when. Maybe you could give me some advice?" With a shrug she always used to find endearing, he said, "I'm clueless."

You can say that again. Why hadn't she taught Rhetta to attack, kill, or something equally dangerous? Instead her loyal dog sat and stared at them, obviously as shocked as her mistress.

Calm. Be calm. She rubbed at the ache spreading from her heart and willed herself not to throw up.

Screw calm. Revenge was always better.

Before she could think of all the reasons not to do it, Samantha grabbed the ring from the box. She had to do something. Anything was better than dwelling on the horrible ache filling her.

"Sam, don't be like that—"

"Don't be like what? You, you . . . A-hole!" She gulped and swiped at her angry tears. "You've been living with me, sharing my bed. My god, we just had sex!" The psychological fist sucker punched her again, causing her to gasp. "When were you planning to tell me you'd found someone else?" she managed to say on an emotionally strangled wheeze.

"Don't make a scene." Until she noticed the direction of his gaze, she'd forgotten she held the ring in a death grip. He couldn't take his eyes off a damned ring he'd bought for another woman, and he was telling her to not make a scene? Who the hell did he think he was?

"Don't make a scene? Don't make a *scene*? I'll show you a scene!" she screamed, blinking furiously at the fresh tears blurring her vision as she quickly scanned her kitchen for a weapon. Something, anything she could use to inflict pain. He deserved to feel some pain.

"I planned to tell you tonight—"

"Oh, was that *plan* for before or after you screwed my brains out?" She slapped her free hand on her forehead, barely feeling the touch through her outrage. "Oh, wait! Obviously after, right? One last roll in the sack?" Her eyes narrowed. "You lowlife, lying, cheating sack of—"

"I'm in love with Bambi, Sam, and nothing you say, no amount of name calling, is going to change that." The *A-hole* had the audacity to look offended.

"Bambi? Her name is *Bambi*?" She tried to keep her shriek down to a moderate decibel. "Does Bambi have a last name, or is she just Bambi, like Cher or Madonna?"

He mumbled something.

"What? I didn't hear you." She visually searched the counter.

Why did she have to be so neat? Where was a knife when you needed one?

"I said her name is Bambi Donner." He glared at her when she snorted in her attempt to swallow her snicker. "Don't be juvenile, Samantha."

"Come on!" Her lips quivered. She was having a bad dream. It had to be a dream. "Who has a name like Bambi Donner? Is it a made-up name? Because, in my opinion, it sounds made up. What is she, a stripper?"

"She's the woman I love and plan to marry. That's all you really need to know."

"Oh, well, excuse me!" She nodded, refusing to let his declaration hurt—well, refusing to let him know it did, anyway. "I get it. She's good in bed. Probably into kinky stuff, right? I bet she does anything and everything you want. Better than me, huh?" She held up her finger, eyes wide with mock surprise. "Hey, was tonight a comparison?" She knew she was being snide, but couldn't help it.

"Don't be a bitch. It's none of your business, but Bambi plans to remain a virgin until her wedding night. I have decided I can wait until then to consummate our relationship."

Sam blinked and swallowed around the lump in her throat. She refused to let him see her cry, but . . . dang, could her night get any worse? "You're kidding."

He shook his head. "It's what Bambi wants, and I respect her too much not to honor it."

Humiliation flared, heating her cheeks. "Well, thanks a damn lot! What was I, the warm-up act?" Talk about a verbal slap in the face.

He took a step closer, his gaze locked on the ring fisted in her shaking hand. "Give me the ring, Sam."

"Oh, I'm sorry!" she yelled. "You want the ring? Go get it!" Her hand whipped out, throwing the ring in much the same fashion she'd once performed in fast-pitch softball.

The ring pinged off the window, banked on the tile back-splash and chinked in a slow, scraping circle on the porcelain of the sink until it fell through the black rubber rim to land with a final clunk in the disposal.

Sean wasted no time diving for the ring, his hand following the bauble down into the disposal.

Samantha was faster, leaping across the counter and stretching for the switch as his hand disappeared through the rubber opening.

Her fingers closed around the plastic angle of the switch, the stainless-steel electrical plate cool against the palm of her hand.

Their eyes met.

2

The air-conditioning clicked on, swirling coolness over her heated skin, the only sound in the quiet apartment—except for Sean's labored breathing.

Her eyes locked with his, she waited a heartbeat. Another.

A sweat bead trickled down his nose, hung on the tip for a second, and then dripped down onto his lips. Lips that had kissed hers so passionately less than an hour ago.

Cheating lips. Lying lips. She wished she could rip them off his face.

Her mouth firmed into a tight line. Determined not to let him see her cry, she swallowed and let her hand fall from the switch. "You're not worth the effort it would take to clean up all the blood," she finally whispered, her throat raw. "Get out."

His shoulders slumped in almost comic relief, and then he groped in the disposal until he found the ring.

Spotting her favorite baggy Texas A&M sweats in the laundry basket by the door to the utility room, she walked through the kitchen on shaky legs, not stopping until her toes touched the sharp edge of the plastic basket. Leaning against the wall, she stepped into the burgundy sweatpants, turning her back to shuck the tunic and pull the voluminous sweatshirt over her nudity.

She was only slightly surprised to turn and find Sean staring at her.

"Do you still have the list you made when I moved in?" he asked, his voice hard as he replaced the ring and snapped the box shut before stuffing it back into the jacket pocket. "Are you going to compare it to what's left after I leave to make sure I don't take anything that isn't mine?"

"I can't deal with this now," she told him, after a beat, ignoring the pain his cruel words inflicted as she looked for her purse. There was nothing wrong with lists or being orderly. He was obviously just trying to hurt her more—as though that was possible. "I'm going out for a while. I expect you to be gone by the time I get home." She met his cold gaze, wondering what she'd ever seen in him. "Anything of yours left here will be destroyed, most probably burned." She stalked to the door and stuffed her cold feet into the garden clogs she wore to walk Rhetta.

Gripping the oval doorknob until it dug into her palm, she turned, blinking back more stupid tears, and choked out, "Leave your key on the table."

It took great restraint not to slam the door on her way out.

She'd been dumped at Christmas, her favorite holiday. Ho-ho-ho. And, in case her dignity hadn't taken enough of a beating, it was for some bimbo with the unlikely name of Bambi Donner.

Two hours and twice as many margaritas later, Samantha's key echoed in the lock. She stepped into the quiet of the darkened apartment, dropping her bag by the door. "Rhetta? C'mon, girl, let's make a fast trip to the doggy run. Rhetta?"

Silence greeted her.

Must be asleep in my bed again. Sam made her way through the darkened living room to the door of the bedroom and flipped on the light.

The rumpled bed was empty. The stale smell of sex permeated the air, turning her stomach.

"Rhetta?" She made a clucking sound as she walked to the kitchen to rattle the dog's bag of food—always a sure way to get her attention. Maybe doing mundane things would help ease the incredible sadness threatening to drag her under.

Bending to reach into the cupboard for the food, she froze.

The dog dishes were missing. So was the food.

Running now, she skidded to a stop at the door of the guest room.

Rhetta's bed and kennel were gone.

It took a moment to command her fingers to hit the correct speed-dial keys to call Sean's cell phone. His voice mail clicked in. Three times.

After leaving three semi-obscene messages, her phone chimed "Born to Be Wild." Sean's name appeared on the tiny screen.

"Where's my dog, you lying scumbag?"

"Don't be such a drama queen, Sam." Sean's hated voice stung her ear. "Rhetta's fine."

"Give her back!" Sam blinked back tears as she paced around her living room, averting her eyes from the glowing lights on the Christmas tree. "She's *my* dog," she half whispered, choking the words out.

"She's both of ours. We picked her out together. And, if you want to get technical, she's more mine because I paid for her spaying and medications. I just let you name her, which is how she ended up with such a stupid name."

"Bring. Her. Back." She ignored his jab about Rhetta's name. He'd made it abundantly clear how he felt about the name, and she wasn't going there again.

"This conversation is over. Bye, Sam."

Numerous calls connected with Sean's voice mail.

Fumbling, she finally managed to send a text message. Within seconds, her phone dinged with his reply.

Get another dog, Sam, and get on with your life.

Her fingers flew on the miniscule keys. I don't want another dog. I want Rhetta.

B.F.D.

Bring her home.

N.W. U R going to have to put it on your famous to-do list. Get a new dog. Rhetta has already moved on. She & Bambi have bonded.

You S.O.B! Bring her home. Now.

Anguished tears streaked down her cheeks, her pulse pounding in her ears while she waited for a reply that didn't come.

Tossing her cell to bounce on the couch, she ran to her laptop and powered it up.

If what Sean had said was true, he had taken Rhetta when he went to see Bambi. If Rhetta was already with the home-wrecker, Bambi must live close. At least within a hundred-mile-or-so radius of Houston.

Samantha clicked on the *White Pages* icon.

"Hang on, Rhetta," Sam murmured, flipping on the printer. "Mama's coming to get you."

How many Bambi Donners could there be?

Only one was listed. Samantha's heart plummeted. Just what she needed to make her holiday season suck even more.

Bambi Donner lived in the little Gulf coast town of Christmas, Texas.

3

Sam called and left a voice mail for both dental practices where she worked as a hygienist, telling them to cancel her appointments until further notice due to being called out of town on a family emergency. It was true—Rhetta was her family, and it was definitely an emergency.

After entering Bambi's address and phone number into her cell, she took a quick shower and haphazardly packed, throwing clothes and toiletries into a tote bag, and then grabbed the printed map and headed for the door.

According to the Internet, Christmas, Texas, was a very small town. With luck, Sam could drive into town, grab Rhetta, and leave before anyone knew she was there. Worst-case scenario, she could have a heart-to-heart with good old Bambi and convince her to relinquish Rhetta. After all, Bambi had Sean. Wasn't that enough?

With those thoughts firmly in mind, Samantha hopped in her beloved BMW 330i and headed south on State Highway 249, taking the elevated entrance to Beltway 8 at breakneck speed. I-59 south came up, and she set the cruise control as she shot out of the entrance ramp. No point in getting a speeding ticket. She had more important things to do.

Breaking for the exit an hour later, she saw the Gulf of Mexico in the distance, the morning sun dancing on the surface. She turned toward the Gulf and saw a big white-and-gold filigreed sign edged in tiny painted evergreens welcoming her to Christmas, Texas, population 867, THE MERRIEST TOWN ON EARTH.

"Oh, please." She glared at the nauseatingly cheerful sign, sponsored by the First Bank of Christmas. *Probably the only bank of Christmas.*

Flicking on her turn signal, she shook her head and sighed. Population 867. Talk about a proverbial dot on the map. How on Earth had Sean even met the bimbo homewrecker?

Sadness once again washed over her when, a few minutes later, she turned onto the town square.

Despite its name, she hadn't been prepared for the extent of the town's holiday display. Hadn't really thought about it. Until now.

Old-fashioned lampposts lined the square, their ornate posts wound to resemble candy canes. Festive wreaths adorned each storefront. Christmas lights and garland stretched across the streets at eight- to ten-foot intervals, forming an arch for cars to pass under. An old-fashioned red brick courthouse, complete with huge white towering pillars dripping with garland, loomed from the center of the square. At the base of the front steps was an elaborate manger scene with real animals secured behind a white picket fence.

The pièce de résistance was the stereo system blaring Christmas carols throughout the square. *Honest-to-goodness Christmas carols before eight o'clock in the morning.*

In her present state of mind, it was enough to make her puke.

A left on the far side of the square took her to Fifth Street. Fumbling with the map printout, she cringed again at the address. Her jaw set, she grimly flipped on her right signal and turned onto Sugarplum Lane. *Gag.* How was she going to get through this?

She had to get through it.

Bambi Donner lived in a small Victorian-style blue frame house, complete with white gingerbread trim that glistened in the morning sun.

While Sam sat in her car and contemplated the best way to gain entry, the front door opened, its Christmas wreath swinging against the leaded glass.

Samantha sank lower in the gray leather bucket seat and pushed her sunglasses up on her nose.

Two people stepped onto the front porch. One of them was Sean. He gazed lovingly into the eyes of a tall, statuesque blond woman. Big surprise—Sean always gravitated toward blondes. This one was dressed in obvious designer clothes and laughed at something he said.

Samantha's on-the-road breakfast of a pumpkin cream-cheese muffin and gingerbread latte threatened to reappear. Sean had never looked at her like that. She watched as they paused by the white picket fence and shared a sweet kiss before Sean opened the door of his car for the bimbo. Something else he'd never done for Samantha. Numb, she watched them drive away while she tried to regulate her breathing. She would not cry. She refused to cry. She had too much to do.

She had to break into a house.

Samantha would have bet, living in a quiet, small town like Christmas, Texas, that Bambi would have been more trusting. But, no, the bimbo/homewrecker/dog thief had her little house locked up like she was protecting the crown jewels or something. Other than Rhetta, Samantha would bet Miss Bambi didn't have much worth stealing. Yet even the stupid little wooden gate was locked, forcing Sam to consider climbing the fence.

A casual glance around confirmed the lack of witnesses, so she swung her leg over the fence and stepped over. Unfortunately, the cuff of her slacks caught on the point of a picket. The abrupt cessation of forward momentum caused her lead foot to slip back, wrenching her ankle as the stiletto heel of her boot slid sideways.

She bit back her yelp of pain as she hopped to disentangle her pant leg. Another quick glance brought relief. No one had watched her humiliation.

As casually as possible, she strolled up the front steps, crossed the porch and pushed the ornate doorbell.

A chime rendition of "Winter Wonderland" echoed in the empty house.

She rolled her eyes and muttered, "Give me a break," then rattled the locked door.

From somewhere toward the back of the house, Rhetta's deep, distinctive bark called to her. It sounded muffled, she thought, as she walked around the side of the house, testing windows and glancing over her shoulder as she made her way toward the backyard. Poor baby was probably locked up in her kennel.

Dang. The back door was locked, too. Where was the infamous trust of small-town folk? She glanced up, wondering if the rose trellis next to the back porch would hold her weight. The homewrecker may have forgotten to lock the attic dormer.

"She ain't home," a gruff voice called from the next yard. A head, sporting a green-and-yellow-billed cap advertising a tractor supply, appeared over the top of the fence. The man's weathered cheeks were grizzled with white stubble. "Miz Bambi's out. Something I can help you with?"

Crap.

"Um, ah, I was just wondering if she still had the, um, room for rent. I thought maybe I could see it."

The old man frowned. He removed his hat, scratched his

thinning hair, and then carefully replaced the hat, adjusting the brim. "You new to town?"

Swallowing around the lump of pure fear threatening to cut off her air supply, she nodded as she tried to stand partially hidden by the post on the porch. No point in letting the old man get a good enough look at her to identify her in a lineup.

"Didn't know Miz Bambi was rentin' out a room." He turned and spit, making her already nervous stomach want to revolt. "I have a nephew who's been looking to rent a room." He nodded. "He wants to move to the city. Says he's tired of the country. Wants to rent b'fore he commits, though."

Samantha could only nod in a vague manner. The guy's nephew considered Christmas the *city*?

She hedged toward the edge of the step. "I'll come back later." Like when it was dark and there were no witnesses.

The man smiled. It was a kind smile and made her feel incredibly guilty. "I'll let her know you were here."

"No! I mean, that's not really necessary. She doesn't know me—we've never met. She didn't know I was coming." Sam stepped back off the porch. "I'll contact her later."

His eyes narrowed. At least, she thought they did. With the shadow of the hat, it was difficult to tell.

She wiggled her fingers in what she hoped was a friendly, nonguilty manner and wobbled back around the side of the house, not stopping until she regained the relative safety of her car.

Sweat trickled along her hairline. Her ankle throbbed. She turned the key to start the car and broke a nail, pain searing her fingertip.

What a crappy way to start the day.

4

_____

"I can't tell you how much Paige and I appreciate this, Bret."

Bret Bayne slumped down farther in the scarred office chair and frowned at his cousin, Ed, sheriff of Christmas, Texas. "It's only temporary, understand? I have a job to get back to after Christmas break." Teaching seventh-grade science may not have been everyone's idea of a career, but it was the only one he'd ever wanted, and he was good at it.

"I know, I know." Ed held up his hand. "I'm just saying I appreciate you filling in for me while Paige has the babies. And don't worry. It's always pretty quiet around here. More so during the holidays." He tapped his pockets. "I keep feeling like I forgot something."

"Paige? Don't you need to take her to the hospital?" Bret bit back a grin.

"Smartass." Ed grinned back and reached for his hat on the rack behind the desk. "She's being induced, so there's no hurry. You want to go over the list again?"

"Ed, it's not rocket science. I come here and sit at the desk for a few hours a day, less an hour lunch break. I lock up and go home and come back again the next day and so on until you get back. Oh, and if someone breaks the law—like that's going to happen around here—I arrest them and lock them up."

Ed nodded. "That's about it. Judge McVay, the circuit court judge, comes through town every second Wednesday of the month, so he won't be back until after the New Year."

"Tell Paige good luck and give her a kiss for me." Bret stood and ushered Ed toward the door.

"I deputized you, right?" Ed paused with his hand on the knob.

"Right. And I have the magnet for my Jeep." Because Christmas had only one patrol car, and Ed's truck was unreliable, Bret had volunteered to use his Jeep. Ed had finally agreed to have a magnet made for the doors instead of an official paint job, for which Bret was grateful. After all, standing in for his cousin was only a temporary thing, even if he had been deputized to make it official. Christmas was a tiny coastal town and didn't need more than one officer. Everyone knew where Ed lived if they needed him during off hours.

After Ed left, Bret sauntered back to the office in the tiny jail and settled into the creaky office chair, his feet propped up on the desk. Two hours until he could go home. He tilted his Stetson to cover his eyes. Just enough time for a nap.

Samantha wiped her sweating palm and rang the bell on the ornate desk of the Christmas Inn Bed-and-Breakfast for the third time. Hers was the only car in the little parking area. How busy could they be?

"Will you kindly stop abusing my dang bell, young lady? I heard you the first two times." A rotund gentleman with a full head of snow-white hair and matching neatly trimmed beard shuffled into the foyer. He was dressed in a plum paisley print jacket with black velvet collar and cuffs, a silky black scarf at his fleshy throat. The coat was cinched in at what should have been his waist by a black tie belt. Crisply pressed black trousers and coordinating plum velvet slippers completed the ensemble.

Her first thought was he looked like a *GQ* Santa.

"Can I help you? Speak up, woman, I'm missing *Oprah*."

"Um, I called earlier about a room? Samantha Harrison?" Maybe if she focused on him and concentrated on the conversation, she would be able to ignore all the Christmas decorations threatening to close in on her.

"Right." He nodded, late afternoon sunlight streaming through the leaded glass transom glinting off his hair. "You're the one who didn't want a room that had anything to do with Christmas." He narrowed his blue eyes. "You Jewish?"

"No. I'm just . . . not in the Christmas spirit, I guess you could say."

He chuckled, his belly going up and down with each sound. "Missy, you are definitely in the wrong town if you don't have Christmas spirit." Twinkling eyes observed her. "If that's so, why on Earth did you come to Christmas, Texas?"

"It's a long story." She waved her hand when he began to open his mouth. "Don't ask." She started to remove her platinum card and then paused. Better not to leave a paper trail when you planned to commit a crime. But was it a crime to steal your own dog? For that matter, was it really stealing? Instead she pulled out the cash she always kept for emergencies and paid for two nights. When the man just stood looking at the money she placed on the ornate writing desk, she bit back a sigh. "What's wrong? Don't you take cash?"

He stared at her for so long she thought he was going to tell her to take her money and leave.

Finally, he gave a faint nod. "Oh, yes, ma'm, I just hadn't seen any gen-u-ine cash in a while." He turned and took an elaborate key from an ivy-draped hook. "I'll just show you to your room." He glanced behind her. "Where's your luggage?"

She held up her leather tote bag. "I don't plan to stay very long," she explained when his snowy eyebrows lifted. "And if you'll just give me the key and tell me which room, I can find it myself." She closed her hand over his and tugged at the key ring; then she smiled what she hoped was her most sincere smile. "I wouldn't want you to miss any more of *Oprah.*" After pulling the key from his hand, she paused at the base of the stairs. "Thanks, anyway. Which room is it?"

He recovered quickly. "Second door on the left."

Upstairs, Samantha paused, staring at the shiny brass plaque. "Great. Just great." She would be staying in the bowels of hell, otherwise known as the *Jingle Bell Suite.*

She stepped into the room and relocked the door as she flipped on the light to alleviate the impending darkness. The cheerful strains of a bell-chorus rendition of "Jingle Bells" filled the room. Her hand shot out to douse the light. Thankfully, the grating sound of about a million bells also ceased.

Her temples began to throb. Rubbing her stiff neck, she shoved up her sleeve to check her watch. Bare arm greeted her. Her mind flashed to her watch on the tray by the kitchen sink, where she'd placed it while cleaning up from dinner. Crap. Her life just kept getting better and better.

A soft knock sounded on the polished cherry door.

"Go away." She didn't know anyone, so it was okay to be rude because the knocker obviously had the wrong room.

"Miss Harrison?" It was the old fat guy from the front desk. "Is everything all right?"

"Is there a way to turn off the bells?"

She thought she heard him chuckle.

"Oh, yes, of course, there is," his muffled voice assured her. "Simply turn off the light. Anything else I can help you with?"

"No, I think that about does it. Thanks," she added as an afterthought.

When she was sure he was gone, she flipped the light on and off several times, wincing at the bell chorus.

Just shoot me now.

5

Samantha blew out the cinnamon-smelling candle by the white wrought-iron bed in her room and then licked her forefinger and thumb and touched the sizzling wick to make sure it was out. No point in burning down the only place she had to stay at while on her rescue mission. She sneezed. Candles did that to her but were still preferable to the noise that accompanied the light.

She squinted at the elaborate curlicue clock by the bed. Her stomach growled. Almost eight. It had been dark for a while. Would the bimbo be home by now? With the way Samantha's luck had been running, not only would the homewrecker be there, she'd be doing the wild monkey dance with Sean.

Samantha gave a derisive chuckle. Despite what Sean said, she knew—she just knew—there was more going on than an *affair of the heart*. The alternative—that Samantha just hadn't been good enough, pretty enough, sexy enough for Sean—was too ugly to contemplate.

Bambi, bimbo/homewrecker/dog thief, could have Sean,

Samantha thought as she pulled on the rest of her all-black out-fit. Good riddance.

Samantha was going to get her dog back.

Bret jumped, startled awake by the jarring ring of the phone clipped to the utility belt at his waist. Where was he? Oh, right. Acting sheriff.

He finally unclipped the unit and connected. "Sheriff's of-fice. What? Who did you say you were?"

"This is the Jingle Jangle Alarm Company. Who is this? Where is Sheriff Ed? We have an alarm!"

From the thrilled sound of the woman's voice, it could have been their first. Bret bit back a chuckle. This was one of the rea-sons he'd moved back to Christmas. He loved small-town life.

"This is Bret Bayne, Ed's cousin. I'm acting sheriff while he's gone. He—"

"Hi, Bret! I heard you were back in town. It's Autumn, Au-tumn Summers—remember me? We were in the same biology class together in high school."

"Of course I remember you." Despite her unfortunate name, Autumn had been homecoming queen their senior year. "How have you been?"

"Fine, fine. Married Ronnie Mays after graduation and had three kiddos—bang, bang, bang."

He winced. "Congratulations—"

"Don't bother congratulating me—Ronnie was the same creep he was in high school. I—oh, listen to me! Going on like that when I'm supposed to be conductin' business. We have an alarm! Now, where did you say Ed was?"

"He took Paige to the hospital this afternoon—"

"Oh, my! Is it time already? How's she doing?"

"Okay, I guess. Ed called a little while ago. When they began to induce her, they realized there might be a problem with the twins, so they transferred her to a hospital in Corpus. Something about needing a neonatal unit. Now . . . what was that you were saying about an alarm?"

"Oh! I durn near forgot about that! A silent alarm came in a few minutes ago. Fourteen-oh-three Sugarplum Lane."

Bret scribbled the address on the notepad and then tore off the page. "I'll get right on it."

"It's probably just their cat again. She sets off the motion detector every year about this time. I think the lights from the tree get her hopped up, and she jumps more than usual. But since they pay for our service, I figured someone should take a drive over there."

"Yes, ma'am. I'm on my way."

"Rhetta?" Samantha called softly to her dog. No point in Rhetta barking and drawing unwanted attention.

Her shin scraped painfully against the edge of a coffee table, causing Samantha to bite back a yelp. Dang, it sure was dark. Even the puny gas street lamps, though pretty, gave off no appreciable light.

Her friend Meg was right. When it gets dark in the country, it gets *dark*. With a capital *D*.

Before she realized it, she walked directly into what had to be a Christmas tree, judging by the scratchiness and scent. Luckily, she caught it before it toppled.

A sound came from the back of the house.

"Rhetta?" Samantha called in a whisper.

The blinding light of a powerful flashlight shone on her.

It wasn't Rhetta.

"Put your hands where I can see them!" a booming voice commanded.

Oh, crap.

6

The first thought in Bret's mind on seeing the petite woman whose lush curves were clad entirely in black was that it wasn't a cat that had set off the alarm.

The second thought was: now what? He really, really didn't want to arrest anyone. Ed had assured him it wouldn't be necessary. If he arrested someone he'd have to fill out all the stupid forms and go online and set up a hearing date. He'd have to arrange for them to be fed. This was supposed to be his Christmas vacation. He'd planned to spend it relaxing and unpacking the boxes still remaining from his recent move.

The woman chose that moment to turn and run toward the front door.

Then again, he was being paid to serve and protect.

He took off after her. Despite her size, she was a surprisingly fast runner. Or else he was out of shape. Or both. He sucked in a breath and picked up his pace.

"Stop!" he called as she hurdled over the nativity scene by the front porch.

She took a flying leap over the lighted sleigh and reindeer in the middle of the yard and would have made it if her heel hadn't caught on one of the antlers.

The predicted rain had started to mist everything, making the grass slippery as calf snot beneath his boots. She got to her feet and would have escaped had her own boots not slipped on the wet grass, taking her down with a bone-jarring thump.

Before she got away again, he closed his hand around her upper arm and pulled her none-too-gently to her feet.

"Breaking and entering is against the law," he told her between wheezing breaths.

"I. Didn't. Break in." She jerked and twisted, but he held firm. "Let go!" What he could see of her pretty face contorted in a wince. "You're hurting me!"

"Sorry." He immediately relaxed his grip.

Just as immediately, she slipped away and hit the sidewalk at a dead run.

Now that he had his wind back, he easily caught up to her. He swung his arm around her middle, pinning her back to him with his forearm as he lifted her off the pavement. His hand touched a softness it took a moment to identify. Immediately, he lowered his hand from her breast, hoping she hadn't noticed. He wasn't cut out for this line of work. He was a teacher, not a deputy.

"Let go!" She squirmed, her firm little backside grinding against the part of him that was doing its damnedest not to notice.

"Can't do that." He grunted when a sharp high heel connected with his poor shin bone. Ed wasn't paying him enough to take this kind of abuse.

He winced as another kick met its mark. If Ed weren't his cousin, Bret would type up his resignation and leave it on the unguarded desk.

Unfortunately, he was. And Bret had agreed—given his word.

"Stop resisting arrest," he said through clenched teeth while he attempted to gather all the flailing arms and legs in order to stuff her into his Jeep.

Her back stiffened. She braced her booted feet on each side of the door and locked her knees.

No doubt his Jeep would bear battle scars before this whole mess was over.

"This isn't even a real police car!" She pointed at the magnet on the door while managing to keep her knees locked. "Who are you really? I have Mace! Let me go!"

"You don't have Mace. You don't even have a pocket in that getup. Where did you put your keys? Did you drive here?"

"I refuse to answer until I talk to my lawyer! I know my rights."

"Lady, you're just making things worse—"

"Worse!" Her shriek echoed in his left ear. "How could it get any worse?" She went limp and sniffed, wiping her nose with the back of her hand as he settled her into the bucket seat and buckled her seatbelt. "It was already the worst Christmas of my life. Now this."

"Aw, c'mon, it can't be that bad." He plastered a smile on his wet face, determined to remain filled with the holiday spirit if it killed him, and climbed from the rain-soaked pavement into the relative dryness of the driver's side.

Before he could turn the key in the ignition, her seatbelt clicked, and he turned in time to see her scramble out of the car.

"Damnit! Get back in the Jeep!" Yelling was dumb, he knew that, but he hoped she'd stop.

Instead she broke into a run, heading for Fifth Street. If she made it to the square, she could duck into any one of the stores and lose him.

Swearing under his breath, he released his own belt and took off in hot pursuit.

She bobbed and weaved like a running back, only with a

much more attractive backside, he noticed. He'd always told his students there was a logical process to just about everything, so he watched for a pattern to her moves and was able to intercept her.

She grunted when he tackled her. He immediately rolled to take her weight and possibly protect her from the worst of the muddy patch of city property.

They rolled to a stop at the edge of the curb just as it began to rain harder.

She wiggled, doing her damnedest to get away again.

He tightened his grasp, crossing his thigh over her legs to prevent leverage. "Get your bony elbow out of my rib cage," he growled in her ear.

"Let go of me and I will!" Her breath was hot against his ear.

It should not have excited him.

"No way. I'm not taking a chance on you running away again. You're under arrest."

In response, she nipped his earlobe with her sharp little teeth.

It should not have excited him either.

No doubt, he had to get control of the situation, not to mention his sex-starved body.

Rolling to his feet, he pulled her along with him. "Let's try this again. I'm taking you in."

"I thought you were arresting me." She tried to tug away, but he held firm. She winced, so he eased up. She took immediate advantage and bolted.

This time, he was ready for her. Within three steps, he was on her, trying to keep his weight off her as they rolled to bump against the streetlight.

Their gazes met, panting breath intermingling as they lay, heartbeat to heartbeat.

The drizzling rain surrounded them, enclosing them in an

intimate cocoon. The cool air swirled, causing their body heat to make steam.

At least, Samantha wanted to believe the steam was caused by their heat versus the cooler, saturated air. Instant chemistry-slash-attraction was definitely something she did not need, had not planned on, and was absolutely something she did not want.

But, dang, whatever cologne the guy wore made her mouth water.

"I've had about all the excitement I can stand for one day," Bret grumbled, slipping a handcuff over her slender wrist and snapping it shut. Before he met her gaze, he clicked the other end around his own wrist. "Now. Let's go."

She lagged back, forcing him to half drag her to the Jeep.

"Get in." He waited while she slid into the seat, swallowing a yelp when his right arm jerked sideways.

"It'd be easier for you to drive if you'd uncuff me," she pointed out in a snippy-sounding voice.

"I can manage. Get back out and come with me."

"Maybe I don't want to."

He scooped her out of the car. "I wasn't asking."

He stalked to the driver's side, opened the door, and half tossed her over the gearshift as he followed her into the car. "Buckle up."

"I can't—"

"Sure you can. Just use one hand."

"Not all of us are as adept as you at using one hand," she sniped, but he refused to respond to her innuendo.

Instead he swallowed a growl of frustration, clicked his seat-belt and then finished snapping hers.

She tugged, but he finally was able to turn the ignition and shift into gear.

"What's your name?" He downshifted and turned onto the square.

"What do you care? What's next? Are you going to ask how old I am or where I go to school?"

He pressed his lips together to keep from laughing at her absurdity.

"No offense," he finally said when he could control his voice, "but I think you've been out of school for quite a while."

"Gee, thanks." She slumped in the seat, jerking his arm along with her.

"Hey, I need that hand to drive." He tugged until he edged her closer to the gearshift. "And I need to know your name because I just arrested you, remember?"

"You didn't read me my rights." He didn't need to look at her to see the look of triumph.

"You've been watching too much TV. Not necessary." He wheeled into the parking space in front of the courthouse marked SHERIFF and turned off the engine; then he smiled sweetly at his prisoner. "No witnesses. It'd just be your word against mine."

While she sputtered, he grasped her shoulders and pulled her out of the car. It had been a long time since he'd had a date—that was the only reason he'd developed a fascination with watching the rise and fall of her breasts beneath the snug-fitting black turtleneck. Of course, he could have done without the rain activating the citrus scent of her wild blond hair.

"Take your hands off me!" She jerked away and would have fallen, taking him down with her, had he not grabbed her shoulders to steady her.

"Could we please stop the drama and just go in and get the booking process out of the way?"

"Sure." She lagged back when he started walking. "As soon as you uncuff me."

Couldn't happen too soon, as far as he was concerned, but he'd be damned if he'd give her another opportunity to escape.

"Which I will do," he assured her, "as soon as we get inside the office. It's raining. I'm wet and tired and don't want to chase you down again. Now walk. Please," he added in a softer tone. His grandmother had always told him he'd catch more flies with honey than with vinegar. Wouldn't hurt to try.

"If you're arresting me, will I at least have a chance to shower off all this mud?" Trotting along beside him, she looked more like an eager date than a prisoner. Which was entirely not what he should be thinking.

"Yes, ma'am." Standing aside, he allowed her to walk into the miniscule sheriff's office ahead of him. He may have humiliated her by rolling her around in the mud and arresting her, but at least now he could afford to be a gentleman.

"Really?" She glanced around at the combination desk/booking station, coatrack, and low oak railing separating the cells from the office. "A place this size has separate shower areas for men and women?"

"Didn't say that." He bit back a grin. "Aw, don't go getting all bristly on me. You're the only *perpetrator* in custody at the moment. So, for the time being, it's the women's shower."

Her sigh sounded pitiful, but he hardened his heart.

"I'm too filthy to argue. Just uncuff me and point me in the direction of the shower."

Instead he urged her toward the desk. "First I need to book you."

Digging her heels in, Samantha tried to put her hands on her hips and attempted to look fierce. Judging from the giant officer's expression, she hadn't succeeded. That had always been her problem: no one seemed to take her seriously.

Not even Sean.

The thought was sobering. Not that she'd really wanted Sean to take her seriously—it just would have been nice to have had the option.

"Ma'am?" *Dudley Do-Right's* smooth voice crashed her pity party, catapulting her back into her current sucky situation. "Name, please?"

Under other circumstances, having a hottie like the one before her asking her name might have thrilled her. However, when said hottie had tackled her, handcuffed her, and was now in the process of arresting her . . . not so much. Dang, could her day—her life—get any worse?

She rubbed her aching wrist. Despite what old *Dudley* may think, she wasn't acting. She wouldn't be surprised to see a bruise when he finally took off the cuffs.

"Couldn't you take this off? Please? How about if I promise to stay put?"

Green eyes observed her for several heartbeats. Finally, he nodded, recessed light reflecting from his soft-looking dark hair. "I reckon." He stood and reached into the pocket of his snug jeans.

Then he patted the other pocket.

"Damn," he said under his breath. He scanned the floor around the desk and glanced at the entrance.

Their eyes met.

"I don't suppose you see a key lying over there, do you?"

Suddenly, *Dudley Do-Right* lost all his allure, becoming a real *Goober*.

Curling her fingers into her palms until her short nails dug into the flesh, she mentally counted to ten. Then to twenty.

It didn't help.

"Un-freaking-believable! You lost the key, didn't you?" She jumped up and leaned across the desk to grab his collar with their joined hands. "Didn't you?"

"*Well,*" he drawled with a slick-but-insincere-looking smile, revealing straight, white teeth, "I wouldn't exactly say that."

"Oh? And what exactly would you say?" How the heck was she going to take a shower shackled to the Greek God disguised in jeans and a soggy broadcloth shirt? Just when she'd thought her day couldn't get any worse . . .

He turned up the wattage on his smile. "I'd say *we* lost the key. After all," he hurried on when she began sputtering, "we both were rolling around on the ground while you were resisting arrest. I figure you're at least equal in blame."

She would not further degrade herself by arguing. Besides, it would get her nowhere. "Please tell me there is a spare key."

"'Course there's a spare." He opened and shut every drawer in the desk. Twice. "It's got to be here somewhere."

When another thorough search failed to produce a key—big surprise—he picked up the phone.

"I'm calling Ed. He's my cousin, the real sheriff. I'm just sitting in for him while he has a baby. Well, he isn't having a baby, of course. It's Paige. His wife." He smiled, his attention on the voice vibrating through the handset. "Hey, Ed! How's Paige? Great! Say, Ed, I have a little problem." He winked and turned his back as much as their linked arms allowed and then lowered his voice.

For pity's sake. Like she wanted to listen to his conversation. She began whistling, looking everywhere but at the man behind her.

"Very funny." His voice told her otherwise.

"What?" She turned to find him staring at her. Funny, his eyes looked more green than they had just a few minutes ago.

"You were whistling the theme from *The Andy Griffith Show*."

She attempted a sincere smile. "Sorry. Did he tell you where the spare key is?" He nodded. "Well?"

"It's at the hospital in his pocket."

"What do you mean, it's in his pocket? Go get it!"

"Can't. They discovered a problem with the babies and transferred her to the big hospital in Corpus Christi." He rounded the desk. "Now, don't get upset—"

"Don't get upset! My boyfriend dumped me for some bimbo, right at Christmas, and then steals my dog. I don't care about him, I just want my dog back. Was that too much to expect?" Before Bret could answer, she sniffed and rattled on. "I came here to get Rhetta back—"

"Rhetta?"

"That's my dog. Long story. I wanted a dog named Rhett Butler, but when I saw her, I couldn't resist her. So . . . I named her Rhetta." She took a deep breath. "I drove here to get her—"

"Are you sure she's in Christmas?"

"Will you stop interrupting? Yes! I'm sure she's in Christmas. Why else would I drive all the way down here from Houston? Where was I?"

"You drove to Christmas to get your dog back." He settled

against the edge of the desk, sticking his free hand in his pocket to keep from acting on the insane urge to stroke her hair away from her expressive face.

"Right. I found the house, but she—the homewrecker who stole my dog—was there. I—"

"I thought you said your boyfriend took the dog."

Her eyes narrowed; her nostrils flared. He wouldn't have been surprised to hear her teeth gnashing.

"So," she continued in a hard voice, carefully pronouncing each word, "I checked into my room and waited until dark. But Rhetta wasn't there. Then you came in." She shrugged. "You know the rest."

"You were still breaking and entering. That's illegal." At this point, he'd like nothing better than to just let her go. But he'd taken an oath. Besides, the alarm company had a record they'd called the alarm in to him.

"No!" Her blue eyes flashed, drawing him back to their conversation. "I wasn't breaking in. Well, I was, but I wasn't going to steal anything." She waved her hands as she talked, slinging his through the air in the process. "I mean, it's not stealing if what you take is rightfully yours, is it?"

He sighed. "Do you have proof of ownership?" If she did, he could dismiss the arrest as a mistake, fill out the appropriate forms, and go home.

"Yes!" She sat up straighter and then wilted, flopping back in the chair. "Well, no. Not with me."

"So I'm supposed to just let you break into the Wileys' on your word you were looking for a dog that may or may not be there and may or may not be yours."

Her pale brows furrowed and then she once again shot to her feet. "Wiley? I thought her name was Donner."

"Donner?" He shook his head. The woman was obviously confused. "Bambi Donner lives next door."

"Crap." She sank down again into the oak chair next to the desk and buried her head in the crook of her elbow. "I can't do anything right."

"Full name, please."

"Okay, Miss Harrison," Bret said, working the kink from his shoulder from typing one-handed. "I logged you in and set up your court date."

She raised her head and looked at him with bleak eyes. "Now what?"

"I have to keep you in custody until the circuit court judge comes back through town. Unless you have someone here who would vouch for your integrity." He arched a brow at her, not surprised when she shook her head. "He comes through here the second Wednesday of each month—"

"So you're telling me he won't be back until after Christmas?" She sat up straighter, pushing the already tight knit tighter over her breasts. Not that he noticed. Well, he didn't want to notice, which should count for something.

He shrugged and tried not to look guilty. "Actually, he won't be back until after New Year's. Sorry." He touched her arm. "Are you sure about Bambi? We went to school together. I can't believe Bambi Donner would steal anything, especially a dog. As for being a homewrecker, well, that's about as big of a stretch. There must be some mistake."

"No, no mistake." Samantha stood and stretched while Bret averted his eyes. "My rat-fink ex-boyfriend told me so. Trust me, I didn't misunderstand a word. He made it painfully clear." She looked at the drying mud caked to her black jeans and sweater. "Any idea when the key for the cuffs will show up?"

"Ed promised to drive it back as soon as Paige delivers, first thing tomorrow morning, at the latest." He bent his knees to look into her blue eyes. "Would you like to shower off some of that mud?"

Her small smile looked grateful. "Great. Then it can be your turn. No offense, but you're a mess."

"None taken. I'll call my grandmother—she's the cook for the jail—and have her bring over some food as soon as she finishes supper at the bed-and-breakfast she runs. Gram should be here by the time we get cleaned up." He dug in his pocket for his cell and punched in numbers.

Samantha narrowed her eyes. "She doesn't, by chance, run the Christmas Inn B and B, does she?"

Bret laughed. "Naw, that's her old rival, Nick. Gram's place is the White Dove. Don't tell me you're staying with Nick? I'm just kidding," he said when she looked alarmed. "It's a nice place. Bigger than the Dove, but, of course, the Dove has better food." They slowly made their way to the back of the jail. "Hey, Gram, it's Bret," he said into his phone, "I have a prisoner here and would surely appreciate it if you could bring us some supper." He frowned. "No, I'm not kidding. I'll tell you about it later. Thanks, see you soon."

Samantha stopped just inside the shower-room door as he laid his phone on the property desk, jerking Bret's progress to a halt. "I can't shower in there." She turned wide eyes on him. "It's just a room. There's not even a shower curtain."

"It's not like you'll be naked," he said, lifting their joined arms. "These things make undressing impossible. Now what? It's clean, if that's what you're worried about."

"No. It's just that, well . . ." She took a deep breath, during which Bret averted his eyes. Well, he should have, anyway. "So you're telling me I should shower in all my clothes? Then I'll be all wet."

"You're not exactly dry now. And you're also covered in mud. I figure at least this way you could get some of the mud washed off."

After some effort, they removed their boots, but it was clear his prisoner still had misgivings.

"I could catch cold sitting in wet clothes in the cell all night waiting for your cousin to bring the key," she pointed out.

"Not likely," he said through clenched teeth. "Colds are caused by a virus. Being wet and/or cold has nothing to do with it. Believe me, I know these things. I'm a science teacher."

"You said you were a deputy." Her eyes narrowed again. The woman had a suspicious streak a mile wide.

"No, I said I was acting sheriff while my cousin was off. He deputized me, but I'm Bret Bayne, a seventh-grade science teacher *in real life*. Nice way to spend my Christmas break, don't you think?" White teeth flashed at Sam when he grinned.

He reached past her to turn on the multiple showerheads.

Steam and warm mist enveloped their feet.

"I can't do this," Samantha said, stepping back, the momentum dragging him along with her. It was bad enough just being so close to the man, inhaling the mouthwatering cologne. Water would only increase its potency . . . and possibly make her do things she normally would not do. "I'll just stay in my muddy clothes until your cousin gets here."

She watched a muscle in his jaw flex. He reached out with his free hand as he stepped back and pulled her into the warm shower spray.

Samantha shrieked and then choked on inhaled water.

"Suit yourself," he said in a clipped tone, "but I want to get some of this mud off me." He made a big production of scrubbing at the muddy streaks on his jeans.

She narrowed her eyes against the stinging spray and then quickly rubbed as much mud from the front of her sweater as possible, given the short amount of time her jailer allowed.

Bret knew he should look somewhere, anywhere else. But his eyes had a will of their own and were locked on the small hands scrubbing at a rack that made his mouth water like a bluetick hound. Despite the steam and dark fabric of her sweater, he could clearly see the pebbled tips of her breasts. At least, he thought he could. Which was the problem. Where Samantha Harrison was concerned, his imagination was working overtime.

He swallowed a groan and as discreetly as possible rearranged his expanding package as he reached across her to twist the controls to the off position.

"That's about as clean as we'll get." His attempt at a jovial tone echoed in his ears. "May as well go back to the office to wait for supper." He strode past her, eyes averted, tugging her in his wake.

Trotting behind his broad back, slipping and sliding on the tile, Sam had the urge to stick out her tongue. She was the wronged party here. He had no business arresting her for simply trying to get her dog back. Cuffing her to him was overkill. He wasn't even a real policeman. Then, to make matters worse, he'd gone and lost the stupid key to the handcuffs. She stretched and tried to ease the knotted muscles in her back without tugging on his arm.

He tossed a threadbare towel over his shoulder to land on her head. She grabbed it before she lost her balance, wiping as much moisture from her face and clothing as she could without breaking stride.

Yes, sir, it was turning into an all-around crappy start to Christmas.

8

"Evening, *deputy*," a small woman with wild white hair said with a sassy smile as she elbowed her way through the front door half an hour later, carrying a huge wicker basket. "I just heard all about your apprehension of the *dangerous felon* out at Wileys' place."

She walked to the desk, where they'd been playing cards, rising on her toes to plunk the basket on the surface. "Move those things before the whole basket falls plumb off onto the floor." She glanced over his shoulder at Samantha. "That the *perp*?" She made a sound that was suspiciously close to a snort of laughter. "D'you think it's safe to allow her to roam free out here like that?"

He shot her an annoyed look and silently raised their cuffed arms, tugging Sam to his side. "Not a problem," he said.

"Aren't you the cutest little thing?" the woman said, stepping closer. "You don't look like a hardened-criminal type."

"I'm beginning to think she's a professional gambler," Bret grumbled. "She's already won all my money."

"Don't pay any attention to him," the woman said. "He never could play cards worth a damn. What's your name, sweetie?"

"Samantha Harrison." She straightened to her full five foot one and a half inches. "And I'm not a professional gambler *or* a criminal," she declared with all the sincere dignity she could muster. It was difficult to radiate sincerity when one was dripping wet and handcuffed. "I was just trying to get my dog back. She was dognapped."

The old woman's eyes, which bore a striking resemblance to the ones of her arresting officer, widened. "Mercy! Who on Earth would steal your dog?"

"She claims Bambi has it," *Dudley* supplied.

"Bambi! I've never known Bambi Donner to steal anything." She leaned closer, her peppermint-scented breath wafting out to envelope Sam in a sense of well-being. "Are you sure it was Bambi, honey?"

What the heck was so great about Bambi-the-homewrecker/dog-thief Donner that everyone was so willing to leap to her defense?

Sam swallowed her outrage and unclamped her jaw to say in a quiet voice, "Yes, ma'am, I am. Sean—he's my scumbag ex-boyfriend—told me he'd fallen in love with her when he broke up with me." She blinked back tears she didn't try to hide. "I had to get out of the apartment."

"Of course you did, honey." The old woman patted Samantha's shoulder. "You poor little thing."

"I told him I wanted him to pack and get out while I was gone." Sam sniffed. "When I came home, Rhetta was gone, too."

"Rhetta's her dog," the deputy interjected.

"Of course it's her dog, silly, I got that. What I don't get is why on Earth Bambi would get mixed up with such a lowlife as Samantha's boyfriend."

"Ex-boyfriend," Sam and Bret said at the same time.

The woman shook her head as she reached into the basket to begin unloading. "I still can't get my mind wrapped around Bambi doing such a thing. Why, I've known the Donners since before Bambi was born. Fine people. Upstanding, God-fearing—"

"I get it." Samantha interrupted, earning a startled look from the woman and a glare from her grandson. "You don't believe it. No one believes it." She shrugged and reached for a piece of fried chicken. "I don't mean to be rude, but it's true." Searching for an end to the uncomfortable silence, she bit into the succulent drumstick, its flavor exploding on her tongue. She swallowed her moan of pleasure along with the meat. "This is wonderful. You're a very good cook, Mrs.—I'm sorry, I don't know your name."

"Oh! Where are my manners?" The woman set down a covered bowl and swatted Bret before reaching for Samantha's hand. "I'm Hannah Strong, Bret's grandmother. And you said your name was Samantha?"

She had a strong handshake for an old lady. Samantha appreciated it and smiled as she shook the woman's hand. "Hi. Yes, ma'am. Samantha Harrison."

"What a lovely name." Hannah glanced meaningfully at her grandson. "Don't you think so, Bret?" She leaned closer. "You and your boyfriend recently split up, is that right?" Sam nodded, earning a dazzling smile from Hannah. "So you're not currently seeing anyone?"

"Gram!" Bret's cheeks looked distinctly ruddy.

"What? I'm just getting to know your little friend."

"She's not my friend," Bret said through clenched teeth, a muscle ticking along his jaw. "She's my prisoner. I arrested her for breaking into the Wileys' house."

"Oh, pooh." Hannah waved her hand in a dismissive gesture. "You're not even a real deputy—"

"I am, too! Ed deputized me before he left—" Bret's hand gesture sent Sam's chicken leg flying across the room.

"Hey!" Sam elbowed him. "I was eating that!"

"Sorry." He didn't look sorry.

"Bret, pass your friend another piece of chicken. And don't you think you would be safe to uncuff the poor thing?" She clucked at her grandson, shaking her head. "I think you're taking this whole thing a little too seriously."

"He lost the key, and his cousin has the spare," Sam supplied, earning a scowl from Bret. "We're stuck like this until at least tomorrow morning."

"Of all the lamebrain stunts." Hannah began picking up the dinner and repacking the basket. "Bret Hadley Bayne, you get that poor thing something warm to cover up with and march yourself home right this minute."

"Gram, I can't go home. Remember?" He held up their joined arms, waving a little for emphasis. "I'm not any more thrilled about spending the night in jail than she is, believe me."

"Then take her home with you. Don't look at me like that. You know you'd both be much more comfortable at your place, not to mention warmer."

"But as an officer of the law—"

"Oh, Bret, dear, put a sock in it. No one is here. No one will know or care." She hefted the basket. "If you want any food, it will be on your kitchen table."

"Wait!" The idea of spending any time in the privacy of Bret's home struck panic in Samantha. "Bret said you own a B and B—maybe we could stay there with you?"

Hannah shook her head. "Nope. Sorry. Full up. What with the holidays and the parade on the Gulf, I've been booked for months. In fact, it would be a help to me for you to stay at Bret's place. I don't really have time to cook for the jail right now. He has plenty of food and knows how to cook." She reached for the door and shot her grandson a pointed look. "I'll expect you to follow directly as soon as you can get the place locked up for the night."

Bret and Sam stared at each other after the door clicked shut.

"Well." Sam broke the silence. "Looks like we can either starve or you have a houseguest. And as I just realized I'm famished, lead the way."

9

Samantha lagged behind Bret's broad back as much as possible to protect her face from the stinging rain. Making him more miserably wet than they already were was just a perk.

"Why can't we drive?" she asked again, tugging his wrist with the cuff in an effort to renew circulation to her own wrist.

He turned and circled her shivering shoulders with his warm arm. Being handcuffed caused their bodies to bump against each other in a most disconcerting way. Before she had a chance to decide if she should be outraged, he tugged her a little closer. It would be so easy to cuddle up to the warmth he offered. Heck, who was she kidding? It would be so easy to take him up on just about any offer right about now.

Sleep deprived. That's what she was, and it had to be the reason she was noticing all the things she should not be noticing about her arresting officer. Yes, she definitely needed to voice her objection.

But before she could think of anything to say, any stinging rebukes, he beat her to the punch and started talking.

"Because we're already here."

Immediately, she noticed two things. All right, three, but the fact that he was incredibly hot and smelled so good she wanted to lick him didn't count because she'd noticed that before. The first thing was he hadn't been pulling her into his embrace—not that she'd have allowed it—he'd been leaning to open his door and dragged her along with his momentum. Because of the second thing, she felt compelled to say, "This is a bank."

"No, it's not." Was it just her, or did he sound more than a tad irritated? "It used to be a bank. F.B.C.—First Bank of Christmas—built a big, new place out by the interstate back when I was in high school. This place has been vacant ever since, so, naturally, when I decided to move back and found out it was still available, I bought it."

"Oh, yeah, naturally," she mocked. "We all have an unbearable urge to live in an old, abandoned bank." She stepped through the open, ornate, beveled glass double doors, squinting in the darkness while her eyes struggled to adjust. "There aren't any rats or anything, right?"

"Not anymore." He reached and flipped a switch. Lights blazed, causing Samantha to recoil.

Once she was reasonably certain her retinas weren't burned out, she glanced around.

"Wow. You actually live in a bank . . ." Beneath the elaborate chandeliers, marble floors gleamed despite their obvious age. "The floor is . . . spectacular." She met his gaze. "You don't find things like this anymore."

He seemed pleased, nodding as he looked around with obvious pride. "No, you don't. That's why I had to buy it. I remember coming into this bank with my grandmother when I was a little boy and thinking it was a palace." He pulled her farther into the open area, pointing to several medallions inlaid into the marble. "That's where the deposit-slip desks used to be."

To the right was a cozy-looking sectional with a big, square, padded ottoman facing a large flat-screen television mounted on the wall over a dark wood console cabinet. To the left of the TV was a round, ornate brass door.

"Is that the safe?" Sam wondered if he'd let her see inside it.

"One of them. There's another one upstairs—it's a little smaller than this one—in what used to be the bank president's office and a small one through the French doors at the end of the room in the old loan offices. I use this one as a bar and wine cellar. I'll open it up and show it to you after supper."

"What's over there?" Samantha pointed to the row of gleaming brass bars inserted into a half wall and wondered if there was a back way out. Maybe she could escape once the handcuffs were off.

He walked with her when she tugged. "It's the old teller cages. There was a break room directly behind this area, so it was easy to make it into my kitchen and the teller area a dining room." He flipped another switch as they walked through a swinging oak gate. "The counters the tellers had used work well for a serving area, and I built storage underneath."

"You did that yourself?" She ran her free hand along the worn wooden counter, trying not to be impressed. In spite of his attractiveness, she needed to remember the man was not a potential boyfriend or even a friend. Escaping was not personal. Heck, he probably wouldn't even care because he was just subbing for the real sheriff. But it wouldn't hurt to play nice and be sociable. Maybe he'd let his guard down. "You did a great job. I never would have realized they weren't attached to the counters originally."

"Thanks. The actual kitchen is in the old break room, right through this door." They skirted around a gleaming banquet-sized table, and then he pushed open a swinging door with his free hand, flipping another switch. "I had to totally gut and re-build. Took me most of the summer before I transferred here."

"So you just moved here? I'm confused. I thought you said you'd come into this bank as a little boy."

"I did. Born and raised in Christmas. After college I took a teaching job in Corpus Christi."

"Corpus is beautiful. Why would you want to move?"

He shrugged. "It just made me homesick for the beach I grew up on and all the people who know me. Then I found this place and couldn't wait to make the move. I think this is my favorite project." He gestured, drawing her attention back to the kitchen.

Espresso-colored cabinets with gleaming black granite countertops outlined the large room. Beneath a lone window was an oversize triple stainless-steel sink with an industrial-looking faucet. A professional-looking cooktop graced the top of a wide island. Assorted stainless-steel appliances winked at her from around the room.

"Do you cook?" She shook her head before he could answer. "Sorry, stupid question. Of course you do." What she wouldn't give to have a kitchen like that one. Of course, she'd also like to win the lotto so she could stay home and enjoy it. And that wasn't likely to happen.

"Not as much as I'd like," he said, drawing her back to the conversation, "but I do my share. Christmas is a really small town. There are two restaurants on the square and about four little seafood shacks down by the bay. They all serve great food, but it can get monotonous. And my grandmother has enough to do without cooking for me."

He nodded toward a mahogany pub set at the end of the kitchen against an exposed brick wall. His grandmother had obviously been there, judging by the amount of food covering the square table. "I eat most of my meals right there." He glanced down at their cuffed wrists. "I'm really sorry I lost the key." His green eyes told her it was the truth. "As soon as we finish eating, I'll call Ed again to see if he can't get here sooner."

Samantha's traitorous stomach chose that time to rumble, the sound echoing from the tall ceiling.

Bret laughed, exposing dimples along with the straight, white teeth she'd noticed earlier.

Samantha temporarily forgot about food. How would his mouth feel on hers? Goose bumps rose at the thought of his teeth nipping at her skin.

"Let's get you fed and then I'll make that call." Bret said, jerking her back to the present.

"Okay, but then I want to see the rest," she protested while jockeying for position at the table. "Could you have found any taller chairs?"

"I think you need a booster chair, shorty." He grunted when her elbow met its mark and then lifted her to sit on a pub chair. He dragged another one close and sat, reaching for the plate of fried chicken. "Dig in."

The evening passed in companionable conversation. Had it not been for the handcuffs, it might have been a date. It was getting more and more difficult to remember it wasn't and keep on guard for an escape route.

Cleaning up after eating proved to be difficult, but they finally managed to get it done and resumed the tour.

The line of old-fashioned cubicles that had formed the loan offices were still intact, their wooden-framed, frosted glass separating each space. Bret used one as his office and one as a little library, and the last one housed a treadmill and some kind of all-body workout contraption that looked more like a torture rack Sam had seen in old movies.

While watching an action-packed movie, complete with buttered popcorn from the old-fashioned popcorn maker in the vault, Samantha fell asleep.

Snuggled to Bret's warmth, she drifted. . . .

* * *

Warm. It was so warm. No wonder—she and Bret were on the beach. He kissed her, each kiss deeper, more thrilling than the last.

His hand toyed with her aching nipple. When did they get naked? She made a mental shrug. Who cared? As long as he kept doing what he was doing, she didn't care if they were naked, even in public. Heck, when his hot mouth covered her breast, sucking her nipple deep into his wet heat, she realized she didn't care if they were being watched by the entire town. Besides, she knew, on some level, it was a dream, so she went for it.

Bret rose above her. Somehow, though still on the beach, they were now lying on a bed, the satin sheets caressing her back while Bret caressed her front . . . and everywhere in between.

He bent, rubbing his smooth, firm chest against her achy, needy one. By the time he bent his head to suckle again, she thought she would scream in frustration.

Never, never had she been so turned on, so responsive.

His voracious mouth covered hers. She clasped her hand around his iron-hard erection and guided him to the place weeping for him.

His warm hands gripped her shoulders. . . .

"Samantha?" His voice filtered through the echo of her racing heartbeat. He shook her shoulder.

"Samantha," Bret said again as he yawned and stretched in his sitting position, the action bringing Sam up off hers. "Wake up."

He stood, pulling her up with his movement. "Let's try to get some real sleep. I left a message for Ed to text me when he's on his way."

There it was, the moment she'd been dreading all evening. Sure, it wasn't technically a date—she was, after all, under arrest. But, dang, sitting all snuggled up to Bret's firm chest while watching a movie, it had felt more like a date.

And she liked it more than she cared to admit. Especially what had come afterward. Wait. That had been a dream. Hadn't it? Or had her captor been diddling with an unconscious woman? No, *Dudley* wouldn't do that. It was obviously a dream brought on by her recent stress. She was grieving for a lost relationship, and Bret was a convenient replacement for her subconscious. Yes, that was it. It had to be.

And now she had to sleep with him. Well, not *sleep* with him, sleep with him. Crap. Why did he have to be so cute and nice and smell so good?

She was so confused.

"Wait." She grabbed the edge of the sofa, halting their progress. "I didn't get to finish the tour."

"That's what I'm doing now. Samantha—"

"Call me Sam." She shrugged at his raised eyebrow. "Everyone does."

He gazed down at her, so close she could count the little crinkly lines around his green eyes. His scent engulfed her.

Their breath mingled.

Was he going to kiss her? Would she let him? Would she kiss him back? And where would their kiss lead if she did? And did she want to go there?

Her heart pounded, making taking a deep breath almost impossible. A viselike pressure filled her chest. Was she having a heart attack?

"You don't look like any Sam I ever met," he said in a soft, intimate voice. "I'll call you Samantha." His warm breath brushed her forehead. Or was that his lips?

He walked them to the vault and pressed an ornate brass button she hadn't noticed. A grinding motor sound filled the room, followed shortly by a deep, vibrating clunk.

The marble wall to the right of the vault slid open to reveal a small brass elevator, complete with a retractable gate.

Bret slid back the gate and tugged her into the elevator. He cranked the gate shut and pushed another button to begin their ascent.

Suddenly Sam understood the fantasy of sex in an elevator.

She had to get out. Fast. Before she acted on the instant fantasy she'd just created.

"Aren't there any stairs?" Her voice cracked. "This looks like it may be the original elevator."

Bret grinned down at her. "Probably is. The only stairs lead up from the back of the kitchen. The elevator is easier and closer. Relax, I take it every day."

While she was thinking about a rebuttal, the door swished open. Bret slid open the gate and pulled her out of the elevator.

His bedroom was huge. From what she could see, it took up the entire second floor. She wanted to ask if he'd made his bedroom furniture because it resembled the workmanship she'd seen downstairs, but she was struck mute by the predominant feature of the room: his bed was massive, up on a pedestal, bathed in the spotlight of a recessed light directly above. It looked like a sacrificial altar.

Bret's hand on her shoulder turned her to face him.

He leaned close, his scent wafting around her, making her dizzy.

"Samantha?" His voice was low, sexy as all get-out. "Are you ready to go to bed?"

10

_____

"What?" Sam's voice squeaked, and she had to struggle to remain upright. Did anyone actually swoon anymore?

"Unless you need something else? Do you want to use the bathroom? It's right through there." He glanced down at their cuffed wrists. "I can close the door of the water closet as far as possible and stand out here."

She'd limited her liquids all evening, anticipating just such a problem, but, dang his hide, now she had the urge.

She halted their progress at the bathroom door. "I don't have a toothbrush. Or floss. All my stuff is at—where I'm staying." Better not to remind him of where she was staying. That way, it might take him a while to find her, which would be beneficial if Bambi, the bimbo/homewrecker/dog thief, made a scene when Sam rescued Rhetta. Unless Bret tried to find her for more personal reasons, which would be totally ridiculous, and she wasn't remotely interested. Well, okay, she might be interested. Crap, he was looking at her like she'd lost her mind. "I can't sleep without brushing and flossing," she explained in what could only be described as a pathetic whine.

"No prob. I have extra toothbrushes and just about every flavor and type of floss you could want."

"You floss?"

"Don't sound so surprised. Not all guys are pigs."

"I didn't mean—"

He laughed. "Sure, you did. But it's okay. After what your boyfriend put you through, you're allowed. Just remember, we're not all like him."

"Ex," she whispered as he ushered her into a bathroom roughly the size of her entire apartment. "He's my ex-boyfriend."

Relieving herself with one arm sticking through a partially closed door was humiliating, to say the least.

She quickly discovered brushing teeth while handcuffed was more than difficult. Especially when one person was left-handed and the other was right-handed. Flossing was even worse.

"Ow!" Sam elbowed Bret's hanging forearm. "You're smacking me in the face," she said around the fingers holding the floss.

"You're doing it yourself," he fired back. "I can't help it if my hand moves when yours does. Ever heard of equal-and-opposite reactions?"

Finally finished and headed into the bedroom, she averted her eyes from the bed dominating the room. "I don't suppose you'd consider sleeping on the floor?"

He snorted. "You supposed right. The bed is too high. Neither of us would be comfortable. It's a big bed. There is plenty of room for both of us." He folded back the burnished gold spread, revealing lush-looking burgundy sheets. "Slide on in, Samantha."

"This isn't very professional," she felt compelled to point

out, suppressing a shiver that must have been because of the coolness of the sheets. It certainly wasn't because of her bed partner.

"Neither was losing the key." He pulled the covers over them and loomed over her.

"What do you think you're doing?" Could she fight off a man his size while handcuffed to him? Would she want to?

"Turning off the light." His voice did not sound amused.

"Oh." A few seconds passed with her listening to him settle beneath the covers, seemingly ready to go right to sleep while she was acutely aware of his every move as well as the heat radiating off him like a blast furnace. "It's kind of hot in here, don't you think?"

He huffed out a breath in the darkness. "You're the one who insisted we sleep in our clothes."

"You're the one who said it would be impossible to get them off anyway." Let him try to deny it.

"True . . . why are you trying to argue?"

"I'm not. It's just . . . well, I guess I'm still sort of irritated to be under arrest. And the handcuffs aren't helping the situation." She rolled to her side. His face was half shadowed in the moonlight. If anything, it made him better looking. Sexier. *Stop.* "Maybe I'm on edge because I realize if you wanted to take advantage of the situation, there isn't much I could do about it. Especially all alone with you here in your house. It's sort of unsettling."

He rolled to face her. She braced her knee on the mattress to keep from rolling into him.

"Is that an invitation?" His voice was low, sexy, intimate.

And irritating.

"What!" She tried to jump up, but his weight attached to her wrist held her down. "What planet are you from? Because there is no way on Earth that was in any way, shape, or form an invitation!"

"Good." He rolled to his back, his free hand behind his head.

"Good?" she sputtered. "Why is that good?"

"You're not my type."

"Ha! That's a big, fat lie! I'm every guy's type—I'm female, under eighty, and breathing."

"Lady, I don't know what kind of men you've been around, but trust me, you are not my type."

She flopped back on her pillow, blinking back stupid, irrational tears. Maybe he was telling the truth. Maybe she wasn't anybody's type.

If Bambi was any indication, Samantha sure hadn't been Sean's type.

Always too curious for her own good, when she was reasonably certain her voice wouldn't wobble, she asked, "Why not?"

"Why not what?" The jerk sounded half asleep.

"Why am I not your type?"

The bed dipped again as he rolled toward her. "For one thing, you talk. A lot. For another, you're too skinny. I like my women with meat on their bones."

I could gain weight if I ever had time to relax and enjoy my food. Wait. Why would she want to gain weight for *Dudley Do-Right*? As soon as she was released, she was grabbing her dog and escaping Christmas. "Is that it?"

"Well, there's one more thing, but there's nothing you can do to change it."

"What is it?" She raised a tentative hand to his shoulder. His shirt was dry now, sort of stiff and scratchy, but it didn't mask the hard muscles and hot skin beneath. His heat zipped through her fingertips to pucker her nipples. Dang physical reaction. Good thing it was dark. "Tell me," she said in her sexiest voice.

She'd turned on lesser men with that tone of voice. Not that she necessarily wanted to turn Bret on, but it still stung to hear him say she wasn't his type. "Tell me," she repeated. "I really want to know."

"You're too short."

11

Too short? Had he actually had the nerve to tell her that not only was she not his type but she was too *short*?

Sam refrained from slapping him upside the head. She also showed admirable restraint by not gouging out his eyes or pinching and twisting a plug out of his muscular arm.

But a way to get back at him did occur to her.

She scooted closer and ran her bare foot up the inside of his calf. Did she dare? Oh, yeah.

"I can think of some things where height doesn't matter."

"Oh?" His voice sounded tight. "Like what?" He'd better not laugh in her face. She wouldn't be responsible for whatever bodily damage she might be forced to inflict.

And there wasn't a female judge in the state who would convict her.

Despite her urge to run—face it, that couldn't happen anyway—she scooted as close as possible, given their cuffed hands between them.

"Like kissing." Before she lost her nerve, she stretched forward and brushed her mouth across his lips.

"Kissing's okay," he conceded. "I'm not sure I'd call that a real kiss, though."

His free arm circled her waist and dragged her against his hard, muscled body.

Mercy, she'd never had a science teacher with a body like that. Maybe junior high science would have held her interest.

"Samantha?"

"Hmmm?" It took an effort to keep from purring her words with his heat and scent enveloping her.

"Try it again." He pulled her closer still. "Kiss me." He breathed the words against her lips.

She felt the vibration clear to her toes.

Okay, maybe she wasn't his type. Maybe he wasn't her type either. Oh, who was she kidding? She honestly could not think of a single one of her friends back home who wouldn't positively drool over *Dudley*. He was everyone's type.

Even hers.

All the reasons it was a bad idea to get involved with someone she would never see again once she left town flashed into her mind. She quickly made a mental list: The first was the most obvious—she wouldn't be hanging around Christmas once she retrieved Rhetta. Second, they'd just met. Third, they'd not only just met, it was definitely not under the best of circumstances, which brought her to number four: he had arrested her. There was probably some kind of law or rule against them getting together. And, number five, she wasn't a one-night-stand kind of girl, and living in different cities made anything else impossible.

But the reasons that trumped all the rest were she would never see him again once she left Christmas, it was the holidays, and she was feeling bluer than she ever would have thought possible.

Then again, men had casual sex all the time, she rationalized. Why shouldn't she? Besides, it wasn't like they could actually go all the way—they couldn't get their clothes off. And it might help lower his guard, making her escape easier. Plus, she wanted him.

Bret chose that time to caress her behind, his touch threatening to send her jeans up in flames.

He wanted her to kiss him. She wanted to kiss him more than she wanted to take her next breath.

She dragged her tongue across his lip, biting back a smile when she felt a little shiver run through him. Her teeth nipped lightly on his lower lip before she gently sucked on it.

He growled deep in his throat, the sound unbelievably sexy. It spurred her to slip her right leg over his lean hip and slide over to straddle the hard ridge of denim before she could think too much about why it might not be a good idea.

He arched his hips, doing a slow roll, grinding his hardness into her.

Her lips sought his. If she was only going to kiss him once, she wanted to pack as much punch as possible into it.

His teeth were smooth and slick against the tip of her tongue. Their minty-fresh breath mingled as the kiss deepened.

His grip tightened. Good, he wasn't as immune to her as he'd let on.

Rubbing her aching nipples shamelessly against his chest, she climbed his body, her free hand raking through his hair. It felt smooth, silky. She wanted to bury her face in it and inhale his unique fragrance. She wanted to fist her hand in it and bite his neck. Her breath came in gasping pants as she licked his face, his neck, all the while rubbing harder and harder in a vain attempt to alleviate the building ache deep within.

Ravenous, his mouth claimed hers. Her bones seemed to melt into the mattress as he deftly flipped her beneath him, their cuffed hands now clenching each other above their heads.

While he feasted on her mouth, his hand was busy. Before

she could take a breath, he had her turtleneck pulled up and over her head to lay like a warm armadillo around her left bicep.

Her bra was freed to slide down her arm to join her sweater.

On fire. She was on fire. Making inarticulate sounds, she writhed beneath him, bucking her hips to encourage him, to show him what she wanted.

His mouth trailed flames down her neck over her collarbone. Downward, aching millimeters at a time, he slowly made his way to the breasts aching for his touch.

A half shriek, half sigh escaped her lips when his tongue circled her erect nipple. She arched her back in an attempt to force it into his mouth. Instead he continued torturing her, laving first one and then the other, coming close, so close to sucking it into his mouth, only to kiss his way back to the other one.

Just as she was on the border of becoming violent in her sexual greed, heat enveloped her nipple.

She sighed, feeling his suction deep down in her womb. Restless, wanting to savor every little nuance of sensation, she moved her legs against the sheet, bucking with each pull of his mouth.

Her back arched, eyes squeezed shut. Ripples of sensation flowed over and through her. Every hair follicle stood on end. Colored lights flashed behind her eyelids as her entire body convulsed, sending waves of heat washing over her, moisture gushing to dampen her still wet panties and jeans.

Bret paused, holding Samantha's limp body crushed against his thundering heart. Damn, the little tease had not only climaxed in her sexy jeans, she'd done it without him.

That would not do.

He ignored the little voice in his head that sounded suspiciously like his grandmother telling him what they were doing— or about to do—was probably against some rule for deputies.

But he wasn't a real deputy, so it didn't matter. Besides, he'd been way too long without a date. Longer still since he'd had a willing woman in his bed.

His cock threatened to go off at the idea of what had just taken place in his partner's pants.

His hand shook, but luckily Samantha was still coherent enough to cooperate and lifted her hips. Within seconds, they were both naked from the waist down.

His hand skimmed over smooth skin and the hard jut of her hip bone. The muscles of her abdomen vibrated against his fingertips as they slid toward her welcoming wetness.

She moaned, spreading her legs, and lifted her hips in time to the rhythmic movement of his fingers, embedded now within her slick heat.

His cock throbbed, the muscles in his butt and thighs tightening into painful knots along with his balls.

Rolling on the condom turned into a two-person job.

With a silent promise to pleasure her more next time, he canted her hips and plunged home.

12

Impending dawn bathed the room in a gray haze when Samantha opened her eyes.

Where was she? Why was she so hot? Sweat dripped from her hair along her neckline.

Whatever she was lying on was smooth and radiated heat.

She felt around with her hand. The activities of the previous night came instantly to mind, hitting her between the eyes with the force of a two-by-four, giving her an instant headache.

Her warm, human mattress grunted and moved a little.

Oh, ick. Their sweat-slicked chests were stuck to each other.

The air-conditioning clicked on, chilling her bare back. How did she get naked? Of course, she remembered Bret stripping her pants and thong from her eager and willing lower body. But the removal of her turtleneck and bra were encased in her memory by remnants of a sexual fog.

As she'd suspected, sex with Bret had been hot and frantic. It was amazing they hadn't ripped each other's clothes off in their mating frenzy.

She started to ease off her latest mistake—and, really, it had been a mistake. Neither of them was to blame, they were just too strangers whose hormones got the better of them while thrust into an intimate setting.

Thrust was probably not the word she needed to be thinking at that moment.

Her eyes closed briefly. Lordy, what had she been thinking? She had veered from her plan. She was in Christmas to get her dog back, not to do the horizontal mambo with a science teacher. No matter how great it had been and how much she'd love an instant replay.

A hard length between her legs caught her attention as she started to move again.

Now what? Morning-after protocol really wasn't among her talents. There had never been a need.

Oh, great. Now he was rubbing her side, his fingers caressing the underside of her breast with each pass of his hand.

She held her breath. It would be so easy to relax against his warmth, to push her now aching breast into the comfort of his palm.

But it would be wrong.

Maybe she'd just lie there a little while longer and move again after Bret went back to sleep.

Rough fingers rolled her nipple. Her breath hitched. Moisture surged, causing her to squirm a little.

Tactical error because the little squirm realigned her opening with the hardness she'd been trying to avoid.

But, dang, it felt so good when he touched her.

His hand left her breast to splay across her buttocks, guiding her to the proper position for his entry.

Her body went on autopilot. It was the only explanation why one moment she was thinking, and the next she could only feel, reveling in the tactile sensations streaking through her, leaving her languid yet eager for more.

He maneuvered her to sit astride him, his hips revolving in lazy, mind-blowing circles.

In the semidarkness, she could barely make out his face, but she returned his satiated smile.

He raised both hands to caress her breasts, the action bringing her hand up as well. Because her hand was hanging out around her breast anyway, she pinched and rubbed her nipple while he squeezed and massaged her breasts.

His heated gaze told her the action turned him on every bit as much as it did her.

"We probably shouldn't be doing this," she whispered, slipping and sliding with each movement of his lean hips.

He made a noncommittal sound and slid their hands between her legs. He held her hand away with the back of his while he ratcheted up her pleasure by rubbing and plucking at her clitoris.

Close, she was so close to an orgasm her toes began to curl.

Faster and faster she rocked, rubbing her engorged folds against him while he continued to pleasure her from within and without.

Her breath came in short, gasping pants; her hips moved with frantic purpose. Her nipples puckered into tight, painful buds that tingled, the sensation shooting to her extremities.

She was on sensory overload. It was too much yet not enough.

Working around his hand, she was able to stroke the tips of her fingers along her slick folds.

Her back snapped into a hard arch, her knees convulsing to slam her down, her pelvic bone grinding against his with each hard thrust of their hips.

Then it happened.

Her climax rushed over her, drowning her in lovely waves of sensations. Beneath her, Bret stiffened, every muscle rigid. He gripped her hip bone, halting her movement while he ground against her. Heat exploded in her pelvis.

She collapsed on his chest, their breathing sounding unnaturally loud, echoing from the high ceiling.

Sam knew she should say something. They couldn't keep having sex if she expected to escape Christmas with her heart intact. Yes, it was just sex—for now. But Samantha knew if they kept doing what they were doing, she would end up with a broken heart.

Samantha Harrison did not have meaningless sex.

And she'd tell Bret so . . . as soon as she could draw enough air into her lungs to form the words.

Their hearts pounded against each other, Bret stroking her back while they struggled to regain their breath.

A rattling sound echoed in the quiet old bank.

"Hello?" a male voice called from down below, the sound echoing from the marble tile, easily wafting over the open banister into the bedroom. "Bret? You awake? Yo, Bret!"

The distinctive rumbling sound of the elevator vibrated the bed.

Heart pounding—and not in a pleasant way—Sam tried to scramble off Bret and the bed. She succeeded in doing neither.

His hand jerked the cuff against her wrist while his other hand gripped her upper arm. "Where do you think you're going?"

"Shhh! He'll hear you."

"Sweetheart, you're not going anywhere." He held their joined arms aloft. He jingled the cuffs for effect, which only irritated her more. He lowered his voice to match her whisper. "Besides, we could yell, and he wouldn't hear us over the racket of that old elevator."

The sound of the elevator door opening had Samantha diving under the covers.

"Don't let on I'm here," she whispered, squeezing her eyes shut, wishing she could make herself invisible.

Cooler air wafted across her face. She peeked through her eyelashes to find Bret grinning at her. "Drop the sheet! He's coming!"

"Samantha, it's my cousin Ed probably bringing the spare key. He knows you're here," he explained patiently. "That's the reason he's bringing the key."

Humiliation burned her cheeks. "I still would rather not face him. Please?"

"Suit yourself." He dropped the edge of the sheet and said, "Hey, Ed, how're Paige and the babies?"

"Good, good. Despite all the dire predictions, the birth was fast and uncomplicated. I should be able to bring them home by Christmas."

Bret shifted on the bed and nodded at his cousin.

"Things all right down at the station?" Ed stared at their boots and then at the pile of jeans and underwear on the floor and grinned. "Need me to do anything for you while I'm here?"

Under the sheet, Bret tweaked Samantha's nipple, earning a tiny squeak. "No, I think I have it covered. Thanks anyway."

"Heard you had a little excitement. How's your prisoner?"

"A little ornery—ow!" He shifted and grinned. "But I'm working on improving her disposition."

Ed nodded and stepped back toward the open door. "I'll just leave the key here on the dresser. I promised Paige I'd be back in time to help her feed the babies."

"I didn't realize you could lactate, Ed, you old dog."

"Very funny. She did tell me to give you a message when I saw you. Something about this being your harbinger?" He held up his hand, palm out. "Hey, don't shoot the messenger. Play nice, children. I'm outta here!"

Samantha waited until she heard the front door close before fighting her way out from under the covers. "I'm not ornery! And it wasn't fair to fondle me when you knew there was nothing I could do to stop you."

"Sorry." He grunted as she crawled over him, shoving bony elbows and knees into every soft—and one not so soft—place on his anatomy. But he still managed to enjoy the view.

"Do you think he suspected we had . . . you know?" While she talked, she tugged him to his feet.

He gazed pointedly at their pile of discarded clothing. "I think he may have had a clue or two."

Her shoulders slumped when she saw where he was looking. "Oh, crap!"

"Hey," he said, bending his knees to look her in the eye. "Don't worry about Ed. He never was one to carry tales. Besides, he's not all that bright." He flashed a tentative smile. "There's a chance he didn't put two and two together." A very slim chance. Very slim. Ed may not be the sharpest branch on the Bayne family tree, but even he couldn't have missed the clues. But if it made Samantha feel better, Bret had no problem telling a slight fib, as Gram liked to say.

"Whatever." She pulled her sweater back over her head, her bra leaving a misshapen lump by her armpit, and bent to retrieve her underwear. "Let's get out of these cuffs so I can go to the bathroom alone. Then I need to go back to the B and B and get cleaned up."

"Ah . . . you can't do that." He turned the tiny key, freeing their wrists from cohabitation. Funny, his felt sort of lonely. He rubbed at the rapidly cooling skin. "You're still under arrest. I can't let you go."

"That's ridiculous! I didn't do anything wrong, and you know it."

"Breaking and entering is a crime, even in Christmas, and it doesn't matter if the perpetrator doesn't have criminal intent. You did the crime, now you have to do the time."

"Oh, that's real original." Tugging up her jeans, she stomped to the bathroom door. "Will you at least take me to pick up some clean clothes and get my car?"

"Sure. You never did tell me where you put your car keys." He waggled his eyebrows. "Inquiring minds want to know."

"Could you possibly come up with any more clichés?" Huffing a sigh, she leaned against the doorjamb of the bathroom. "I left them on the front porch while I went in to get Rhetta."

"That wasn't too bright."

"Add it to my list."

Bret's Jeep rolled to a stop at the curb in front of the Wileys' home. "Where's your car?"

Sam pointed at a black BMW parked on the other side of Sugarplum Lane and reached for the door handle.

He grabbed her elbow before she could hop out. "Wait. I'll go with you."

She looked at his hand on her arm and then up at him with what his dad had always called a rattlesnake stare. "That's not necessary. I'm just going to grab my keys and take off."

"Yeah, that's what has me worried. The taking-off part."

"I know, I know, I'm still under arrest. I meant I was taking off from here and going back to the jail."

He'd just bet she did.

"You're not going back to the jail. You're staying at my house. For now, anyway."

They got out of the car at the same time.

Samantha glared at him across the hood. "If you're that worried, you can just wait and follow me."

He rounded the Jeep and took her elbow, walking her up the

sidewalk. "Oh, I'm not worried, Samantha." He propelled her up the steps to the front porch. But instead of stopping to allow her to get her keys, he continued to the front door and rang the bell.

"What do you think you're doing?" Sam wrenched her arm away and tried to take a step back. "My keys aren't in the house! The owners will know we're here," she finished in a strident whisper.

"That's the idea," he fired back, ringing the bell again. "Don't worry, I'll be right here while you apologize to the Wileys for breaking into their house."

13

"Well, that was humiliating." Sam jerked away from Bret the Traitor's touch as they walked down the steps of the Wiley home a few minutes later.

"It never hurts to apologize for a wrongdoing." He reached her car before her and opened the driver's side door. "Do you know the way back to my house?"

She sighed and tried to unclench her jaw. "Yes, I know the way. You live on the town square. It would be almost impossible to get lost."

"Okay, then. I'll follow you back, get you settled before I take off." He shut the door.

Immediately, she buzzed down her window. "Wait! You're leaving?"

"I'm technically on duty." He shrugged. "I'm still acting sheriff. I have to spend time at the office."

She knew that. Well, she should have known that. Would have known it, had she thought about it. It was the break she needed to escape Christmas with Rhetta. So why wasn't she gleefully planning instead of watching *Dudley* walk to his car, admiring his lean hips and long legs?

It was just rebound sex. She knew it; Bret knew it. Yet it had felt . . . like more. How desperate and pathetic was that?

She started her engine and pulled away from the curb, surreptitiously glancing in the rearview mirror and then jerking her attention back to the road when she saw him smiling at her. She didn't want him smiling at her. It messed with her head. It messed with her to-do list.

It messed with her heart.

No, it didn't. Her heart had absolutely nothing to do with the feelings chasing each other through her mind and body. Rebound sex would do that to anyone. It had caught her off guard, that was all.

When you were arrested for breaking and entering, you certainly didn't expect to experience the best night of your life between the sheets with your arresting officer.

Another glance in the rearview mirror had her groaning. Her hair was a mess of tangled waves. And with no makeup, her face wasn't much better. Rhetta had dragged in better-looking stuff from the garbage.

Sam tapped her brake and stuck out her arm, motioning Bret to come up beside her at the stop sign at the corner of the square.

"It's four buildings to your left," he said with a smile.

"I know that! I was just wondering if we could swing by the B and B for my stuff. I could really use some clean clothes."

"Sure. I was just thinking you might like to go watch the Christmas parade tonight. Did you bring anything warm to wear?"

"I have a heavy sweater and a jacket in my bag. But if the parade is here, can't we watch it from your place?"

"It's the Harbor Lights Parade out on the bay. All kinds of boats, decorated and lit up. You'll love it. Trust me."

After a quick stop at the Christmas Inn, he motioned her

into a parking place in front of the old bank and pulled into the space in front of her.

She watched him hop out of his car and amble toward hers, a big smile gleaming white in his tanned face.

Trust me.

Oh, crap, she could be in so much trouble for Christmas.

Sam stepped into the shower and almost groaned at the wonderful feel of warm water on bare skin.

She'd just shampooed her hair when cooler air touched her back.

"Move over, short stuff." Bret's cooler hand against her shower-warmed skin made her jump.

"What do you think you're doing?" She swiped at the shampoo threatening her eyes.

"Taking a shower before I head to the office."

"The shower is occupied." She closed her eyes and tried to regain the tranquillity of a moment ago while the water rinsed out the shampoo.

Maybe if she ignored him, he'd go away.

Big hands covered her breasts, slick with shampoo, and gently squeezed and rubbed them to aching awareness.

Maybe not.

"Go away," she said, but it came out sort of breathless.

"You don't mean that," he said in a low, sexy voice right next to her ear, sending goose bumps chasing each other down her body.

"Y-yes, I do."

"Liar." He nipped her earlobe. "I can feel your heart racing."

"It's fear," she lied. "I'm afraid I'll slip and fall. It's too crowded in here."

In reply, he lifted her, holding her high against his shower-fresh body, probing the part of her that didn't want to be probed. Okay, maybe it *shouldn't* want to be probed.

Dang, that felt good. She couldn't help it. She wrapped her legs around his waist. Purely for safety measures, of course.

He kissed his way up her neck, not stopping until he covered her mouth in a deep, wet kiss that had her shimmying against him, practically begging him to take her.

And he did.

Either she was really excited or he was a little soapy or both. The end result was he slid into her way too easily, her eager body accepting him more readily than was probably proper.

Heat. All around her and deep within her, all she felt was heat. Flames of passion licked her from within while Bret took care of licking the outer part.

Higher. Each thrust was higher, penetrating deeper, taking her breath.

Cool tile met the heated skin of her back, the grout a gentle abrasion with each deep stroke of his heated length.

Bret pressed Samantha against the wall of the shower, his hips helping to hold her up as he trailed kisses down her neck across her chest to her breast. He had to take it slow, make it last. If he kept pumping into her wet heat, that wouldn't happen.

She whimpered and wiggled her sweet ass, her smooth legs grasping him closer while her pussy sucked him deeper.

The muscles up the backs of his legs began to tighten. *No! Not yet!*

He pumped harder, their skin making a soft, slapping sound with each thrust. *No, no, no, not yet.*

He sucked her nipple deeper, rolling it on his tongue, grinning when she groaned and gushed around his cock. Holding the rigid tip between his teeth, he ran his tongue back and forth, rewarded when she shivered, her inner clampings beginning.

In an effort to stave off his climax until hers ebbed, he counted to ten. He silently sang the alphabet song. He tried to remember the names of all his science teachers.

Finally, he could ignore the sensuous suction no more. With a roar, he pumped once, twice, three times, grinding into her soft flesh while he experienced *la petite mort*.

On shaking legs, he held her limp body close as he lowered her to stand on the tile of the shower stall.

He had the insane urge to tell her he loved her. She wouldn't want to hear that. He wouldn't want to say it.

Not yet.

Sam hummed as she made Bret's bed and then stopped midsmoothing of the sheets. Why was she feeling so content she had the urge to be domestic?

Sex. Mind-blowing sex. The best sex of her life, to date. But, still, just sex. And rebound sex at that.

But it hadn't felt like that when Bret had kissed her goodbye. Of course, he'd made her promise to stay in the house. *House arrest.*

Because, technically, it was a bank, in her opinion she was free to go anywhere she chose. As long as she got back before he came home.

Okay, so she was looking forward to the parade. It wasn't like it was a date or anything.

She squirmed a little at the thought of how their evening might possibly end. So what if it was just rebound sex? She deserved a little sexual gratification.

She still didn't believe for a second that Bambi bimbo/homewrecker/dog thief and Sean weren't doing the deed. Sean's sex drive may not have been anywhere near Bret's, but even he couldn't go without sex for long. He'd just told her they were abstaining to tick her off, she thought as she finished blow-drying her hair and picked up the heated straightening iron.

Strains of "Born to Be Wild" filled the bathroom as she slid the first clump of hair through the iron, the styling products hissing against the heat. Speak of the devil—Sean was calling.

She stood, gripping the iron, and stared at the phone. Why was he calling now? Had he changed his mind about Bambi? Did it matter now?

While she debated, the phone went silent. A second later, it rang again. Again, it was Sean calling. It must have been something important. Did she care?

When it rang a third time, she answered. "What?"

"Where are you?"

She gripped the iron handle harder. "What do you care?"

"I thought I saw your car."

"Where are you?" she fired back.

"It doesn't matter where I am. I don't want you making a scene. Just answer the question, Sam."

"Fuck you." It wasn't something she'd ever said, but it seemed appropriate. Feeling smug, she hit the disconnect and then glanced around to see if anyone had heard her.

That was when she noticed she still held the straightening iron in a death grip. Followed closely by noticing the smoke.

With a shriek, she pulled the iron out of her hair. Or tried to pull it out. It was kind of . . . stuck. She pulled harder, and it came out.

Unfortunately, so did a rather large clump of her hair.

"Oh, crap!" She leaned closer to the mirror, blinking back tears as she surveyed the damage.

A hank of hair about three inches wide clung tenaciously from the edge of the smoking iron. Flipping the dial to off, she yanked the plug from the wall and then leaned in again to look at her hair.

None had grown back since the last time she'd checked.

From about an inch from her hairline across a good three inches of her scalp, nothing but singed stubble, less than two inches long, had survived. The stubby patch was roughly the size of her cell phone.

A quick glance at the clock confirmed she had a few hours to do damage control before Bret came back.

Sure, she'd promised to stay under house arrest, but this was an emergency.

Even *Dudley Do-Right* would understand.

There was a combination barber shop and salon just off the square, right around the corner from the old bank. Maybe they could take her right in and do something to even it out.

Sunglasses on her nose, she glanced up and down the deserted sidewalk before stepping into the afternoon sun. *So far, so good.*

She'd just rounded the corner when she spotted Hannah, Bret's grandmother, getting out of a white Lincoln Town Car. Dang! Sam hopped back and peeked around the corner. Hannah was walking into the barbershop/salon, which Sam now saw was named Nola and Ed's Swirl, Cut & Curl.

Slumped against the warm brick, Sam scanned the storefronts along the square.

Luck was with her. A few stores down, perpendicular to Bret's, was a plateglass window with pink café curtains. In a gold-lettered arch were the most beautiful words Sam had ever seen: THE HAIR HUT, and, beneath that, WALK-INS WELCOME.

With a quick glance at the jail, she hurried toward the Hair Hut, praying someone could fit her in. Performing a miracle would be nice, too.

Familiar smells and sounds greeted her, along with the little brass bell above the door. There was just something so comforting about a salon.

"I'll be right with you, honey! Just let me get Mildred under the drier," a heavy east-Texas-accented voice called.

Relaxed, Sam sat on the pink velvet couch by the window and idly paged through an old hairstyle magazine. Everything would be okay. She'd get her hair fixed and be back well before

Bret. He'd never know she was gone. She wondered if the Hair Hut did pedicures.

"Hey, sweetie." A petite woman of eighty, if she was a day, with flaming red hair teased to an inch of its life rounded the corner. She picked up a Diet Coke from the counter and took a swig. "Damn, that's good! How can I help—oh, my lord! What did you do to your hair?"

"Believe me," Sam said with a dry chuckle, "it wasn't intentional."

"I should hope not." The woman circled her like a red-headed vulture. She reached to touch the damage. It made a crackling sound and broke off in her fingers.

"Can you fix it?" *Please, please, please.*

"Not me, honey, but you're in luck. The only-est person here who may be able to salvage it just had a cancellation. She's taking a break." The woman looked at a huge watch strapped to her tiny wrist. "She's about done. Let's get you shampooed. Tina, the shampoo girl, is right through those curtains. By the time you're done your stylist will be waiting."

The woman walked to the end of the counter and bellowed, "We got a nine-one-one! It's a gen-u-ine hair emergency. We need you pronto, Bambi!"

14

Samantha's heart stumbled. She may have even screamed. *Bambi? Bambi? Please, Lord, don't let it be that Bambi!*

A teenage girl stuck her head through the curtains, her bright yellow and orange hair done in spikes that stood out from her small head, giving her the appearance of a startled rooster. She popped a huge purple bubble. "You okay?"

"What?" Sam glanced back at the counter. "Oh, yeah, I'm just great. Did she just say Bambi?"

"Yep," the girl said, leading her behind the curtain to the row of shampoo bowls. "Sit here." With a flourish, she whipped a nylon drape over Sam's semireclining body and then gingerly touched the damaged section of hair before patting Sam's shoulder. "I'm going to use the heavy-repair rinse. Don't worry. If anyone can fix this, it's Bambi Donner."

Sam's heart sank while her stomach lurched. The roar in her ears drowned out the shampoo girl's amiable chatter.

What had she done to deserve such bad luck?

The redhead peeked through the curtains. "Oh, good, you're

done. Bambi's at her station waiting for you, sugar. It's the last one on the right. I'd walk you, but I have a customer."

"I can take you over," the shampoo girl chimed in.

"That's okay," Sam said around the lump of dread in her throat. "I'm sure I can find my way. Thanks anyway."

With slow steps she walked through the busy salon. All around her, conversations droned while driers hummed, their heat wafting the smell of styling products, hairspray, and perfume. Under normal circumstances she would have found it all comforting and inviting. Today it was oppressive.

Never taking her eyes from the blonde who was easily a head taller than the surrounding stylists, Sam concentrated on placing one booted foot in front of the other until she reached her destination.

In hindsight, she didn't know what she expected, but it certainly was not the warm, almost shy smile of the gorgeous statuesque woman who stepped forward to meet her.

"Hi, I'm Bambi. What's your—oh, sweetie, what did you do to your poor hair?" Bambi's husky voice sounded genuinely distressed. She clucked her disapproval as she walked around Sam, occasionally turning Sam's head one way and then another. "I can fix it, but it's going to be short. Are you okay with that?"

"I don't think I have a choice."

"Here, have a Coke." Bambi shoved the cool silver can into Sam's hand an hour later. "Whew! I need a break! We'll just let the deep-root conditioner set for a few minutes and then shampoo you again and style it."

Sam took a grateful sip, savoring the cool, carbonated treat. She didn't want to, but found she liked Bambi. Under different circumstances, she might have become friends with the hairdresser. Truthfully, she couldn't understand how such a sweet person could get mixed up with a slimeball like Sean.

But that didn't mean she wasn't going to take her dog back.

Bambi leaned a hip against the counter, facing Sam after her last shampooing, and smiled. "So, tell me, Samantha, what brings you to Christmas?" She chuckled. "As if I didn't know." She winked a heavily made-up eye, her thick false eyelashes fanning her perfectly sculpted cheekbones.

Sam's heart tripped. "Wh-what do you mean?" If Bambi knew about her attempted break-in, it would be just that much harder to get to Rhetta.

"I think you came here for a certain science teacher." Bambi turned and reapplied her cherry-colored lip gloss and then smiled at Sam in the reflection. "I can't blame you. Bret's a doll. I've known him since first grade. You'd never find a nicer guy."

Sam couldn't help but wonder exactly how well Bambi knew Bret. Not that it was really any of her business.

"How did you, I mean who—"

Bambi laughed, the deep, rich sound forcing Sam's lips to curve into a smile. "That's the only drawback about Bret—his grandmother is the biggest gossip in town, bless her heart. I know she's been worried about Bret ever since he left and was relieved when he came home to settle down. And she's been fretting about his lack of dates. You can't blame her for being thrilled he found you."

"But he didn't find me. I—" She clamped her big mouth shut before she spilled the truth about why she was in town. "I mean, we sort of, um, found each other. I . . ." Her voice trailed off when she saw the picture of Rhetta being hugged by a radiant Bambi in an ornate silver frame on the counter.

Bambi blotted Samantha's hair with the towel and then finger combed through the short curls. "Pretty, isn't she? Her name is Lassie. My honey gave her to me." She splayed her left hand in front of Sam's face, wiggling her fingers, the diamond on her ring finger flashing light. "He also gave me this. I'm engaged! Can you believe how lucky I am?"

"No, I can't. I mean, congratulations. Your ring is very pretty. Um . . . Lassie?" Why in the heck would anyone name a Lab Lassie? Besides, her name was Rhetta. Always had been, always would be.

"Yeah, Lassie the Lab. Kind of cute, don't you think?" *No.* Oblivious, Bambi went on. "It was my honey's idea. He's so funny." She got a dreamy look on her made-up face that made Sam want to hurl.

"I need to get going." Sam tried to peek around Bambi's side to see her new hairdo in the mirror. "I want to be back before Bret gets home."

"Hot date, huh?" Bambi giggled and fluffed Sam's hair some more. "Where's he taking you?"

"Huh? Oh, um, he said something about some kind of parade." Inspiration struck. "Are you going to the parade tonight?" If so, it might be the perfect time to grab Rhetta and make their escape.

"No, we went last night. They have the light parade on the bay every night for two weeks before Christmas. Have you ever seen it?" Sam shook her head. "It's spectacular. I go every chance I get. Always have. Imagine every size and kind of boat decorated and lit up." She sighed. "All those twinkling lights reflected on the water, it's just beautiful. And," she added with a smile and another wink, "it's also romantic when you're with the right person."

Bambi twirled Samantha's chair around and dramatically whipped off the cape. "Ta-da! What do you think?"

Sam stared at the stranger in the mirror. Her current bobbed style was the shortest her hair had been since the time in third grade when Ron Kozak had cut a hunk out during social studies.

She slowly reached up with a shaking hand and touched a glossy curl. Soft-looking hair fringed her face, hugging her entire head in a halo of loose golden curls. "I think you're a genius," she said in an awed whisper.

Bambi squeezed Sam's shoulder. "I had a good base to work with. If you want it straighter, do me a favor and do not use another straightening iron! Just a little gel, worked through it, should do the trick."

Sam stood and slipped the hairdresser a more than generous tip, ridiculously grateful.

"Have a great time tonight!" Bambi called as Sam walked away. "Hey, if you're not doing anything tomorrow, I get lunch at noon. Why don't you come by and we can grab a burger or something?"

"Um, I'll see. I've been kind of . . . busy"—under arrest—"but I'll try," she assured the crestfallen Bambi. With any luck, she would have grabbed Rhetta and be on her way back to Houston. Assuming she could work her way around the pesky arrest thing.

Sam took a flying leap onto the sectional just as Bret's head appeared above the half shutters along the old bank's plateglass windows.

"Oh, hi," she said as he stepped into the marble entry.

"Hey. Ready to go to the—what did you do to your hair?"

Running nervous fingers through her hair, she forced her mouth to smile. "I cut it," she said in what she hoped was a chirpy, upbeat tone. "I, um, had a little mishap with my straightening iron and burned a chunk off. I'd been thinking about cutting it, anyway, so—stop laughing!"

He pulled her up into his arms. "I can't help it. You look so cute, all flustered. Were you afraid I wouldn't like it?"

"I don't give a rat's ass if you like it." She tried to back out of his arms, but he held tight. "I was merely answering your question."

"Aw, don't go getting all bristly on me." He nuzzled her neck. "I like your hair."

"Y-you do?" She arched her neck for better access for the kisses he trailed along the sensitive skin.

"Mmmm-hmmm," he whispered in her ear. "It's sexy."

"Bret," she said against his mouth.

"Samantha," he breathed into hers and then kissed her.

Her heart, which had just regained normal rhythm after running back from the salon, took off again.

A step took the backs of her legs to the edge of the sofa, knocking her off balance.

He followed her down onto the plush cushions, his mouth devouring hers, his hands pushing her T-shirt up and over her head to land on the other end of the sectional. Her bra soon joined it.

Despite being naked from the waist up—and with the way Bret's hands were going, she'd soon be totally naked—Samantha was far from cold.

Bret's mouth left hers to trail kisses down to her breast, sending heat streaking to her extremities with the first pull on the engorged tip.

Sam arched her back, offering herself, shameless in her obsessive need for his touch.

Light from the setting sun blasted through the plateglass, hitting her in the eyes.

"Bret," she said, tugging at his equally bare shoulders. "Bret."

"What?" He glanced up at her as if he hadn't just slipped his hand through the open zipper in her jeans to delve beneath her panties.

"The windows!" She stretched in an effort to reach the blanket on the end of the sofa to cover her nudity.

"What about them?" He stood and shucked his jeans and boxers in one move.

She blinked at the bobbing head of his erection and licked her lips, her thought process temporarily disrupted.

Evidently mistaking her silence, Bret dropped to his knees between her legs and began tugging off her pants.

"The windows!" she said again. "Someone will see us."

"Only if they're about seven feet tall," he shot back. "Okay. I'll close the blinds." As he stood, he pulled her pants the rest of the way off.

Instinctively, she clamped her thighs together, but Bret was having none of that. With a warm hand on each knee, he pried them apart.

Their gazes met.

He smiled a smile so sexy, so wicked she had to struggle not to squirm. "I need something to give me incentive to hurry and draw down the blinds," he said in a low, smooth voice that sent goose bumps along every centimeter of her exposed skin.

He pushed her knees down and then ducked to swipe his tongue along her exposed folds.

As quickly as it had happened, it was over. She lay sprawled on the sofa, watching the play of muscles on his bare butt as he sauntered to each window and lowered the solar shade, throwing the room into shadows.

He dropped on the sofa a few feet from her and began crawling toward her. Stalking her.

Claiming her.

She reached for the blanket again only to have him pull it from her grasp and toss it aside and then move closer. "You don't need that," he said, his eyes never leaving hers as he grabbed a condom from the ottoman.

"I thought we were supposed to go to a parade," she whispered, scooting back a little.

His hands shot out to grab her ankles, spreading her legs wider as he pulled her closer, wrapping her legs around his waist.

262 / P.J. Mellor

The tip of his sheathed erection tickled her opening.

She bit back a groan and tried to wiggle closer.

He stopped her by reaching down to roll each distended nipple between his fingers, gently plucking and pinching.

"Later," he whispered, aligning the head of his penis and flexing his hips, filling her with his heat.

15

_____

In the growing dimness, she could just make out his handsome features. But it didn't matter, she decided, shutting her eyes, as long as he kept doing the things he was doing to her. As far as she was concerned, he could wear a bag over his head, as long as he kept pounding her into the cushions. And playing with her breast. And flicking her nub. _Oh, yeah, baby, just like that._

Bret watched Samantha's face while they made love. Yes, it was making love. He'd told himself it was just proximity sex and/or rebound sex last night, but in the light of day, while he'd been at work and missing her like crazy, he'd realized the truth.

He'd moved back to Christmas to find Ms. Right and raise a family. When he'd first encountered Samantha, she would have been his last choice. Now he couldn't imagine growing old with anyone else. Which was really crazy. He knew all about pheromones, knew there was probably a scientific explanation for their instant attraction. Chemistry was not a foreign concept. And he knew sexual chemistry was not a myth. But when he thought about Samantha, he also knew it went way beyond any scientific explanation. Was it love? Was it possible to fall in love with someone so quickly? Maybe that was where the pheromones kicked in.

He didn't know. But he did know, if it was love, it would be emotional suicide to open his big mouth. He needed more time.

But time was running out. The circuit court judge had left a message saying his plans had changed, and he would be in Christmas the next morning. If things went well, Samantha could be free by the afternoon. Free to take her dog back. Free to leave Christmas. Free to leave him.

Samantha's inner muscles began squeezing, milking him of his staying power. Her back arched, and she did a little shiver, her breath hitching, her moisture dripping around him.

Stay. He increased his tempo, pounding into her harder in an attempt to get deeper, so deep she could not leave him.

Mine. Tell me you're mine. Say it. Tell me I'm more to you than a convenient fuck. He pounded into her, earning a little satisfied-sounding grunt. *Tell me. Tell me you feel what I feel and want to stay and see where it leads.*

Sweat dripped from his hair, splashing onto his hands where they were braced on either side of Samantha's head.

He gripped her shoulders, pulling her to him for closer contact as he convulsed, his climax wringing him dry, zapping what little strength he had left.

They collapsed on the cushions, their labored breathing echoing in the quiet room.

Tenderly, he kissed her neck, her eyelids, her cheeks, brushing his lips across her mouth, her chin.

After a few minutes, she moved her hands, smoothing them over and down his back, over the swell of his buttocks.

With great reluctance, he pulled back, kissed her forehead, and sat up.

"I need a shower—"

"May I join you?" Samantha had a soft smile on her kiss-swollen lips.

It ripped his heart out to know he could cause her smile to fade.

"That's probably not a good idea, Samantha." Without looking at her, he scooped up their clothes and tossed hers to her. "I want to get to the beach in time to grab something to eat before the parade starts. If we took a shower together, that wouldn't happen." He knew damn well what *would* happen, and it most likely would end with him spilling his guts, begging her to stay.

"Where are we going?" Sam trotted along beside Bret, clinging to his hand, wishing they were back at the bank in Bret's bed. In bed, she knew what he wanted, what he expected from her. "I don't see anyplace to get something to eat."

In fact, she couldn't see much of anything. It looked as though the entire town of Christmas was on the beach. Her bare feet were moving so fast, in her effort to keep up, she wasn't even getting to enjoy the tactile pleasure of her toes in the still warm sand.

Bret pointed, but, with so many people standing on the beach, she couldn't see where he was pointing. She had to assume he knew where he was going. He leaned close and said in her ear, "Over there." Then he tugged her to the right.

She dug in her heels. "That's a motor home," she felt compelled to point out. "And it looks empty."

He said something that sounded like "It damn well better be," opened the door, and lifted her in.

"Wait while I get a light." The sound of a lighter filled what she now saw was a compact living room. He lit several candles placed on the peninsula of the kitchen, the bar along the far wall, and on the little coffee table in front of a built-in sofa. Her eyes immediately started to burn and water.

"Is this yours?" She rubbed her nose to keep from sneezing.

"In a roundabout way. It belongs to my grandmother. She's a big NASCAR fan and likes to travel the circuit."

Sam peeked through the blinds by the table. "Will we be able to see the parade from here?"

"Not likely. There's an observation deck on the roof. As soon as the parade starts, we'll head up there. There are lawn chairs on top."

"Oh. Do you mind if I blow out some of these candles? They're making my nose run." When he shook his head, she blew out the candles and then walked into the kitchen and opened the small, well-stocked stainless refrigerator built into the wall. "Wow. All the comforts of home."

He chuckled. "More, probably, than mine. Gram isn't much into roughing it."

She took a few plump grapes from a dish on the refrigerator shelf and popped one into her mouth. "Who takes care of the B and B when she travels with NASCAR?" Another grape went into her mouth.

Lucky grape.

He tore his gaze from her juicy mouth. "Ah, my sister and brother-in-law. They live just outside the city limits, so it's fun for them to come stay in town. My sister, Ashley, says it's like a little second honeymoon." He winced and looked at his feet. "Too much information, if you ask me. But that's Ashley for you. Anything to make my life uncomfortable."

"Is she older or younger than you?" Sam popped another grape in her mouth and chewed appreciatively.

"Older." He swallowed a profanity and lunged. "Enough with the grapes! What are you trying to do, torture me?"

He plucked the remaining grape from her hand and backed her against the cool door of the refrigerator.

"Watching you eating those damn things, all I can think about is what I want to do to you."

"Do?" she asked with a squeak in her voice.

He nodded, enjoying the feel of her body pressed so intimately against his excited one.

"Yeah, like this."

She watched in fascination while Bret bit a tiny piece of skin off the grape and outlined her lips with the cool juice.

He lowered his head and lapped the juice from her mouth with the tip of his tongue. "And that's not all I want to do with the damn grapes," he said in a low growl.

"What else?" So excited now she could barely force the words out. It required too much air.

"I want to do this." He reached between them and pushed aside one cup of her halter, baring her breast. Her nipple immediately puckered in the cooler air.

Their breathing grew shallow, faster.

"And this," he whispered, squeezing the grape to drizzle juice over her.

Sam sucked in a breath as the cool juice ran over and around her nipple, setting off sparks zinging to her abdomen. She had to lock her knees to remain upright when Bret closed his mouth over her, licking and sucking every drop of juice from her excited body.

He repeated the process on the other side, causing her to wonder, again, if women actually swooned anymore.

With shaky hands, she reached for the fly on his cargo shorts. "More," she managed to whisper. "Tell me, show me, give me more."

"After the parade. It'll start in a few minutes."

"Please?" She used her finger to outline the shape of his erection through his shorts while she shamelessly rubbed her hardened nipples against his chest, bare now because she had shoved up his shirt.

"It will have to be hard and fast," he warned.

"Do it." She pushed him away long enough to strip off her clothes. "Hurry!"

He scooped her up and laid her on the cold, hard peninsula bar and then turned to take the bowl of fruit from the fridge.

Desperate, she grabbed his hand and placed it on her weeping flesh, even going so far as to push his finger into her wetness, silently begging for gratification.

She didn't want to think about her actions or the possible ramifications. All she wanted was to feel, to experience everything she could with Bret before she left Christmas.

"You're trembling." His soft voice floated from afar through her passion-fogged senses. He petted her breast and then brushed his lips across the puckered tip.

She was having none of that. If they had only a few minutes to pleasure her, he danged well needed to get the show on the road.

Grasping his head, she pushed his face into her aching breast. "Suck it!" she demanded. "Suck it hard. Harder!" She released her hold and writhed on the countertop, shoving his hand lower in a silent attempt to tell him what she wanted. What she desperately needed. "More," she whimpered, almost weeping with need.

She cried out when he released her. Within seconds, he pulled her to the edge of the counter, placing her legs on his shoulders. She purred her approval and arched her hips in anticipation. She'd never been a big fan of oral sex but found she was more than ready for Bret to go down on her. In fact, she craved it.

Coolness filled her. She raised her head to watch him stuff a plump grape into her weeping portal and then delve in to pluck it out again with his tongue. Once, twice. Before he could try for three, her orgasm ripped through her, so powerful it surely registered on the Richter scale. Had Bret not held her securely, she would have arched right off the counter.

Before she had a chance to float back down, he pulled her legs back onto his shoulders and licked every drop of grape residue from her engorged folds, spearing her with his tongue until she came again. And again.

Limp, she was barely conscious when he lifted her and carried her to the sink to spray off any remaining juices—her own or the fruit.

She leaned heavily against him as he pulled and tugged her clothing back onto her exhausted body.

"Wake up, Sleeping Beauty, or we'll miss the parade and fireworks. C'mon!"

"I'd rather stay in here and make our own fireworks." Did she really say that? Rallying a little, she climbed, with Bret's assistance, up the ladder to the deck on top of the motor home.

The chairs were padded and comfortable. Sam would have easily drifted off to sleep had the parade not started.

The crowd cheered as each colorfully decorated and lighted boat floated into view on the little bay, regardless of the size.

"It's beautiful," she said, wiping a sappy tear from her eye. And it was a truly spectacular sight, a reminder of why she loved the Christmas season so much. True, her current one had started out as her all-time worst. But she'd met Bret and had phenomenal sex, the best of her life. And the little town of Christmas, Texas, was a truly wondrous place at the holidays. If only she had Rhetta back, her Christmas would be complete.

16

—————————

"Look!" Sam pointed. "That boat has a Santa on a surfboard being pulled by dolphins! Can you imagine how many lights it takes for that, the palm trees and waves, not to mention the animation? It's amazing!"

Bret just looked at her and grinned before taking a swig of his beer. "That's Roscoe's boat. He's the Grand Master of the parade, which means"—he hurried on when she opened her mouth to ask just that—"that's the end of the parade."

She stood up to leave, but he tugged her back down. "It's not done yet."

"But you just said that was the last boat." She sank back into the warm cushion and rubbed her arms. Now that the sun had set, the breeze off the water had a definite chill.

"Keep watching," he said, pulling her up and over to sit on his lap. "C'mon over here. I'll keep you warm."

Santa had just rounded the end of the cove when the first boom sounded. The sky exploded into thousands of twinkling lights. From below, the crowds oohed and aahed.

Sam wiggled down lower against Bret's warmth and was rewarded by his hands slipping under her top. It was difficult to concentrate on the dazzling display of pyrotechnics with Bret's hands sliding around her ribs to cup her breasts.

Moisture immediately pooled, causing her to squirm against the hard ridge in his shorts. She canted her head for him to better kiss the side of her neck, sending desire shooting straight to her core. Who knew neck kisses could bring on such strong reactions?

One of his hands left her breast to slide lower. He opened her fly just enough to gain access.

She held her breath, sucking in her stomach for greater access, hoping he would do what she thought he intended. Happily, she was right.

Bret's long fingers rubbed her clitoris to aching awareness before slipping over her slick folds. He played with her for a while, building her frustration to fever pitch before sliding two fingers deep within her.

She gasped, arching off his lap, anchored only by his fingers, embedded, stroking, taking her higher, hotter.

Fireworks exploded behind her eyelids, setting off brilliant shards in every color of the rainbow. Whether they were from the force of her orgasm or the fireworks display on the beach, she had no idea.

And she was too weak and sated to care.

Bret continued to lightly stroke her as she floated back to reality.

She became aware of people walking past the base of the motor home, a few of them calling greetings to Bret as they passed. He replied, still petting her.

A delicious tingling began as she felt her nubbin begin to swell again. She captured his wrist, stopping the sensuous torture, and leaned her head back on his shoulder to look at him.

"I want more," she whispered, "I want you inside me. All of you," she insisted when he tried to move his fingers downward. "Now."

"Now?" His voice cracked in an endearing way.

She glanced around at the almost deserted beach and then back up at him. "Now. Right here, right now."

He groaned, burying his face in her neck. "You're killing me, Samantha. All the condoms are at home."

She turned and straddled him as much as the arms of the chair allowed, slipping her arms around his neck and touching foreheads. "We're in luck. I stuck a handful in my purse."

He slowly shook his head. "I'm not sure I am in any condition to fetch them right now."

Right now, she was so consumed with lust she doubted she could make it into the motor home either. But she'd try. "Will the chair hold us?" She gave an experimental wiggle.

"Doesn't have to. I have options." He set her on her feet, kissing her belly before pulling her shirt back down. Before she could question him, he walked to the storage box he'd taken the chairs from and pulled out a massive comforter. "This is old, but it should do. Why don't you grab the condoms while I get things set up?"

By the time she returned, he was waiting for her. After folding the comforter in half, he flipped open the edge. "Get in, woman, before I embarrass myself. Clothing is optional. It's not like it will stay on long, anyway."

Sam grinned and, after glancing around, stripped in what was surely a new land speed record before crawling between the soft layers. She snuggled down to enjoy watching Bret all but rip off his clothes, inhaling the scent of fabric softener, her nipples hardening with each breath as they rubbed against the flannel of the comforter.

But, instead of climbing on top of her and finishing what

he'd started, after kissing her, he slid lower beneath the cover.

Sam lay waiting, eager to see what he would do. She didn't have to wait long.

Warm kisses trailed from her knee up the inside of her leg. His breath ruffled what little pubic hair her recent waxing had left.

She waited in breathless anticipation only to be disappointed when he left the spot literally weeping for his kiss to trail kisses up the other leg. Once again, his breath teased and tickled her.

His thumbs massaged the outer sides of her labia, his hot breath taunting her aching folds.

When his tongue stroked the length of her, she almost screamed, her every nerve ending pulsing, waiting for his touch.

Finally, finally, he dragged his tongue upward, the slight abrasion of his stubble making her senses scream until his teeth clamped around her clitoris.

He held it between his teeth, probing it with the tip of his tongue, the pressure of his thumbs preventing her from bucking her hips in a wild effort to gain satisfaction.

Just as she was sure she was having a heart attack and would die unfulfilled, he sucked the morsel deep into his hot mouth and continued sucking until he'd wrung three earth-shattering climaxes from her.

This time, she knew the fireworks were not all on the beach.

Panting, she lay there, commanding her wet noodle muscles to obey her commands to move. They obviously were not listening.

But when Bret slid up her depleted body, his eyes feverish, her moisture still glistening on his lips, she reached deep within to find the strength to take the lead.

It took some effort, but she managed to flip him to his back. Straddling him, she trailed kisses over his face, down his neck, and across his sexy chest, all the while teasing the tip of his penis with her moisture. She wiggled her hips, taking wicked pleasure in feeling his erection twitch with each swipe of her swollen labia.

When he tried to grasp her hips and impale her, she slapped his hands away and maintained her distance.

Slowly, ever so slowly, she kissed her way down his beautiful body until she came to the part literally leaping to attention.

After an initial kiss, she took the bulbous tip into her mouth, swirling her tongue round and round smooth skin, occasionally taking light nips on the top.

Bret groaned and arched his back, thrusting higher into her mouth.

She smiled around his fullness and pushed on his pubic bone until he was once again flat on the makeshift mattress. She'd never done this before, but she'd read a lot about it and listened when her girlfriends talked. She'd always been a fast learner.

Sam slid to Bret's side in order to get better leverage as she sucked him deep into her mouth.

Immediately, she gagged.

Plan B was not to take him quite so deep and increase the tongue action while sucking.

It worked very well. Maybe too well, because she realized she was also turning herself on. Of course, when Bret's hand found her wet core, playing with her while she pleasured him, her libido elevated to stroke level.

Although Bret had not yet climaxed, he was breathing hard, his magnificent body shaking and covered in a light sheen of sweat.

She released him to kiss her way back up. He rolled on a condom in record time but when he again grabbed her hips, she glared at him and moved his hands to her aching breasts.

He squeezed rhythmically while she circled the head of his penis with her wetness.

When neither could take any more, she slowly lowered onto his shaft until their pelvic bones met.

They both groaned and enjoyed their private fireworks display.

17

"What would you like for Christmas, if you could have any-thing in the world?" Bret asked a couple hours later as they lay naked, cuddled up in his big bed after another earth-shaking bout of lovemaking.

Yes, she could now admit, at least privately, it was lovemaking, not rebound sex. In fact, what she shared with Bret was unlike anything she'd ever experienced. It made her suspect her previous encounters had been the just-sex kind.

"Samantha? Are you asleep?" He traced the shell of her ear with tiny kisses. When she shook her head, he asked again, "What would you like for Christmas, if you could have any-thing you wanted?"

You. Forever. But that would make her sound like a pathetic loser, not to mention desperate.

People didn't fall in love in less than three days. Did they?

Stalling for time, she rolled to her side, slipping her leg over his thigh, resting her foot between his legs while she traced lit-tle circles over his heart with her fingertip.

"Anything?" She shrugged, pretending to think. "The same

thing I've always wanted, I guess. I want to get my dog back and go home. I can't think of a better Christmas present," she lied. "What about you?"

He hugged her close and kissed her forehead. "I already got it. But I do have a surprise for you. The circuit judge left a message today. He'll hear your case tomorrow afternoon at one. You may get your Christmas present early—well, at least part of it. Good night, Samantha."

She lay in the dark, cold despite the heat Bret radiated, long after his breathing told her he slept. She should be happy her "house arrest" was drawing to a close. With any luck, she could get Rhetta back and be home in time for Christmas.

Sam hurried along the sidewalk of the square. According to the old clock on the courthouse, she had to be back in three hours. After much searching for a meaningful Christmas present for Bret—just to thank him for all he'd given her, of course—she'd finally decided to go for light and frivolous. After all, if she was leaving town, there was no point in tipping her hand. It was too risky.

If she took this gamble, she could lose her heart.

The next gamble was the most she could manage.

The bells chimed merrily when she pushed open the door of the Hair Hut.

"Hey, sugar—Merry Christmas!" The redhead she now knew was Nadine smiled at her when she walked in. "Your hair still looks darlin'. Don't you just love it?"

Sam touched the curls. "I really do." She glanced around. "Is Bambi free? We talked about going to lunch. She hasn't left yet, has she?"

Nadine shook her head, little dangling Christmas tree earrings swinging with the movement. "No, she called in sick today." She leaned over the counter and whispered, "I think she's having personal problems, if you know what I mean."

Sam didn't, but she nodded.

Nadine glanced around and then whispered, "I heard her having words with her guy when he picked her up last night. Why don't you go see her? I'd go myself, but I'm booked. I can give you her address."

"Ah, no, that's okay, I know her address." Bambi might be more receptive to giving up Rhetta if they could have the discussion Sam had planned in private. It could work out.

She hurried back to Bret's to make sure he hadn't come home for lunch to surprise her. Everything was as she'd left it. Tamping down her guilt, she plucked her keys out of the bowl by the front door and headed to the lot behind the building to her BMW.

She had to take the car, she rationalized, shifting into drive and flipping on her turn signal. It was the only way to go see Bambi, have their talk, pick up Rhetta, and still get back in time for her hearing. Bret would agree. Or at least understand.

She hoped.

Walking up Bambi's front walk, Sam cast a worried glance at the Wiley house. Mr. Wiley, the old man she'd met the first day, liked to talk. She sure hoped he hadn't talked to Bambi.

After suffering through two choruses of "Winter Wonderland," Sam worried Bambi wasn't home. Or, worse, what if Sean was in there with her?

Sam turned to leave as the front door opened.

At first, she didn't recognize Bambi. Gone was the perfectly coiffed and made-up model type. Her hair was sticking out in frazzled-looking clumps around her swollen, tear-streaked face.

"Bambi? Are you okay?" Maybe she needed to go to the hospital.

In response, the taller woman threw her arms around Sam, practically buckling her knees, and wailed, "No, and I'll never be all right again! My life is over!"

Fresh tears began soaking through Sam's last clean turtle-neck. "I'm sure it's not that bad," she said, awkwardly patting Bambi's shoulder as she walked her backward into the foyer and closed the door.

Where was Rhetta? The dog was manic about barking and running to the door to greet visitors. That tendency made her a rotten watchdog because she'd never met anyone she didn't like. Fortunately, due to her size, her bark was usually sufficient.

"Where's . . . your dog?" Sam couldn't bring herself to call Rhetta by another name, especially a lame one like Lassie.

Bambi looked up through teary eyes and sniffed. "Oh, don't worry, she won't bite." She broke down again but regained control. "Poor baby won't even come out of her little bed, her daddy scared her so much!"

Anger flared, but Sam fought it back. Sean may have been a lying, cheating sack of doo-doo, but even he wouldn't hurt Rhetta. "What did, ah, *he* do?" Okay, she could not bring her-self to call Sean Rhetta's *daddy*. Even her deception had its lim-its.

Bambi's blue eyes filled with tears. She took two giant sobs. "W-we broke up. He-he left me!"

It probably would have been crass to point out to Bambi how she'd dodged a bullet. Bambi was way too good for a guy like Sean. Heck, anybody was too good for a guy like Sean.

"I'm, ah, sorry?" She patted the sobbing Bambi again. "Is there anything I can do?" *Say no.* "I'm a pretty good listener." Not that she really wanted to know, but maybe it would make Bambi more receptive to listening to her plead for Rhetta.

"I just made some coffee." Bambi turned on her ridiculous high-heeled slippers and walked toward the back of the house, her brightly printed silk robe flowing out behind her.

Sam followed, glancing around as she went. Bric-a-brac and

knickknacks covered every available surface. Sam had always preferred minimal decorating, and the sight of Bambi's excess made her itch. How could Sean, who had professed to like Sam's style, stand all the clutter? Then again, if Bambi was what he wanted, no wonder he'd left Sam.

Bambi finally got control of her tears after the first cup of the strongest coffee Samantha had ever tasted.

"Sean—that's my boyfriend—well, my ex-boyfriend, I guess, now. Anyway, I thought . . . I thought—" She fanned her eyes while she shook her head. When she regained her composure, she continued, "I thought he loved me. He-he said he understood about me wanting to wait until my wedding night before—" She dissolved in unladylike sobs.

Sam reached across the tiny, cheerful yellow table and patted Bambi's hand. "It's okay. You don't have to explain. I can fill in the blanks."

"B-but when I told him the real reason I had to wait, he, he . . . left m—me!"

Crap, Sam thought, how could she take Rhetta away from Bambi at a time like this? It would be a double whammy, thanks to that rat-fink Sean.

"What the hell are you doing here?"

Speak of the devil.

Sean stood in the kitchen doorway, one arm braced on the doorjamb in a white-knuckled fist.

"Sean!" Bambi stood up, bosoms heaving.

Sam noticed they were also pretty impressive bosoms. Yet another reason Sean had left her for Bambi, no doubt.

"This is my friend, Samantha, and you have no right talking to her like that."

Oh-oh. The jig was up. Sam inwardly cringed, waiting for Sean to tell Bambi exactly how he knew Sam.

"I should have known!" Sean bellowed, sneering in a most

unattractive way. Really, what had she ever seen in him? "I'm just picking up the rest of my stuff, and then you two can be alone."

What the hell did he mean by that? Did he think Sam had been so broken up over losing him she'd gone to the other side?

"Daddy," Bambi whined in a sickeningly pathetic voice that made Sam want to tell her to shut up. "Please, come home. We can work it out. I love—"

"Shut the fuck up!" Sean drew back and punched Bambi square in the jaw, knocking her to the tiled floor.

"Sean!" Samantha scrambled up from the table, scanning the little kitchen for a weapon. "Since when do you hit women? She—"

Sean gave a derisive laugh. "Check under her skirt. She's no woman. I'm outta here."

After the front door slammed, Sam went to help a whimpering Bambi up. "Do you need a doctor?"

Bambi shook her head. "No, I know how to take a punch." She grinned and winced, gingerly patting the little cut on the edge of her lip. After giving Sam a quick hug, she stepped back. "Thanks for coming over. Don't look so worried. I'll survive. I own my own home, have a career I love, and a town full of friends and family. And I have a great dog to love and take care of, so I can be thankful for that, can't I? It's best to find out about Sean now than after we married, right?"

Sam nodded. "Right. But . . . he said such mean, hateful things."

"You mean about me not being a woman?" Bambi poured another cup of coffee.

Sam nodded.

Bambi took a delicate sip and sighed, dabbing an errant tear. "That's the irony of it all. If he hadn't pushed, hadn't challenged me to prove my love, I would have been a woman before our wedding day. I had the hormone shots, the money saved, and the surgery date set." She sighed again. "Don't tell me you didn't suspect? Samantha, think about it, there are very few women my size."

"Um, do you plan on going through with the surgery now?" She couldn't believe she was having this conversation.

"Of course! I'm still me, still trapped in the wrong body. The surgery was planned long before I even met Sean. I'm doing it for me, not for him or anyone else."

"Well, good luck." Sam took a step toward the door. "I was just worried when you weren't at the Hair Hut when I went to meet you for lunch."

"Do you still want to go to lunch? I can get changed and cleaned up."

"Thanks, but I have to be somewhere at one. I'm going to be here for at least another day or so. How about a rain check?"

"Really?" Bambi smiled for the first time since Samantha had been there and then frowned. "You don't have to, you know. I'm fine."

"Well, I'm not. I may need a friend, not to mention a cheese-burger, after I talk to the judge. How about tomorrow?"

"It's a date. Well, not a date, but—"

Sam laughed as she stepped onto the porch. "I know."

Sam waved good-bye as she opened the car door. Still smiling, she slipped onto the leather seat of her car and turned the ignition.

Click. Click. The engine wouldn't start.

Crap.

18

"Don't be mad," Sam said to a silent Bret as he drove. "I had to talk to Bambi." She glanced at the muscle ticking in his jaw. "I thought you'd understand."

"And I thought you understood the meaning of house arrest." He glared across the Jeep at her. "What else have I been wrong about, Samantha?"

"Nothing!"

"Oh, that's good, because I thought maybe I was wrong to think you cared enough about me, respected me and my authority enough, to stay where you promised you would stay."

Ouch. "It has nothing to do with how I feel or don't feel about you or even respect. If I get the charges dropped, I could leave Christmas this afternoon, tomorrow morning, tops. Don't you see? I had to go talk to Bambi to try to get Rhetta."

He arched a dark brow and looked pointedly around the Jeep. "How did that work out for you? I don't see a dog."

"Yeah, well, when I got there, Bambi was a basket case. Sean, scumbag that he is, had dumped her, and she was heartbroken." She narrowed her eyes. "You don't seem surprised. Wait. You said you grew up with Bambi. You knew. Why didn't you tell me? You let me go on about everything and didn't say a word."

Bret navigated into a parking spot in front of the courthouse. "Wasn't mine to tell." He heaved a breath and turned off the ignition, turning to look at her. "Growing up, Bambi was Bill Donner. When our class saw the *Bambi* movie in first grade, he announced he wanted to change his name to Bambi."

"That must've gone over well."

"Actually, I don't think any of us were all that surprised. The adults probably thought he'd grow up and forget about it. But by junior high, we all knew he was different. But he was also our friend." He shrugged. "Bill deserves to be happy, and if being a woman named Bambi does that, that's his business."

"You know, I kind of get that," she said as he helped her out of the car and they walked toward the courthouse. "A month ago, if I'd discovered Sean had left me for a transsexual, I would have considered it cosmic justice. But now . . . I feel sorry for Bambi."

"So sorry you decided to let her keep your dog?" He held the door open for her and pointed to an elevator.

"Not quite. But I didn't want to kick her while she was down. I'll try again."

"And when you get your dog back?" He removed his cowboy hat and nodded at the receptionist, who seemed a little too happy to see him. "Afternoon, Lissa. We have a meeting with Judge McVay? The Harrison case."

"Go on in, Bret," Lissa said, motioning to an open door on the right of her desk with a smile that was so syrupy it would rot teeth. "He should be back any minute."

"When I get Rhetta back," Sam said, picking up their conversation as they entered the judge's chambers, "I'm going home." She flicked a tiny ornament on the miniature Christmas tree sitting on the massive desk. "I've had about all the Christmas I can stand."

"Tonight's the Christmas caroling on the square. I thought, after that, we could have a nice dinner. I bought you a Christmas present," he added with a smile.

She thought of the present she'd bought him and wished she'd had more money to spend. "You really didn't need to buy me any—"

"I know I didn't *need* to—I wanted to do it." He nudged her elbow. "Here's the judge. Stand up."

Samantha wasn't sure what she'd expected, but it wasn't the short, round gentleman with a white beard, fishing waders, and a hat covered in what she assumed were fishing lures. What was it about the town that all the old men looked like Santa Claus?

"Sit, sit," Sportsfishing Santa said with a wave of his hand as he took his place behind the desk. He flipped through the open file and then looked up at Sam, his blue eyes like truth-seeking lasers. "Says here you broke into a house. That so?"

"Well, yes, but I—"

"Breaking and entering is a crime. Even if you didn't take anything."

"I wasn't going to steal anything! And I didn't even mean to break into the house." She leaned forward, ignoring Bret's hand on her elbow. "Judge, do you own a dog?"

"'Course. Finest hunting dog I've ever had. But what does that have to do with your case?"

"My dog, Rhetta, was stolen." She dug around in her bag and then pulled out a photo she'd had taken at the pet store last Easter. "That's Rhetta. My ex-boyfriend took her while I was out and gave her to his new girlfriend—"

"The Wileys have been married longer than you've been alive. I don't see Mrs. Wiley carrying on."

"I know! I was confused and thought their house was her house." Tears welled. She choked out her plea. "I just wanted to get my dog back, and it all went terribly wrong."

"Did you ever think of just asking the woman for your dog?"

"Your honor," Bret interjected, "she was under a lot of stress. The breakup was a shock. I'm sure, in her state of mind, she went for the simplest solution." Samantha nodded. "She just wanted her dog back and didn't realize she was breaking the law."

"Well, because the Wileys appreciated your apology and don't want to press charges and nothing was harmed or stolen," the judge said, scribbling on the papers, "I'm going to dismiss the whole thing." He looked up, smiling, the light from the window reflecting off the dancing lures on his hat. "And, because it's Christmas, I'm not charging court costs." He stood. "Now go have yourself a Merry Christmas and let me get back to my fishing."

"Oh, thank you! I—"

"Ho-ho,-ho! *Merry* Christmas!" the judge called as he walked down the hallway.

"Did he just say ho-ho-ho?"

Bret shrugged. "It's a Christmas thing." He settled his Stetson on his head and ushered her toward the elevator. "When you called me to come get you, I called the service station about your car. We can swing by there on our way home. It's just on the other side of the square. Then I need to go back to work for a while."

Sam pulled to a stop across the street from Bambi's house and prayed her car would start again with its new battery. She glanced at the clock. Just enough time to appeal to Bambi and possibly get Rhetta before she had to be back to the bank for dinner and caroling.

She paused with her fingers clutching the car door handle. *Crap, this cannot be happening!* She watched as Bret made his way up the steps of Bambi's house and rang the doorbell.

Was it some kind of curse that the men in her life were attracted to Bambi? There was no reason for Bret to be there.

Yes, in her heart she knew Bret was nothing like Sean. If he had gone to see Bambi, there had to be a good reason. She hoped.

A sick feeling in the pit of her stomach, she drove back to the bank and parked. Tomorrow would be soon enough to get Rhetta and leave Christmas. Assuming Bret wasn't dumping her, too, she wanted one more night with the sexy science teacher/deputy. She needed one more night. Just to say goodbye, of course.

Dinner was probably wonderful—after all, Bret's grandmother had prepared it—but Samantha was too sad to taste much. True, she'd wanted to escape Christmas—the holiday and the town—but now that the time was drawing near, she discovered she was going to miss it. Miss Bret. Miss Bambi. Heck, she was even going to miss seeing Santa everywhere she turned.

She glanced across the table at Bret. Candlelight may have been becoming for women, but it was not too shabby for him either. Tears burned the backs of her eyelids.

Tonight. She just had to get through tonight.

Her feet dragged when Bret insisted they go watch the carolers on the square. If this was the last night they had, she wanted to spend it in Bret's bed, not standing around watching a bunch of people sing.

However, she soon was caught up in the spirit, joining in on the carols and returning smiles. The caroler stroll culminated in front of the courthouse at the manger, where children gave a wild and hilarious performance of the nativity.

Wiping tears of laughter from her eyes, she walked hand in hand with Bret toward the bank. "Thank you for inviting me. I had a great time."

He chuckled, the sound settling in her stomach. "My pleasure. That suicidal shepherd stole the show!" His laughter echoed again. "I always thought using towels and rope was a bad idea around little boys. I lost it when he started tugging on the rope and it fell around his neck!"

After their laughter subsided, Sam said, "How about when one of the wise men decided to sit in the manger and broke the crib? Somehow a baby Jesus doll, headfirst in a metal wastebasket, doesn't seem the same."

Bret laughed as he unlocked his door. "I can't wait to see my kids up there in a Christmas play someday."

Their eyes met.

Sadness washed over Samantha. His kids. His kids with someone else. Would Bret even remember their time together?

Bret closed the door behind them, pulling her into his arms, his mouth coming down on hers in a hunger that matched her own. Almost.

Clothing seemed to fall away as he backed her toward the sectional. His mouth and hands were everywhere. She clung to him, desperate for the sexual gratification only he could give her. Desperate for him. Desperate for his love or whatever he could give her in the time they had left.

She whimpered when he broke the kiss and pulled back. Clutching at his shoulders, her nails digging into his warm flesh, she tried to pull him back to her eager body.

"What about the shades?" he asked, his breath coming in harsh pants, his hand busy with her erect nipples.

"I don't care. I want you. Now!"

"Well, I do care. And I have a plan, a plan that doesn't include anyone watching what we're doing."

"Oh?" She dragged the tips of her breasts across his chest.

"I've been thinking about what you said, about leaving Christmas."

Her stomach clenched. "We don't have to talk about it now."

"I don't want you to go."

What was he saying? "But I have a life, a job in Houston."

"We have dentists here. They're always looking for good hygienists." He backed her against the arm of the sofa and then surprised her by flipping her to her stomach against the soft microfiber upholstery.

He pushed her legs apart, his hot breath fanning her. The velvet of his tongue, taking a leisurely lap, had her gasping.

"I could come to your office," he said, his voice vibrating against her. His tongue speared her in quick, hard thrusts, withdrawing before she could settle into a rhythm. "We could adjust the dental chair and do this," he said, his hot breath ratcheting her pleasure up a notch before he closed his mouth over her and sucked.

Her climax washed over her, drowning her in sensation. Her nipples puckered into aching buds.

He moved between her spread legs and entered her with a hard, deep thrust she felt all the way to her ribs. "And this," he said in a hard whisper.

After she'd come again, he lifted her and walked into his office. With one arm, he cleared the desk and then laid her on the cool wood, arranging her to his satisfaction. "And you could come to school to visit me after class, and we could do this." He bent to pull her aching clit deep into his mouth and suck.

Sensation shot to her nipples, intensified by the gentle pinching of his hands while he sucked her third orgasm from her excited body.

She'd scarcely had time to breathe before he pulled on her legs, sliding her bottom closer on the slick desk surface, tugging until she sat straddling him on the desk chair.

She returned his kiss with all the passion consuming her,

tasting her excitement on his tongue, breathing in the musky scent of their lovemaking, wild for him. For them, together.

He arched his hips, impaling her, the old chair creaking with each thrust. She tightened her knees, riding him hard while he sucked her breasts with such intensity, she felt it between her legs.

They climaxed together, their panting breaths echoing from the high ceiling.

He swirled his tongue around the tip of one nipple and then gently rubbed it between his teeth before releasing with a soft kiss.

He kissed his way up her throat to her ear. "Ready for your Christmas present?"

She gave a languid stretch, enjoying his intake of breath as she rubbed against him. "That wasn't it?"

"Nope. That was just the warmup. Here." He wrapped her in the throw from the couch. "Wait here. I'll get it."

After watching the enticing play of muscles on his butt as he walked away, she stood and pulled the throw closer as she padded to the sofa to get her present for him out of her bag.

"Hey, you moved." Bret walked toward her, a festive-looking present in his hand. She was disappointed to see he'd donned a pair of boxers. "I was thinking we might see what positions we could come up with on the weight bench or treadmill."

"I think we could come up with some better stuff in your bed." Noticing his hot gaze, she let the throw slide from her shoulders, exposing her breasts.

His boxers had a noticeable bulge when he stepped forward and pulled the throw back up to cover her. "Where's your sense of adventure?" His teeth gleamed white in the dimness. "Here. Merry Christmas, Samantha."

Her fingers shook so badly it took a while to open the little box. "You're going to have to turn on a light so I can see."

While she finished opening her gift, Bret lit a fat candle on the side table, bathing them in a golden glow.

"Oh!" Tears blurred her vision—probably from the candle, because she'd sworn there would be no sentimental tears—as she held aloft a fine gold chain with a tiny pair-of-dangling-handcuffs pendant. "It's beautiful. And very thoughtful. Thank you." She brushed her lips across his, took a deep breath, and handed him his gift. "Great minds must think alike."

His laugh echoed from the tile when he pulled out her gag gift, a pair of purple fuzzy handcuffs she'd found at the little sex shop Bambi had recommended outside of town.

"I love them!" He kissed her and winked. "Want to try them out later?"

"I could probably be persuaded. Keep going. There's more."

"The key to my heart," he read on the sequin-encrusted box.

She held her breath while he opened the box and examined the key-shaped vibrator touted as the ultimate couple's pleasure device.

His heated gaze met hers. "Oh, yeah, we will definitely be giving this a workout tonight." After a carnal kiss, he whispered against her lips, "I just have one more present. Be right back."

"I don't need—" She clung to him, but he managed to step back, silencing her with a finger on her lips.

"Shhh. I promise you you're going to love this one. I'll be right back."

She watched him leave the room, pulling the throw closer to stave off the sudden chill.

The only thing she really loved had just walked out of the room.

Against all odds, she'd fallen in love. Practically at first sight. How stupid was that?

A clicking sound echoed in the quiet room. Wiping away a tear, Sam looked up to see Bret walking toward her, his hand on a leash.

Rhetta gave a joyful bark and rushed toward Sam, who dropped to her knees to receive sloppy doggy kisses.

After burying her teary face in the warm, stubby fur of Rhetta's nape and hugging the dog so tightly she squirmed, Sam looked up through her tears at Bret's smiling face.

His gift proved good guys still existed. Rhetta was the reason he'd been at Bambi's. He'd gotten Sam's dog back for her, even knowing it would mean she could go home, would go home and leave him.

"Thank you," she whispered around the lump in her throat. "I love you," slipped out before she could monitor her words.

The declaration hung in the air between them as the seconds ticked by.

She closed her eyes, humiliation heating her cheeks. How had she been so careless as to let the words fall out of her mouth? Even if it was true, as she suspected, Bret was probably horrified. She wouldn't blame him if he ran away screaming.

Warm lips brushed against her eyelids. Strong hands gripped her shoulders, tugging her to her feet. She opened her eyes.

"Now that you have Rhetta back, how long do we have before you leave Christmas?"

We have dentists here. They're always looking for good hygienists. Bret's earlier words echoed in her head.

She looped her arms around his neck, hoping she wasn't making the biggest mistake of her life. "Oh, there's no real rush. I'm thinking maybe twenty or thirty years."

Bret's green eyes glowed with heat and . . . something else. Did she dare hope?

"I think Rhetta will excuse us while we go upstairs for a while." He gathered Sam close, lifting her in his arms as he strode to the elevator.

As the elevator doors whooshed shut, Sam caught a glimpse of her dog, head cocked to one side as she watched her mistress being carried away by a virtual stranger. Which was very un-Rhetta-like.

Her heart fluttered. Maybe it was a sign her pet agreed Bret was the right one for her.